HANNOKI'S WILL

EMMA K BLACKER

2QT Limited (Publishing)

First Edition published 2016 by

2QT Limited (Publishing)
Unit 5 Commercial Courtyard
Duke Street
Settle
North Yorkshire
BD24 9RH

Cover design:Robbie Associates Ltd.
Cover images: shutterstock.com

Printed in the UK by Lightning Source

A CIP catalogue record for this book is available
from the British Library

ISBN 978-1-910077-93-1

Chapter 1

IT started with the occasional whisper in his head, with feeling upset or angry when he knew he was not, but he ignored it and blocked it out as best he could. David had important exams coming up that he had to study for; nothing was more important to him than getting high scores. Maybe if he did really well, his father would be proud of him and maybe, just maybe, he would let him go to the Federation of Worlds Navy summer camp this year. For the last two years his father had told him he was a failure and his grades were not good enough to earn him any reward.

David leaned back on his chair and rubbed his temples. He looked up at the ceiling where, when it was dark, you could see star constellations. His father did not like how he had decorated his room; he said it encouraged day dreaming. The walls were covered with pictures of the great spaceships, like the *Phoenix* which had been the first deep-space vessel to launch after the nuclear war which had devastated Earth over two hundred years ago.

The *Phoenix* had been named to give people hope. In the aftermath of the war many countries were uninhabitable; food and water were dangerously low and with the pollution in the soil growing more was impossible. All the remaining specialists had come together to build the ship, pooling what knowledge and resources were left, realising that this offered them their last chance for survival as radiation poisoning continued to kill hundreds of people every day. The Phoenix was a generation vessel: families had lived and died on board, and it was responsible for finding the first habitable planet in the Lyra constellation, which had developed a thriving population and it became the first stepping stone into space exploration. There were now five populated planets which were joined together by the federation of worlds.

How David longed to be able to go up in a spaceship, to travel into unknown space for years at a time like the first space explorers. He sighed; for the moment he would be happy to get the right grades and keep his father happy. It would be years before he was old enough to apply for the FWN. Anything could happen between now and then and at the moment it was not an argument worth fighting over. It was worth asking again about going to summer camp, but not fighting over.

∗

David could not believe it as he sat in class and looked at the results on his screen: 100% on maths and 98% on the sciences. He was top of the class and he could not stop grinning; surely now his father would be proud of him, proud enough to let him go away for the summer.

Despite his joy, other emotions started to intrude, feelings of disappointment and worry.

'I can't believe it! My parents are going to kill me. They are going to take away my games.'

'Someone beat me. Who?'

'What I expected, I guess.'

David heard the voices echo in his head. He looked around the room, sure that his classmates must be talking among themselves, but everyone was sitting quietly. Had anyone spoken?

David closed his eyes, took a few deep breaths and rubbed his temples with his fingers. Everything went quiet again.

'David, are you alright?'

'I am fine Mrs Delcani, just a little overwhelmed.'

'You have worked very hard this year. You got what you deserved.'

'Thank you.'

The teacher turned away from him and looked over the class. 'For those of you who are unhappy with the results, you will be given the opportunity to resit the exams in a month's time. If you want to register for this, come and see me by the end of tomorrow. For those of you who have done well, congratulations.' She scanned the faces again before saying, 'class dismissed.'

The classroom was suddenly filled with the sound of chairs moving and students talking. David grabbed his bag and left as quickly as he could. A few of his classmates tried stopping him to ask how he'd done, but he was so keen to get home and tell his parents the good news that he said he would catch them later and hurried out.

All the way home he pictured how it would go. He anticipated his mother's joy and his father's pride, asking again about the FWN and finally being told that yes, he could go. He ran down his street, through the front door and burst into the living room where his mother was sitting.

'David, whatever is the matter with you?'

'Is Father here?'

'Of course not. You know he never returns from his office until dinner time.' She saw the look of disappointment on her son's face. 'What is it, David?'

'I got my exam results. I was looking forward to telling him what I got.'

'He'll be back later but tell me. I take it you did well.'

David grinned and nodded, 'Top of class for maths and

science.'

'David, congratulations! I'm so happy for you, I know you worked really hard this year.'

'Last year Father said he would never consider letting me go to the FWN camp with my results as they were. Do you think he will let me go now?'

'We will talk to him when he gets home. I am sure he'll be as proud of you as I am.'

David listened for his father's return. He had checked after talking to his mother and there were still places at the camp; now he was desperate to talk to his father. Ten minutes before dinner he heard the door open and close and he ran down the stairs in time to see his father walk into the living room.

David followed him in and watched as he poured himself a drink. His father turned. 'Whatever you want, not now.'

'I have something important to tell you.'

'I said not now,' his father snapped. 'I just want ten minutes of peace and quiet before dinner. Whatever it is, it can wait.'

David realised that he would only anger his father if he tried to push, which would not get him what he wanted, so he left the room and waited until dinner.

As he sat at the table, he tried again but was silenced again. His father wanted to eat his dinner in peace and quiet. Was that too much to ask? David looked at his mother, hoping that she would talk about the results on his behalf, but she did not. As the meal came to an end, David tried again.

'However important you think what you want to tell me is, it isn't. I am tired and it can wait,' his father snapped.

'But it can't.'

'You dare to contradict me?'

'You said last year that I could not go to the FWN

summer camp because my grades were not good enough. I got top of class this year, including 100% in maths, and there are only a few places left for this summer,' David said in a rush.

'This is what you consider so important?'

'It is to me.'

'But not to me,' his father said and left the room.

David watched him go then ran up to his room in tears; he could see that all his hard work had been for nothing. His father did not care.

He could feel his mother's pain and his father's anger. His mother had gone after her husband and they started to argue over him. He had caused this, this was his fault. David closed his eyes and tried to block them out, but other voices started to make themselves heard. He tried to block those out too but he was too upset. He could not concentrate and they got louder and louder so he did not hear his father slam out of the house.

David sat crying as the voices went round and round in his head. Finally, in desperation, he put on some music and turned it up as loud as he could but it did not drown out the noise in his head.

'David, what is wrong?' his mother said as she came into the room and saw him curled up tight in the foetal position, his hands over his ears and shaking uncontrollably.

She had been annoyed when she heard the music. Her marriage was not a happy one but she had become an expert at keeping the peace, keeping a smooth-running household. Tonight, for the first time in years, she had challenged her husband about how he treated their son and the argument made her shudder. Now this.

She had tried calling up to his room; when David did not answer, she went to the bottom of the stairs and shouted up. She was annoyed that she had to go to his room and was about to give him a piece of her mind but when she opened the door and saw him, she knew something was very wrong.

'David,' she said again, but he still did not acknowledge her presence. She walked forward and grabbed hold of his hands, trying to pull them away from his ears.

David pulled back from her, horror in his face. 'Please make the voices stop,' he whispered.

Mary turned off the music. 'All you had to do was turn it off,' she said as she sat on the bed next to him and stroked his hair, noticing how wet it was with sweat.

'No, I was trying to tune the voices out. They just don't stop.'

'No one but me is talking, sweetheart.'

'Yes, they are. There are so many people talking and they won't be quiet.'

'Oh my God!'

'Mother, why won't the voices stop? Please, just make them stop,' he begged.

She tried to hold him but he pushed her off and moved as far away as possible, cowering in the corner of the room.

❉

'What is wrong with my son?' Mary Wilhelm demanded of the doctor.

When she was unable to calm David, she arranged for him to be taken to a hospital to be examined. She called her husband to inform him but, after their argument, he had taken a business deal originally assigned to his deputy and was now on his way to another planet. He did not see the need to return. Now she was standing outside her son's room, with no one to turn to, talking to David's doctor.

'There is nothing wrong with your son, Mrs Wilhelm,'

the doctor reassured her.

'Of course there is something wrong with him! He was hysterical and saying he could hear voices where there were none.'

'It is very distressing. Normally, when someone's telepathic abilities mature, it is a gradual process. Did he ever mention hearing or feeling things he did not understand before now?'

'No, there has been nothing. My son is not telepathic. I would have known if he was.'

'Your son definitely is, Mrs Wilhelm. He will need to be assessed by the United Telepathic Association to see how strong he is. They will develop a training program to help him use and control his ability.'

'No, you don't understand. My son is not telepathic, something else is wrong with him. No one in my family or my husband's is telepathic.'

'Mrs Wilhelm, I can understand that this is a shock to you but I need you to trust that what I'm saying to you is true. Though the telepathic trait does normally follow within a family, it can occur randomly. Your son needs specialist help or his ability will drive him insane.'

'No, no, you have to be wrong.'

'I'm not. Your son will be fine when he's given the help and training he needs.'

'Oh God! My poor baby.'

'This is not a bad thing. With help, he will have a normal life and a great advantage over other people. It will just take time for him to get there.'

'When would this training need to start? Would he be able to stay at home as he does now?'

'I have already contacted the UTA and they will be here this afternoon. As to the form of his training, that will be up to them to decide.'

'Can I sit with my son until they come?'

'Of course, though I should warn you that we had to give him drugs to stop him hearing the voices and a mild sedative to calm him down. He will not be very coherent.'

She nodded, went into David's room and sat next to his bed. He turned and looked at her. His hand fumbled towards hers and she took hold of it.

'They're not there any more,' he told her. 'They were going round in my head.'

'So the doctor explained to me. He's getting someone to come and talk to you. They should be able to help you understand what is happening and how to deal with it.'

'I hope so, I just want the voices to stop,' David mumbled, before drifting off to sleep.

*

Mary Wilhelm paced the small side room where she was waiting while the two members of the UTA spoke with her son; they had made it very clear she was not welcome in the room with them. She had tried to call her husband again but had got no reply. She left yet another message, begging him to call her, but for now all she could do was wait. Time seemed to be going very slowly. After what seemed like forever, there was a knock on the door and the two UTA members walked in.

Mrs Wilhelm turned and looked at them in desperation. 'Will my son be alright?'

'Your son will be fine but he is very sensitive, Mrs Wilhelm. It will take time for him to learn how to fully control his abilities,' the one who had introduced herself as Arita Folsham said. The other was called Jarik Yurik.

'What does that entail? Can he train from home, around his normal studies?'

'I'm afraid not. He will have to come to the association for a while, until he has control and can close off other people's minds without help. Once he can do that, his personal needs will be assessed. If it is in his best interests to return home then yes, he can. But he would have to continue to study under the UTA ahead of anything else.'

'Of course. We'll do anything you ask. How long will it take for him to learn control?'

'I don't know, everybody is different and learns at their own pace. As I said, your son is very sensitive. I should warn you that the more sensitive a person is, the longer it takes them to learn control.'

'Can I come with him?'

'No. While he is learning he will be surrounded by other telepaths who can close off their thoughts. You would at best be a distraction and at worst cause him pain. I'm sorry but, until he learns what he needs, you won't be able to see him.' Mrs Wilhelm sobbed at the news. 'You can call him every day and it will only be until he can protect his own mind.'

'But how long? A week, a month, a year? You must have a rough time scale.'

After a pause Arita said 'Six months to a year.'

'He is only ten, I don't want him going anywhere away from me for months. He is my only child.'

'I appreciate how you feel Mrs Wilhelm. It is always hard to be parted from a loved one, whether it is for a month or a year. However, you don't have a choice in the matter. Your son needs to learn control and only another telepath can teach him that. He will be coming with us until he masters the skill.'

'No, he won't. When my husband hears of this, my son will be staying at home.'

'You can call your husband, but it won't change anything.'

⁜

'What is it you want me to do?' Viktor Wilhelm asked his wife when he finally returned her numerous calls.

'I want you to stop them from taking our son away.'

'This is what you disturbed me for?' he asked angrily. 'I can't do anything. The law is very clear that the UTA have the right to take him until he can control himself, for his and our safety. Don't you remember your history lessons about what happened with untrained telepaths? He will only be gone for a while. I don't see what the problem is.'

'The problem is that he is our only son and they are saying he could be gone for up to a year.'

'He will be back. Find something else to amuse yourself with until then.' He cut the connection.

She sat crying, staring at the blank screen, not understanding why her husband would not help her and seeing her life fall apart in front of her. She made her way back to her son's room and, as she stopped at the door, she saw that he was not alone. The people from the UTA were with him. When they saw her they said something to David, who nodded in understanding, then left him and came over to her.

'Can we talk outside?' She nodded and stood with them in the corridor. 'Mrs Wilhelm, it's time that we were leaving.'

'Of course,' she said, relieved that they were going. 'When do I bring David to you?'

'I'm afraid you don't understand. He will be returning to the UTA with us.'

'No! He can't go yet, it is too soon. He is not well and all of his things are at home,' she cried, starting to panic.

'We can arrange for someone to collect his things from your home. David is not unwell and the sooner he starts his training the better. At the moment he is on drugs that suppress his ability – and those can be unpleasant. Our facilities are shielded and he won't need to be on them there so the sooner he comes with us, the better it will be for him.'

'Can I say goodbye to him?'

'Of course.'

They stood aside and let her walk into her son's room. David was awake and turned his head as she walked in.

'David, how are you?' she asked. She went to the bed and took hold of his hand.

'The voices have stopped,' he said. 'But my head feels empty.'

'I know, the doctor has given you something that causes that. But there are other people here who can help you learn how to block the voices out by yourself.'

'I know, they told me. Will you be able to come with me?'

'No, this is something you have to learn without me.'

'How long will I be away? I asked them but they didn't tell me.'

'I don't know. It depends on how long it takes for you to learn to control your abilities.'

'I'll do the best I can.'

'I know you will.'

'I'm sorry but it is time for us to be going,' Arita said.

'Can't you just give us another ten minutes?'

'No, Mrs Wilhelm, the sooner we go the better it will be for David. The drugs will wear off soon and we would prefer it if he was not given another dose.'

'Please, can't you give us a little bit longer?' she pleaded.

'We can't wait.' Arita said. At a sign from her, Jarik picked up David and started to carry him out of the room.

'Please, just a bit more time,' David's mother begged. She followed them into the corridor and grabbed at Jarik and her son.

'Mrs Wilhelm, this is how it has to be. It is only for a

short time, then you can see him again,' Arita said, and blocked her attempts to follow.

'David!' She shouted after them.

'Mum!' David shouted, fighting Jarik's hold and reaching out.

Now security officers had arrived and they stopped her from following her son. All she could do was watch as he was carried out of sight.

'I know it's hard but it is the best thing for him and it's only for a short time,' Arita told her. 'We will send someone to collect his things in the next day or so. If you can have them packed and ready, we would very much appreciate it.'

When she got no reply, Arita turned and walked away.

Seeing the last link to her son disappear, Mrs Wilhelm crumpled to the floor in tears.

Chapter 2

Eight years later.

'ADMIRAL Yoland,' his aide said, as he approached the desk. 'I am sorry to disturb you, sir, but you told me to inform you immediately if there was another attack.'

Yoland looked up. 'Of course. Is it the same as the others?'

'Yes, sir.'

'Do you have the report?' He held out his hand.

'Yes, sir.' The aide handed over the information chip and the admiral loaded it into the computer.

'You can go,' the admiral said and leaned back in the chair. His aide looked startled for a moment but, knowing better than to question his superior officer, turned and walked out of the room, closing the door behind him.

Admiral Yoland rubbed his eyes in frustration as he read the report of the attack. It did not tell him anything new; the scenario was the same as it had been in previous strikes. None of the approved military tactics had worked; Yoland knew that they would not - they had never been effective before. It was another failure for his FWN.

He sent the relevant sections of the report to the scientists working on the problem but he knew that they needed more information on the pirate ships' systems. Nothing in the report would help and their complaints would continue.

'We have never been able to develop cloaking technology

of our own,' the scientists argued. 'How can we detect something we don't know how to make? Capture us a ship so we can reverse engineer the technology,' they advised.

Easier said than done, Yoland thought. How do you bring in a ship that is cloaked and that you don't know about until it is too late?

He knew his answer to the problem but it was not something others had been willing to listen to. Maybe they would now that their tactics had so spectacularly failed.

⁕

'We can't have a telepath on board one of our ships,' Admiral Sucani argued once Admiral Yoland put forward his suggestion.

Yoland's hypothesis was that if science could not detect the ships, maybe a human mind could find the crew. 'They could be the only ones who can help us stop these attacks,' he argued.

'Our scientists will find a way to detect these ships.'

'When? They have no idea where to start. By their own admission it could take them months, even years if we cannot capture a ship for them - and we have not come close to doing that. How many more vessels have to be attacked? How many more killed before you are willing to try something new?'

'We have other tactics we can try.'

'All off which will fail when we can't see our attacker,' Admiral Yoland retorted. 'The number of attacks is increasing; they are getting stronger and more confident. During the last one they killed five people and injured several more. How many are you willing to let die because of an old prejudice?'

'With a telepath on board, the personal thoughts of the

crew won't be personal any more. There is little enough privacy on board a ship to start with.'

'How is it any different having a telepath on board a ship from having one in a room? They are now accepted nearly everywhere but we have held onto our preconceptions.'

'We have to protect our crew.'

'We have to protect the other ships,' Admiral Yoland countered.

'Enough!' A third person joined the argument. 'I agree that we need to look at new ways to deal with this threat. We can't rely on traditional methods because this is a new threat. We are being seen as weak and ineffective. We need to talk to the UTA and see what they can offer us. If they believe they can make a difference, it is something we need to look at.'

'With due respect sir ...' Admiral Sucani started, addressing the admiral of the fleet.

'No, we have done it your way with tried and tested methods and it does not even deter them, let alone stop them. Admiral Yoland is correct: we must try something new. If that means talking to the UTA, then so be it. But we will talk before anything is agreed.'

'Yes, sir,' came the reluctant agreement.

'Admiral Yoland, will you make contact with the UTA? Arrange a meeting with them as soon as possible. Make no promises but see if they are willing to help and if so, how.'

⁜

The call came through. 'Sir, Tali Gregson from the UTA is here to see you.'

'Please send her in,' Admiral Yoland said. He had contacted the UTA as soon as his meeting with the other admirals had ended, keen to get moving before anyone could change their minds. He had not known what to expect from them when he requested a meeting. They were curious and suspicious and wanted to know more, but he was unhappy with the security of the telecommunication system and he wasn't sure who he was talking to, so he had said he would explain the details in person only. He offered to go to them but, to his surprise, they said they would send someone over to discuss his requirements in person.

So an hour after the call, Admiral Yoland was about to meet his first telepath. The door opened and in walked a young, petite brunette who looked as if she had only just left school. It wasn't what he was expecting at all, and it occurred to him that the UTA were mocking him. He quickly supressed the thought, unsure if this girl could read his mind.

'Thank you for coming so quickly, Ms Gregson. I'm Admiral Yoland,' he said, standing up and holding out his hand.

'I'm sorry, Admiral, but we avoid contact when we can. Please don't think I am being rude by not shaking your hand.'

'Of course, I'm sorry. I remember reading that but ingrained habits are hard to break. Would you like to sit?'

'Thank you,' she said, settling herself in the chair opposite his desk. 'I have to confess I and those I represent are very curious. As far as I am aware, the FWN contacting us for a meeting is unheard of.'

'I have to admit that there are those who disapprove of this meeting. However, a growing number are starting to think, like I do, that you may be the only ones who can assist us. I have been given the authority of the admiral of the fleet to open talks with you and see if there is anything you can do.'

'You have me and the rest of the UTA intrigued. Please

explain and I will advise as best I can.'

'Before I start, I know I can't tie you to a confidentiality agreement as we have no agreement with the UTA but I am going to ask that you keep our discussions to yourself. Your discretion would be very much appreciated.'

'The UTA's reputation is built on discretion not contracts. As long as you can assure me that nothing you tell me will undermine the UTA or the Federation, it will stay with the people who need to know.'

'Thank you,' Admiral Yoland said. 'I don't know how much attention you pay to our affairs, but there have been reports in the news that a string of ships have been attacked on various trade routes.'

'The last attack was yesterday where five people were killed. This was the tenth attack but only the third where there have been fatalities. The FWN, though reportedly putting out extra patrols, have yet to prevent an attack and are now coming under heavy criticism. How am I doing?'

'Better than I expected,' he admitted.

'If that is why I am here, I don't know why you think we can help. Surely you have your own processes in place to deal with this?'

'We do, and we have been implementing them but they are not working. Ships are being attacked more frequently.' He paused and then continued, 'What has not been reported is that we cannot detect the attackers' ships. They have gained a cloaking technology that we don't know how to defend ourselves against. Our scientists and engineers are saying that they need a ship so they can reverse engineer the technology.'

'But how do you get a ship if you can't detect them?'

'There lies our problem.'

'Indeed,' Tali said, sitting back in her chair. After a moment of silence, she continued, 'I am guessing that you are hoping a telepath on one of your vessels could sense the ships in space and give you a warning that there is a threat?'

'Something like that, yes. Would it be possible?'

'I honestly don't know. We are not welcome on any deep-spaceships. A lot of liners insist that we are sedated when we travel. What we are capable of in space, if anything, is largely untested.'

'But you have theories?'

'We do. I believe we could help you - but it is only a theory. There is someone whom I would need to talk to, to gain a better understanding of our capabilities.'

'If you could help us, would you be willing to work with us? Help develop these theories?'

'I'm not authorised to make such decisions on behalf of the UTA. I need to discuss this with my superiors. I would not want to make promises or commitments that we, as an organisation, could not keep. I will report back and let you know what we decide.'

'Thank you,' the admiral said, standing up. 'You have my direct contact if you have any questions.'

He showed her to the door. Just before he opened it he said, 'I am surprised you were willing to come all the way down here. I expected this meeting to be at your institute.'

'I wanted to come. I wanted to see if you would actually let me in.' And with that, she opened the door herself and left.

※

'You believe he spoke the truth?' Gareth Longsworth, the principal of the UTA, asked Tali. She had gone straight to his office on her return and now sat opposite him together with some other UTA officials.

'I believe they are desperate. They are considering

us because they see no other solution to the very real problem they have.'

'Can we help them? I have no idea how our abilities are affected by space.'

'David has his theories. He has talked to telepaths who have travelled between planets and he even found a few who were not sedated on the trips,' Tali told him. She had arrived at the UTA a few months before David. They had trained together a lot and his fascination with space was well known among his peers. He had been known to say that his biggest disappointment in life was being a telepath as he could not join the FWN.

'Did you speak to him before the meeting?'

'Yes, sir. He gave me some useful information about current problems so I guessed why they wanted help, but I didn't know enough. It would have been useful if he'd attended the meeting as well.'

'That was never going to happen,' Longsworth said. 'Either he would never have left or he would have agreed to God only knows what.' Longsworth leaned forward and typed a code into the terminal in front of him. 'David, are you able to come down and join us?'

'Of course, I will be right down.' The connection was closed.

'How much do you think he can help us?' the third person in the room asked. Reginald Smith was one of the governing body.

'We won't know until we talk to him,' Longsworth replied. 'But he probably knows more than us and he could at least advise us about who to talk to.'

It was not long before there was a brief knock on the door and David walked in. 'Sir,' he said, acknowledging the principal. 'Mr Smith, Tali. How did it go at the FWN? Was I right? Was the information I gave you useful?'

'Very useful, thank you. You were right about those

attacks.'

'That is why we have asked you to join us here,' Longsworth said. 'I think your interest in the FWN and space will help in what we have been asked to do. Please take a seat.'

'I will try and help as much as I can.' David sat next to Tali. 'Though I obviously have no experience of space travel, I have just researched it for my own interest.'

'Which is more than anyone else in this room has done,' Longsworth commented. 'The FWN can't stop the attacks on the trade routes because the ships are cloaked and they don't know how to combat it with their own resources. They are asking if a telepath on one of their vessels could sense a pirate ship in time and accurately enough to be of use. I know your range is impressive, David, but in space a few miles is no distance at all. I struggle to see what help we can be, but I don't want to reject the FWN's request for assistance unless I am sure we cannot help them. I would be interested in your views.'

'In theory our range in space would be longer as there are fewer minds to obstruct us. How much longer, I don't know. I have never heard of anyone who has tried it.'

'Tali tells me you have spoken to people who have travelled on ships unsedated. What did they say it was like?'

'Quiet,' he replied wistfully. 'They never tried to do anything, they were too worried that if they used their abilities they would be sedated and left at a base the next time the ship docked. I am sorry I can't be much more help. I don't even know who could answer your questions.'

'That is alright, David. It does make coming to a decision harder, however.'

'Are you considering sending someone? If you are, I

would like to be considered.'

'Don't be ridiculous! You are one of the few stable level tens that exist; we can't risk you on what could be wild-goose chase,' Smith stated.

'If it is a wild-goose chase then there should be no risk to me. On the other hand, this is our chance to break though into organisations like the FWN. If we send someone who lacks strength or resents being sent, then the whole mission could be pointless and damaging to our reputation. If you send the wrong person it could undermine everything the UTA has worked so hard to build.'

'We could send you and it could still be pointless.'

'But at least I want to go,' David pleaded. 'I want to try and make this work. If I fail then at least you can argue that you did your best. We need to go to them and be honest, tell them that we don't know if we can help, that what they are asking has never been tried before but we are willing to give it a go.'

'I thank you for the offer, David, but we also need to see who else is willing to take on the role so we can assess who would be best.' David opened his mouth to argue but Mr Longsworth continued. 'I know you wish to go, David, but we will need to balance the needs of the FWN with those of the UTA. This challenge needs to be opened up to all members and the proposal will need to be placed before the board of governors before any decision is made about who will go. Your theories and request will be placed before them. If you can send me any information that would assist, I would be very grateful. Thank you everyone,' Mr Longsworth said, effectively dismissing them all from his office.

As they walked out of the office Tali caught up with David. 'You really want to go don't you?' she said.

'More than anything. I have always wanted to travel in

space. This could be my chance.'

'The admiral I met was nervous around me and did not know how to behave. There was a definite feeling of fear and anger coming from that place, as well. I just could not place who or where it came from.'

'There are always people out there who do not like us.'

'Maybe, but we are not normally stuck in a tin can in the middle of space.'

'I know. But if I know what is coming then I can deal with it. Your concerns are just a better argument for sending a stronger telepath.'

✳

'You want me to take a telepath on board? Father, are you serious?' Mark Yoland responded when his father explained why he had called.

'I am. Deadly serious. It was not easy getting the other admirals to agree with this, and it was even harder getting the UTA to allow one of their telepaths to go on this mission. They fear for the safety of their representative. I assured them he would be posted on our most powerful deep-spaceship and all possible measures would be taken to keep him safe.'

'So you want me to have him because I captain the fleet's flagship, the *New York*?'

'Yes, and because you are my son and I trust you. I need you to support me in this. The UTA don't know if they will be effective; this is new territory for them as it is with us. It needs to be handled with care to avoid what could be disastrous repercussions if this mission fails. The UTA is growing in strength and influence as more companies, organisations and planet leaders accept them and employ them for their skills. We can't afford to alienate them through our prejudices – it would affect us adversely in the long term. The fact they are giving us someone is being seen by some as a step in the right direction.'

'The crew are not going to like it.'

'They don't have to like it, they just have to put up with it and follow orders,' the admiral stated, 'Mark, this won't be for long. Either this telepath will be useless and go back to the UTA, or he'll be successful and get you a ship. Then he still goes back to the UTA.'

'Fine. Where do I pick him up?' Mark asked, resigned to following his father's wishes.

'At star base Amora on Europa, as soon as you can get there.'

'We have just left Delos after a refit. We can be with you in five days.'

'I know. I have already arranged for the telepath, David Wilhelm, to meet you there.'

Chapter 3

A month after Tali's first meeting at the FWN David stood outside his father's home and took a deep breath before pressing the intercom. The UTA had tried to convince him not to come back here, that this was a bad time to start opening up emotional topics, but he was determined to give his father a chance before he left the world.

In the last eight years, his father had never come to visit him. David had to admit that he had not tried hard to engage with his father, either. At first he was too hurt by his father's rejection, then he became accustomed to the lack of contact. He could have visited any time during the last few years but he had not. Now it seemed important before he started the next stage of his life.

He had not been here for eight years, not since the night his telepathic abilities surfaced and his mother took him to the hospital. The last time David saw his father was at his mother's funeral, shortly after he had been taken to the UTA. His mother died as his initial training had been coming to an end; when that happened he would have been allowed to return home and continue his training from there. He had talked to her daily and was excited at the thought of seeing her again,

'They say I can come home next month,' he told her and she was so happy. When he was called into the principal's room the next day, he never imagined it was to be told that his mother had died.

He was allowed to attend the funeral with his teacher,

in case the emotion was too much for him, in which case they could exercise control over his mind.

As he waited for his father to open the door, he remembered the funeral as if it were yesterday. He had gone up to his father wanting, needing, to grieve with him but had been rejected. His father would not even talk to him; he just turned away and walked towards another group of people as if he had not seen or heard him. His teacher had seen what had happened and taken him straight back to the UTA. The next morning David was called back into the principal's office and told that after his initial training he would be staying with the UTA as his father had informed them that he could not cope with him and his 'special needs'. There he had stayed until today. He had spoken to his father on rare occasions over the years but they had not met.

The door was finally opened by a middle-aged lady. 'Can I help you?'

'I have come to visit my father.'

'I am sorry, I believe you must have the wrong address,' she said and started to close the door.

'Viktor Wilhelm no longer lives here?' David asked quickly before she closed it all the way. She opened it again and looked at him suspiciously.

'He does but I have worked for him for the last five years, and I know he does not have a son.'

'If you had worked for him for longer, you would know that he does. Can you please tell him that David is here to see him?'

She paused for a moment, unsure what to think. 'Wait here.' She closed the door on him, leaving him on the doorstep. David was not sure if – or when – the lady would return. It wasn't a good sign that she didn't know her employer had a son. He was wondering how long to wait when the door opened a few minutes later.

'David, what are you doing here? Why are you not at the UTA?' his father asked, having come to the door.

'I tried to call before coming over but I could not get through. I wanted to know if I could stay here for a few days.'

His father looked at him, not sure what to make of his son suddenly turning up on his doorstep after so long. 'You had better come in,' he said finally, not wanting whatever they said to be the gossip for his neighbours.

David followed his father down the corridor to a room he recognised as his father's study. Little had changed; the desk and furnishings were the same and although the walls had changed colour, the pictures had not.

'If it is inconvenient, I can find somewhere else to go,' David said, as his father closed the door.

'No, I just thought the UTA took better care of its members and did not just throw them out.'

'They did not throw me out. I have a few free days before my assignment begins and I have not seen you for eight years, I thought I would take the opportunity to see you again since I don't know when I will be back on Europa.'

'I don't understand. I thought telepaths did not leave the worlds they train in.'

'They do, but very rarely. We normally leave the planet only when we have a specialist skill that is needed elsewhere.'

'Is this a job that only you can do then? It must be something special.'

'Let us say they were short on notice and I was the only one willing. I'm going into space. My post is on an FWN ship called the *New York*. I leave in a few days from the space base here.'

'The FWN does not employ telepaths.'

'They are trialling it with me.'

'So against all the odds, you got want you wanted.'

'Possibly. It will depend on how successful this mission is. It may become something or it may not. I can get a hotel room if you do not want me to stay here. I just thought it would be nice to see you again before I left. Since I will be travelling in space, I might be placed on a different planet after the assignment is over.'

'No, it is fine. It was just a surprise to see you again. You can stay here but I still have to work. It is fine,' he repeated, and for the first time David saw his father flustered.

'Thank you.'

'I will get Mrs Ransom to show you to a guest room.' He pressed a button on his desk.

'What happened to my old room?'

'You have not lived here for eight years. Did you expect me to keep it as your room?' Viktor snapped as the door opened and Mrs Ransom came in. 'Can you show my son to one of the guest rooms. He will be staying here for the next few days.'

'Of course sir. If you will follow me.' She stood to one side, leaving room for David to precede her. As he walked out of the room his father's voice made him pause.

'Dinner is at eight o'clock.'

'I won't be late,' he said and Mrs Ransom closed the door behind her as she followed him out of the room.

⁕

David's few possessions were in a single carry bag which he placed on the bed in the guest room. He looked around him. He did not remember this room; nothing in the house was familiar.

He sighed in frustration and started to unpack his clothes. At the UTA he wore a uniform most of the time, only needing casual clothing on the rare occasions when he went out. David had seen a lot of other students go home to their families once they had learned control; they came to the classes as day students. Those with relatives who lived too far away stayed at the UTA but most of their parents still made trips to see their children and kept in regular contact via com link. The only time David left the campus was when he was invited to stay with the friends he had made there.

It did not take him long to put away his things; he hadn't seen the point of buying many clothes since he would wear regulation clothing on the *New York*, which he was due to pick up when he arrived at the port.

He looked at the time: six o'clock. There was not enough time to go anywhere before dinner but he felt too restless to sit quietly in his room and wait. He decided to explore the house and see what he could remember of it.

As he walked slowly down the corridor, looking at the paintings hanging on the wall, he remembered only some of them. He knocked on, then opened, various doors; he found a bathroom, a few more bedrooms and what he believed was his father's room as it was the only room that looked lived in. He glanced around it quickly from the doorway and saw no sign of his mother, or of any other female. The room was tidy but masculine, with no female touches. David closed the door without going in.

Finally he came to a door that he was sure had been his. He took a deep breath and opened it, not knowing what he was going to see or how he would feel if there was just another neutrally coloured room. As the door swung open, he was shocked. So far there had been no sign in the house that either he or his mother had ever existed. The sense of rejection hurt – but what he saw now changed that. It was his room as he remembered it from the last time he was there. There were the same covers on the bed, the same posters on the walls and the same models hanging from the ceiling. His father had hated his room, yet everything was the same.

David walked in and sat on the bed. He saw a picture of his mother sitting on the bedside table; he picked it up and saw there was no dust under it. Mrs Ransom had not known he existed, so who came in here to clean? Or did she think it was a shrine to a dead child?

He got up and wandered around the room, looking in the cupboards and drawers. Some of his clothes had been sent on to him but the rest were still here. Nothing had been cleared out but some things had been moved in; he noticed a few of his mother's favourite things.

Not knowing what to think he closed the door behind him feeling that even though it was his old room he had intruded on something very private.

⁜

Just before eight o'clock, David made his way down to the dining room. His father was already there with a drink in his hand.

'The bottle is on the side if you want to help yourself.'

'Thank you but I'm fine.'

'Please yourself,' Viktor said, taking another sip. 'Dinner will be served shortly.' They both stood in uncomfortable silence for a few minutes, not sure what to say to each other. Then Mrs Ransom came in and announced that dinner was ready and two other servants came in carrying plates.

David and his father sat down at the table and ate. The silence continued. As the main course finished, David's head started to ache and he leaned back, rubbing his temples.

'Headache?' Viktor questioned.

'After spending so much time in the UTA, I forget how loud everything is outside the facility.'

'I thought the whole point of all this training was so you could not hear anything.'

'The only way I could not hear anything would be if I was not telepathic,' David explained. When he sensed his father's confusion he continued. 'Think about what you can hear every day, all the sounds that surround you constantly. You learn to ignore most of what you hear from a very early age, and you know to acknowledge what is important. Being telepathic is similar. The only way you would not hear what is going on around you is if you were deaf. The only way I could stop hearing all the mental noise would be if I was not telepathic. They train you to block out the noise, to reduce it from the excessive noise that hits you when the skill develops. For me, it was like I was at a rock concert, or in the middle of a riot, and they taught me to reduce the volume level to a dinner party. The voices are always in the background but I can't hear what they are saying; there are a lot of murmurs and nothing else.'

'So you can't hear what I am thinking now?'

'No I can't, not unless I deliberately read your mind. And that would be an offence unless you gave permission, or lawful exceptions apply.'

'What could possibly justify your right to read my mind? It would be the ultimate invasion of privacy.'

'I can read your mind if a court issues a warrant, if a life is in danger or if there is a credible threat against the state.'

'If you are so limited, what is the point of having you on board a spaceship? You can't get a warrant and I seriously doubt they expect murders on the ship.'

David leaned back in the chair and smiled. 'What the FWN needs with telepaths is the business of the FWN.'

'So you are not going to tell me what you are doing on the *New York*.'

'No.'

'Good for you,' his father replied. 'I assume that the FWN will inform me if anything goes wrong?'

'You are my only living relative that I know of. As such, you are my next of kin so yes, they will tell you.'

'I understand that Captain Yoland is in charge of the ship. Have you met him yet?'

'No. We have spoken briefly via com link but I won't meet him until I board next week. Do you know him?'

'I know his father well. My company has contracts with the FWN and I have done business with him on several occasions.'

David wondered if that was one of the reasons why his father was suddenly starting to take an interest in him. Or was he just being cynical, bearing in mind that his room had been kept?

⁜

The week passed quickly, David was able to organise everything he needed for his assignment. He ate dinner with his father most nights and, though he could honestly say they would never be close, they were at least able to be civilised.

On the last day, as David came down stairs with his bag, he saw his father waiting for him at the bottom.

'Are you ready to go?'

'I am. Thanks for letting me stay here.'

'It was surprisingly nice to have you here.'

'Thank you,' David said.

'You know I never approved of your fascination with the FWN. I always wanted you to join me at the company. But despite everything, you remained determined and finally got there. If anyone can make it work it will be you - if only so you can stay in space. I look forward to hearing about it when you come back.'

'I'll take that as a compliment,' David replied, not sure how he should take it.

'However badly put, it *was* a compliment. If you ever find yourself back here, you will be welcome to stay.'

Chapter 4

THE car was waiting for him outside his father's home. The driver, who was in a FWN uniform, stepped forward quickly and took David's bag. 'Is the rest of your luggage inside, sir?' he asked.

'No, this is everything.'

'Very good, sir.' David felt the driver's surprise; he must have preconceived ideas about him, especially considering the elite district in which his father lived.

'I'm due to collect what I need for the ship at the space port, this is where I have been told to go.' He handed over a copy of his instructions.

'Of course, sir, I know where that is, it is the main warehouse.'

It took over an hour to get to the space port. David sat in silence, thinking about what was ahead of him. The last week had been hard; at the UTA the premises were all shielded, which considerably reduced the mental noise he could hear no matter where he was in the facility. This week was the longest he had been away from a shielded facility and he was starting to doubt himself. Most students did not stay as long as he had and he was finding the adjustment difficult.

He had been told that he would find it harder than most other telepaths due to his sensitivity; several people within the UTA had argued that he might not cope with the stress of being away from the institute for so long. Over the years, they had tried to get him outside as much as possible, to get him used to being out in the population, but he always got nagging headaches. They were normal, he was told; he could take medication to suppress them and they were not a sign of instability. It did not make him feel better about having to take medication to cope, or that the UTA insisted on regular reviews on his mental status.

The car pulled into the space port. At various checkpoints he was asked for his ID but eventually the car came to a halt. The driver got out and opened the door for him. 'This is the supply warehouse where you can collect anything that you need. You are scheduled to leave on the *New York* in two hours' time from dock 3. You have an hour and a half before I take you there.'

'You don't need to wait, I can make my own way there.'

'Sir,' the driver said confused. 'It might only take ten minutes in the car but if you want to walk you've already left it too late.'

David flushed slightly in embarrassment as he released how naive he was in not realising how long it would take to walk to places compared to going by car.

'Thank you. I would appreciate it if you waited for me.'

'I'll be here when you are ready.'

Taking a deep breath, David walked into the warehouse. He was not sure what he expected to find in such a large building, but he was surprised when he saw a desk in front of him with three people behind it and a queue in front. David joined the line and waited until it was his turn to approach the desk.

'How can I help you?' the man behind the desk asked.

'I was told to come here and pick up my uniform and supplies.'

'I'll need to see your deployment orders,' he said, bored. David silently handed over his papers, the man scanned them and immediately straightened up. 'Please give me a few minutes, sir, and I'll pick up your uniforms and supplies.'

'Thank you.'

David waited as the man walked through the door behind him. He looked around: everything was white and the lights were harsh. The only relief from the brightness was the publicity posters for the FWN and official notices. He was looking at them when the supply man returned.

'Sir,' he called to get his attention. David turned and saw the pile sitting on the desk. 'I have your things here. I'll need you to sign the requisition order before you can take them.'

'Of course.' David looked at the list; after a brief check he assured himself it was all there and signed the order.

'Thank you, sir. Do you have a lift to your ship or do you need your supplies sent ahead?'

'I have a car waiting outside.'

'Very good. Let me help you carry everything out.' Between them they were able to carry out the large bags. David's driver jumped out and helped them load the items into the car and the supply man returned to the building.

'We still have some time,' the driver said. 'Is there anywhere else you need to go, or do you want me to take you to dock 3?'

'To dock 3 please,' David said, having no idea what else there was here to see or do. The car pulled away smoothly.

David looked out of the window during the short drive. He was amazed at the size of everything. The first space dock came into view; the size of the ships they could accommodate must be bigger than he had anticipated. He held his breath as the car turned the corner for his first view of the *New York*, but there was nothing there. Had the ship been delayed? It could not have left already because he was early.

The car stopped and the driver opened the door for him. David was about to ask about the *New York* when someone walked out of the dock and approached him. 'Mr Wilhelm? I am Ensign Teilgar. I have been assigned to take you to the *New York*.'

'I'm sorry. I thought it was docking here.'

'No, sir. A ship the size of the *New York* does not break orbit unless it's coming in for maintenance or repairs that cannot be completed from a space station. The captain has sent a shuttle to take you up, but first I need to see your orders and ID.' Yet again David handed over his papers. 'Thank you, sir. If you would like to come with me, I'll show you on board.'

'I have some bags.'

'Don't worry about them, the driver will have them loaded.' Teilgar led him inside.

As David walked through the corridors he saw that everything was decorated in the same way as the storage warehouse, making it feel cold and unwelcoming. He wondered if the ship would be the same.

Soon they came to a sealed door. Another person in FWN uniform was standing outside it talking to a man in a jumpsuit. 'Ensign Teilgar,' the uniformed male acknowledged as they approached.

'Ensign Falmar,' David's guide responded. 'Is everything ready?'

'They have finished refuelling and as soon as everything is loaded, we will be ready to go.'

'Good.' Teilgar turned to David. 'Sir, this is Ensign Falmar, the second shuttle pilot. Falmar, this is Mr Wilhelm.'

'A pleasure, sir,' Falmar said as he turned and activated the airlock. 'Once your luggage has been stowed, we will be on our way.'

As David followed them on board the shuttle, he paused and looked around. There were several seats but they all had control panels in front of them and he wondered where he was meant to sit.

Ensign Teilgar looked at him for a moment, puzzled that David had not moved forward. Then he remembered that, as a telepath, David had probably never been on a shuttle before. 'You can sit anywhere other than the pilot chairs,' he offered.

David took the chair behind Ensign Falmar and looked at the harness. 'Let me do that for you, sir,' Ensign Teilgar said and strapped him in.

David gritted his teeth as Teilgar's hands brushed against him; he did not want to show his difficulties with physical contact.

'Before we take off, I need to go through the emergency procedure,' Teilgar said.

David did not need to be a telepath to read their body language. They knew who he was and he made them nervous; they were falling back on their training to get them through this trip. He wondered what they had been told about him. Had they been ordered to treat him with respect, or were they doing so because they were scared of him? How he wished he could break the law and read their minds to find out. But he couldn't, so he would have to go into an unknown situation and take everything a step at a time.

'Your belongings have been stowed in the hold,' Falmar informed him a while later.

'We are starting the pre-flight checks and should be taking off shortly,' Teilgar added, then turned to his colleague.

David watched as their hands moved over the consoles in front of them. He was scared and excited in equal measure. For the first time he was out and making his own way in the universe.

'We are ready for take-off, sir,' he was warned. He heard the engines pick up. 'The *New York* is in orbit so it is a short trip. Are you good to go?'

David realised that he was being asked permission to take off. 'Let's get going.'

He felt a slight change in the cabin pressure as the shuttle moved, but the most startling thing was that nearly everything in his head went quiet. He closed his eyes, leaned back and slowly opened up his mind. For first time since he was a child there was silence, blissful silence. Curiously he expanded his mind further and felt the planet, his home, slowly diminish the further away he moved from it. But it was not long before he detected another group of minds. At first the sensation was strange as they appeared to be floating in space. Then he realised it must be the crew of the *New York*; as they seemed to be approaching rapidly, his suspicions were soon confirmed.

'FWN *New York* from Shuttle *Queens*, requesting permission to dock,' Ensign Teilgar was saying.

'Shuttle *Queens* from FWN *New York*, permission granted, please proceed to docking bay 1.'

'FWN *New York* from Shuttle *Queens*, received with thanks.'

The next few minutes passed in silence and David closed his mind off again, then there was a series of hissing noises.

'Sir, we have docked safely.'

'Thank you,' David said. He fumbled to unfasten his harness, stood up and walked to the airlock as it opened onto the docking bay. As he looked out he saw two officers, a male and female. Taking a deep breath to steady his nerves he walked out to meet them.

'Mr Wilhelm, I am Captain Mark Yoland. This is my

executive officer, Maria Ramerase. Welcome aboard the FWN *New York.*'

'Thank you, captain.'

'From our brief conversation, you said you had never been on a spaceship before. Is that correct?'

'Yes, I have never left the planet.'

'You will find that we have a lot of protocols that must be followed. I did ask that you were sent a briefing docket which should have covered the basics.'

'Yes, sir, I received it. They also sent someone to discuss the most important points.'

'How long were they with you for?'

'A day.'

From the look on the captain's face, David could tell he was not impressed. 'You will find on a ship that theory and practice are different. There are skills you will need that can only be gained through repeated practise, I'll assign someone to talk you through them. I won't have you being a hindrance or risk to my crew. But for now I will have you shown to your bunk. When you have unpacked, please come to the bridge and we can talk further.'

Chapter 5

DAVID looked at the small cabin he had been assigned. He thought that his room at the UTA was small, but it was twice the size of this. At least he had the room to himself; he knew from the books he had read that only senior officers had their own quarters and everyone else shared. Was he given his own room out of respect to his consultant's position or because no one wanted to share with him?

There was a narrow bunk with, as he had been told, emergency equipment strapped underneath. Its use had been explained to him when he was briefed but he hadn't had the opportunity to see or practise with it. A narrow metal locker was bolted to the wall and floor and could not be moved. There were communal bathrooms at either end of the corridor, as well as a gym and recreation room on the deck below.

David opened the locker; it was narrow with a shelf at the top and bottom. At least he only had a few possessions so storing them would not be difficult. He placed his things on the bed and decided to organise them later; he felt that the captain would not want him to take too long before he joined him on the bridge.

Leaving the cabin, he followed the directions he had been given and found the bridge. He took a deep breath and walked onto it. 'Permission to come onto the bridge, captain?' he asked nervously, remembering what he had been told about ship protocol.

Captain Yoland stood up and turned. 'Granted. If you

will come with me, we can talk.' He walked off the bridge through another exit. After a brief pause, David followed him. Once the door shut, the captain turned to him.

'David, I will be honest with you. I have severe doubts about how effective your presence will be on this mission, especially as you have no experience of working in space.'

David tried to defend himself. 'I appreciate your concerns, but what I am here to do is something new and untried - both from the UTA and the FWN perspective. You could not have found someone experienced in this or in being in space.'

'I am aware of that but we are going into space for an unknown amount of time. That in itself can cause problems. We're confined, with no way off unless you want to take a walk in space, and no end in sight. All of my crew are experienced in extended tours and know how to deal with it.'

'I am used to bring in a restricted environment.'

'Whatever you think you know, trust me - you don't,' the captain stated. 'You may think that the comfortable training you had at the UTA prepared you for this but, as you said, this is a new trial. No one at the UTA has a clue what stresses a deep-space mission involves. It will be down to me to deal with you and the political fallout when you fail. Added to which, the prospect of having a telepath on board is causing a lot of unrest on this ship. There are reasons why your kind are not allowed join the FWN.'

'What makes you the expert on the UTA and telepaths?' David said angrily. 'How do you know that the training I had there would not be of benefit? And I'm no risk to anyone on your ship.'

'I know that everyone in the FWN spends four years in the academy training for space. The conditions there simulate as closely as possible what it is like on a ship -

and yet there are still several who cannot face the reality of it,' the captain retorted. 'I do know that you have had no training in ship protocol and you have no idea how this mission is going to affect you. Yes, I know someone spoke with you at the UTA about the basics, but that's no more than minimal use. I'm going to have to find someone to train you so you won't be a danger to this ship, yourself or others. If you can't cope, I have to deal with all the ramifications.'

'I understand you have been placed in a difficult position, but it was felt that with the new cloaking technology we're the only ones that can assist,' David explained. 'There will be no blame if this fails. And I can assure you that I will not cause any problems with you or your crew. I'm not permitted to read anybody's mind without permission or unless a lawful exemption applies.'

'And I just take your word for that?'

'No. While we are still within communication range, you can ask what telepaths are legally allowed to do.'

'Maybe I will,' the captain said. 'In the meantime, it will take us a month to get to the area of space where your skills may be of use. Take this time to learn about living on a ship. When we might need your skills, I will let you know.' And with that David was dismissed.

He went back to his room and started to put away his things. There was a knock on his door. 'Come in.' A young man came in; from the markings on his uniform, David deduced he was an ensign.

'Sir, I am Ensign Jon Falconer and I have been assigned to you to ensure that you are aware of the ship's rules and protocols, especially the use of all the emergency equipment.' He was clearly nervous; he kept putting his hands up to his head defensively. David knew that was a common gesture by those who were uncomfortable around telepaths. It was as if they could stop him reading their minds by covering their heads with their hands.

'Thank you,' David said. 'I was given some information before I left, but not much.' He chose to ignore the unconscious movement.

'Yes, sir. I was told to start with the basics so I'm sorry if I repeat things you already know.'

'Even if you do, the revision would be useful,' David reassured him. 'Can you also show me where everything is?'

'Of course. We will start with the canteen and finish with the evacuation pods. I'll even show you how you place yourself into cryo sleep.' David thought Jon sounded way too cheerful when he said that.

✚

At the end of the day David's head was aching more than usual. When he left the UTA he thought he was reasonably well-prepared, but the amount he didn't know about space travel astounded him. No wonder the captain was so annoyed to have him on board. Other than the fact that he was a telepath, of course.

Although David thought his dreams of going into space had been destroyed when his ability surfaced, it had not stopped him researching and reading as much as he could about it. His fascination was always with engineering and he had looked at jobs in this field, much to the annoyance of the UTA because his telepathic ability would not be put to use. The ongoing dispute over the work he should be doing was the only reason he had not yet taken a job. Any work he took needed the UTA's permission and they had refused to allow him anything he wanted to do, until now. When this opportunity had arisen, he was so keen to take the post. They had not wanted him to but, when no one else volunteered, they were left with little choice. The reality was a shock. He was here because the captain had been ordered to take him; he did not want David and resented his presence.

David knew his job would not be easy. He was the first registered telepath on an FWN ship with a crew who had been taught to distrust telepaths and with a task he was not sure he could accomplish. It was going to be a very long trip, but he was determined to make it work.

The knock came again early in the morning. David opened the door, dressed and ready to go.

'Are you ready, sir?' Ensign Falconer asked.

'I'm all yours.' They settled down to work. It didn't take long for Jon to start to relax in David's company. At the start Jon kept glancing at him expecting, no doubt, that he could read his thoughts. But gradually he relaxed and they got along well.

The days fell into a natural, comfortable pattern, Jon Falconer came to David's room every morning and took him to various parts of the ship, explaining their relevance and importance. David now knew why none of the rooms were en suite; even the captain shared a bathroom with his executive officers. This was because all water was recycled and, for efficiency, the bathrooms had to be communal. He learnt that food was strictly regulated, as were fluids. He was shown the gym, and told he should make use of it. Even though spaceships had artificial gravity, it was not the same as the gravity on a planet; on extended tours it became much harder to move planet side at the end so maintaining muscle mass was important. Jon said he would introduce David to some of the crew who were good at fitness training and could help him devise a program. David was surprised; it was the first time Jon had offered to make him known to anyone else. David had to admit that, as Jon was the only one who spoke to him other than the captain, he was starting to feel as lonely and isolated as he had during his first days at the UTA.

'That would be great thanks,' he said.

'Not a problem,' Jon replied. 'I have also spoken to my commanding officer and he has authorised an emergency drill for you.'

'Sounds ominous. What does that entail?'

'Well, before we run it, you need to know how all the equipment works and be able to use it. We will spend time getting you into the survival suits and moving around in them. When you are reasonably comfortable, we will run the drill and show you how to activate the capsules and put yourself into cryo sleep.'

'Sounds fun,' David said sarcastically.

'It should be. Well, for you it won't be but it will be amusing for me to watch you go through it. It's something that you hope you will never need but will be really glad of if disaster strikes.'

'To be honest I'm surprised we did not do it first.'

'What would have been the point when you didn't know where to go?'

'Fair enough. Have you ever had to do this for real?'

'No, but I've had to do lots of drills. Do you know how to put a suit on?'

'I was told in the briefing before I left the UTA.'

'They told you? They did not get you practising?'

'No.'

'Well, now is your chance. There's a life support suit under your bunk. Since it is the one you are most likely to use, let us practise with that one.'

Once back at the room, David pulled out the emergency equipment and unpacked the suit. He thought it would be easy to get it on but, even remembering everything he had been told, he still got stuck and Jon had to help him. He was made to put in on and take it off again and again until Jon called a halt for lunch.

'Now you know how to do it you will need to practise. You need to be able to do it in under a minute and in the dark.'

'Seriously?'

'You will use one of these if the hull is breached and the ship's systems are failing. Everything will work to maintain life support for as long as possible; everything else will be gone, including all but minimal lighting. This suit is your life support - the quicker you get it on, the better your chances of survival. People have worked their entire careers without needing it, but I would make damn sure you know what to do - just in case.'

'Point made.'

'Good. Now, we need to stow the suit away correctly so it won't get damaged, then we go for some lunch and afterwards I will show you how to use the capsules.'

Jon led him into the canteen, which was filling up. Over the last few days they had collected their food under the watchful eyes of the rest of the crew and taken it to wherever they were studying. David collected his rations and waited to see where Jon would lead him to eat. He was surprised when Jon walked towards a table with several others sitting at it. They all seemed happy to see Jon and David assumed it was his normal team. David held back, unsure of what to do. He looked around but there were no empty tables. He was just wondering if he should return to his room when Jon shouted over to him. 'David, stop hovering and get over here.'

He made his way over and the others moved down the bench to make room for him.

'So you are the telepath that Jon is bunking his duties to teach,' the person he sat down next to said.

'That would be me.'

'I can't believe they let you on board,' someone said

from further down the table.

'Sali,' Jon hissed.

'No, it is alright' David said. 'Everyone has the right to their own thoughts and opinions.'

'But my thoughts are not my own with you here. There is a reason why telepaths are not allowed on ships: no one here will have privacy in their own minds.'

David saw others nod their heads in agreement. He felt their hostility and fear. 'Your thoughts are your own while I'm here, just as they were when I was not.'

'Oh come on! Are you really trying to tell me you can't read our minds?'

'I can read your mind. I can read the mind of everyone on board this ship. No one could keep a secret from me if I was determined to find it out, but there are strict regulations about doing that. If I breached them, I would be forced onto medication which would strip me of my abilities. It would take away half of my senses and leave me crippled and disorientated.'

'So we only have your word that you won't read our minds?'

'Even if our regulations didn't forbid it, why would I want to?' David questioned. 'Do you want to hear the conversation of everyone you have ever met, whether you know them or not? Every conversation for miles around you?'

'Of course not.'

'Then why would you think I want to?'

'What you are saying is ridiculous. We can't hear for miles around. What did you mean by that?' someone else asked.

'I mean I can stand on Constitution Hill on Europa and read the minds of everyone at the FWN base,' David said. 'I'm not limited to being in the same room as a person. You don't trust us, but there is no reason not to.'

He spoke to a now-silent canteen.

'So can you read the minds of someone on another ship? How close would they have to be?'

'I don't know. That is why I'm here, to find out what I can do.'

⸭

After lunch Jon took him to an escape capsule and contacted the bridge to let them know what they planned to do.

'When the call comes to abandon ship, get to one of these capsules. They can be crewed by one person. Each capsule has five cyro sleep chambers but the life support can manage as many as ten. If you can, you wait before launching until it is at its maximum capacity. Unlike with your suit, you can't practise this on your own. As soon as I open the door, an alarm will go off on the bridge which is why I contacted them for permission first.'

'Why the difference in the numbers of people it can hold? If the capsules can hold people without cryo sleep, why go into it?'

'The idea is to get everyone off alive. There are enough on this ship for five people to one capsule. If the call to abandon ship comes, it means it has sustained heavy damage and a lot of capsules could have been destroyed. Cryo sleep will be preferable because, depending on where the ship goes down, rescue could take months. The capsules can take extra to account for any that are damaged or those which are not accessible.' With that, Jon activated the hatch and it slid open. 'Now this is how you use it.'

Chapter 6

DAVID was relieved when he got back to his cabin. Everything he had learned today was necessary but it had brought home the dangers of space travel and unsettled him, especially as he did not know if he would be any help.

He remembered what he had been asked during lunch about sensing people in other ships and cursed himself. He did not know the answer and had not tried once since being on board. He had no real excuse other than being caught up in his training. They were still a considerable distance from where the attacks were happening; he guessed the captain would not bother him till then but there was no harm in trying now.

He pulled off his boots, lay down on the bunk, closed his eyes and concentrated. He felt the familiar buzzing of all the minds on the ship; it had been disorientating when he had first boarded. As he had moved around the ship and the buzzing moved, it was like waves in his mind but now he pushed them aside and moved passed them to nothing.

Silence.

For the first time since his abilities had surfaced, he heard nothing and revelled in it. It was not the same silence he felt when given the medication that suppressed his abilities when he first went into the UTA. Then he had felt as if he were locked in a box, able to see out but trapped and helpless. This was peace; this was solitude. He let his mind drift for a while, enjoying being alone with his own thoughts. He was not sure how long he remained like that before he pushed his mind out as far as he could from the ship, but there was still nothing.

He changed the direction of his focus and slowly moved around the circumference of the ship, but continued to feel nothing. He had no reference points to know how far he was searching, so he narrowed his focus and pushed out further, pushed as far as he could. He slowly swept his mind around the ship and then there it was: a glimmer of conscious minds. David pushed as hard as he could to try and find out more but there was nothing, no overriding anger or hostility.

'DAVID, DAVID!' He jumped and brought his mind back. He heard banging and the buzzer going from his door. He reached over and hit the door release by the bed. Jon and another of the men from the table rushed in.

'Jon, what?' he asked. He put his hands to his throbbing head and felt the sweat that beaded his face.

'You were supposed to meet me for dinner. When you did not come, I tried calling. What happened to you? You look like hell.'

'Thanks.'

'David,' Jon said as he came further into the room. The worry was clear on his face. 'Has someone done something to you?'

'No, this is self-inflicted. I tried to see what I could sense in space and pushed too far.'

'And did you find anything?'

'There is a vessel behind us, I can't tell how far and I was trying to find out more when you arrived, but it was so far away that I could not pick up much.'

Jon went to the communication panel. 'Bridge from Ensign Falconer receiving.'

'Ensign Falconer go ahead.'

'I am with Mr Wilhelm. He says he can sense a vessel behind us, no further details known. Do you have anything on your sensors?'

'Stand by.' Then after a few moments: 'There is a freight vessel eighteen clicks to our rear. There is nothing else in our vicinity at present.'

Jon looked enquiringly at David who nodded. 'Thank you, bridge. He is only picking up that one.' He cut the connection.

Slowly David sat up and swung his legs over the side of the bed.

'You really don't look too good. Do you need me to call a medic?'

'No, I will be fine in a moment. It was just harder than I thought to sense ships in space.'

'Eighteen clicks? It is a very impressive distance. I would not have thought it possible for you to have that reach.'

'Eighteen clicks, that is eighteen thousand miles right?'

'Yes.'

'That can't be right. I don't have anything near that sort of range.'

'Then there must be another ship out there that the sensors are not detecting.' Jon moved back to the communication panel.

'Wait,' David said and Jon paused. 'My range is dependent on how populated an area is. There is no real population in space. What I felt were people going about their regular activities, I felt nothing threatening or hostile.'

'You are sure there is just that one vessel?'

'Yes.' Jon dropped his hand and David pushed himself up off the bed. 'Are you ready for dinner?' he asked and walked out of the cabin.

Jon looked at his colleague as David walked out. 'I will

give you a report for the captain and see what he thinks.'

*

'Mr Wilhelm, please report to the bridge,' the tannoy announced.

David looked at Jon. 'I guess I'd better make my way?' Jon nodded his agreement.

As he walked down the corridors, David did not have to be a telepath to know why he was being summoned to the bridge. The captain had been told about his little experiment yesterday. Should he have asked first?

At the bridge he was about to ask permission to enter when the captain turned and saw him. 'David, thank you for being so prompt. Please come in. I was informed that Ensign Falconer called the bridge last night, asking if the scans were picking up a ship to our rear. You had sensed something but could not give a distance or direction. Is that correct?'

'Yes sir, I was practising before we left the regulated trade routes to see what I could sense. Ensign Falconer wanted to make sure that what I could feel was on the sensors and was not a threat to the ship.'

'I have to be honest, I don't understand what you can and can't do. But the fact that you understand your abilities and limitations and are working towards this mission is a credit to you. This is Ensign Talik and he works navigation on the bridge. Is it possible to work with him to see that whenever you pick up a ship you can estimate the location and distance of the vessel?'

'I would be more than happy to try, sir.'

'Good. There are ships less than eighteen clicks from here at present, which I understand was the distance of the freight yesterday. Are you ready to see what you can achieve?'

'Yes, sir.' David sat down at the navigation terminal

next to Talik, who looked at him nervously.

'Sir, I know where each vessel is in terms of distance and location. I don't know how you can sense them and if there is any way to give direction. The captain is worried that if you sense a threat and we can't detect it, it won't be much help.'

'I'm not sure how to work out distance but yesterday was my first attempt. I can tell the direction in relation to the ship, I just have no idea how to vocalise it other than that way,' David said pointing in a random direction.

'Well, let us see if we can improve on that.'

⊹

'You look as bad as you did yesterday,' Jon said as David joined him at the table in the canteen.

'The captain knew that you called the bridge yesterday about the ship I sensed. He has me working with navigation to try and improve my ability to locate the ships. My brain feels over-extended.'

'I have no idea what that feels like, but I am guessing it is uncomfortable.' David snorted. 'Does this mean that I am not training you anymore?'

'No, it means I'll be called when they are picking up ships close by. Other than that, I'm still all yours. Sorry.'

'Don't be,' Sali said as he sat down with them, closely followed by several others. 'He has been enjoying skivvying from normal duties and shift work.' Jon picked up some food from his plate and threw it at him.

'I thought you said nothing should ever be wasted,' David said.

'Shut up.'

⊹

The next three weeks followed a pattern of sorts. Some days David and Jon worked all day without interruption, other days David was summoned to the bridge to work with the navigation officer. He got better at judging how far away ships were and where they were in relation to himself. He also got better at filtering out everyone on the ship and improved the distance he could sense ships at. When he spent the whole day on the bridge, he often left with a splitting headache and had to stagger back to his cabin. On these occasions, Jon, Sali or another on their watch brought him food in his cabin. He knew this was against regulations and protested because he did not want anyone to get into trouble but they told him it was fine and not to worry about it. David wondered if the captain had given them permission.

On the days when he was not called to the bridge, he sat in his room and practised. If he sensed something he did not like, he called the bridge to clarify if they had the vessel on their sensors.

'You have today off,' the captain told David. 'You need it.'

'So what do I do?'

'Whatever you want. Ensign Falconer reports that you know everything you need to. You can now say where the ships you sense are and your distance has increased over time. We will soon be coming into the relevant area of space so relax today, before the real work begins.'

David spent the morning in the gym, then went back to his room and started pacing. He tried to see if there were any ships, but there was nothing. At lunch time he went to the canteen, relieved to have something to do, and joined Jon at his table.

'So how are you enjoying your free time?' Jon asked.

'I don't know what to do with myself,' David admitted. 'What is there to do? I have been to the gym, I have nothing to clean or organise, I have no work. I have nothing to read as my files at the UTA can't transfer over to the ships systems. I am bored,' he said, sounding very frustrated.

'You just chill,' Sali said unhelpfully.

'I've not shown you how to download books or videos, have I?' Jon said.

'No.'

'Sorry, I was so focused on the operational side, I forgot about everything else. When you have finished eating I will show you what is available for when we have down time.'

'Please do.'

Chapter 7

SIX weeks after they left the regulated trade routes and started to hunt the cloaked ships they still had not found anything. The number of vessels David detected was becoming few and far between. His training with Jon had finished and he had returned to his normal duties, which left him on his own for hours every day. He lay on the bunk and stretched his mind as far as he could but sometimes it was days before he felt anything. When he did he called the bridge and they always had the vessel on their sensors. He knew they were looking for the proverbial needle in a haystack, but that did not stop him feeling frustrated and useless.

He spent a lot of time on his own, often sitting in his room reading or eating alone in the canteen. When Jon's shifts allowed, David met up with him and his watch; the more time he spent with them, the less hostile and suspicious they became. That was helped by his willingness to answer any questions they had about telepaths.

'So you tell us,' one of them asked, 'you are not allowed to read our minds, yet you are allowed to see where these ships are. How does that work?'

'I am not reading minds when I search for the ships. I am searching for minds and the mood.'

'What is the difference? You are still reading minds.'

After a moment, as others waited, David started to explain, 'I am not allowed to read minds. Similarly, listening devices can't be used to listen to conversations without proper authorisation. What I am doing is similar to when you are trying to find a room with people in it and you listen for a rumble of voices without listening to what they are saying. When I say I am picking up a mood, it is like picking up a tone of voice or reading body language. Does that make sense?'

'Sort of. I guess not having any experience in what you do makes it hard to understand the difference. For now, I will accept your word that you won't read my mind,' Jon joked.

'As if he would want to explore your perverted thoughts,' Sali retorted.

'You are a fine one to talk,' Jon said and they all laughed.

✴

David was lying on his bunk, scanning the space around the ship, when the door buzzed. He had been concentrating so hard that for a moment he thought he had misheard; he rarely had unplanned visitors. Then the door buzzed again. David hit the release button by the bed, expecting to see Jon or one of his friends, but was surprised as it was someone he did not know.

'David Wilhelm?' the man asked.

'Yes.'

'Jon Falconer asked me to come by. Can I come in?'

'Of course.' David swung his legs off the bed and stood up. 'How can I help you?'

'Jon seems to think I need to help you. He said that you did not know anything about space and he had to train you in all the protocols. He said he told you about the gym but he does not know if you have been using it and he has not given you any training programs.' The man said nervously. 'Though to be honest, he is not very good at it himself. He knows what he needs to do but nothing more, so I would not trust anything he gave you.'

'I have been there once or twice. I never really used a gym much before, but that does not explain why you are here.'

'It is one of the things I do on the ship. I create fitness programs for the crew and do general health assessments. If there are any warning markers, they get referred to the medical bay for further tests. You are not part of the FWN and are not subject to these regulations but Jon asked me what would happen if you did not exercise so I said I would come and talk to you.'

'Well, thank you, but I exercised a lot on the planet. I plan to do something so my fitness levels don't fall too much. I think I will be fine.'

'But you have always lived on a planet. Though the artificial gravity here is good, it is not the same. If you don't work out probably while on board you could find a planet's gravity crushing when you return. Though running is good, you really need to work on weights and resistance. You need to build muscle mass on board ship.'

'I never heard that this was a problem.'

'It is not normally. From the start of training we are taught what we should do. Once we graduate, we do short assignments in space and if we cannot deal with it we never go on long missions. You have none of these safeguards and none of the training. For you it might be a problem. Exercise is so ingrained into our training that by the time you are accepted onto a ship like the *New York*, training habits are as ingrained as eating.'

'How does everyone else cope? There are private transport ships and cargo vessels.'

'If you work in space, you know what to do and how to train. For passengers on vessels, they are going from point A to B and are rarely in space long enough to be affected adversely.'

'I remember Jon saying I had to go but I did not realise it was that important. I just use the cardio machines. I have never used weights.'

'You need to go most days if you don't want problems when you get back to a planet. As I said, I can help you with training programs.'

'I take it you are available now?'

'Yes, sir, if it is convenient to you.'

'Lead on.' David stood up and grabbed his gym bag, 'I don't know your name,'

'Yelish, Bralik Yelish.'

Bralik put him through hell in the gym that day and for the next few days. Compared to people at the UTA David was considered relatively fit. What a joke! He thought Bralik had never had to train someone as unfit as himself, but the trainer remained patient with him. While they worked Bralik liked to chat to pass the time.

'So this telepath academy clearly does not place any emphasis on fitness. What did you learn there?'

'The main focus was on controlling and developing our abilities. After that it was normal academic studies.'

'What sort of things did you like to study?'

'Maths and engineering mainly, but they never took it as far as I would have liked. Most of what I know I got out of books.'

'If you have an interest in the subject, why not allow you to take it as far as you can?'

'Engineering is not a career that needs telepaths. They would prefer us to go into law and politics.'

Bralik threw his head back and laughed. 'Why does that not surprise me? My partner is an engineer on board. After we are finished here, I can take you down there and introduce you, if you like.'

'Yes, that would be great,' David said, surprised at the offer.

*

After that everything became easier. Before every meal David scanned the space around the ship; if he picked up anything he called it into the bridge, but they were always aware of it. After breakfast he went to the gym for an hour before going back to his cabin and studying the material Kate Jenson, Bralik's partner, had given him. After lunch he went down to engineering and spent the afternoon putting what he had learnt into practice and after dinner, if there were ships close by, he worked with the navigation officer on the bridge.

As time went on and he got to know more people, the crew started to accept him and their perceptions of him changed. Now he always had people to spend time with. If it was not Jon and his friends, it was people who worked engineering or others he met in the gym.

⁜

'You wished to see me, captain?' the chief engineer, Famar Redek, asked as he entered the captain's office.

'Yes, sorry to pull you out of engineering. I wanted to make sure there were no problems with our resident telepath. I hear he has been spending a lot of time in engineering.'

'Yes, sir, he started in there about two weeks ago.'

'Is he causing problems for your crew? It was never my idea to have him here and I will support you if he is causing any disruption.'

'No, sir, he is fine. I understand he has made a lot of friends with other crew members. When they heard about his interest in engineering, he was invited to visit. I think they were curious about him but I understand that he is very bright and is making himself useful. Are you concerned about him working with the ship's systems?'

'No. I was concerned that his presence would cause unrest but that hasn't happened. If you and your crew are happy for him to work there then he can stay. If there are any problems, let me know straight away.'

'Of course,' Famar said. 'Though I will say I am surprised by him. Like you, I was not happy with having him on board and neither were my crew, but they certainly accept him now. He has made several good friends.'

'Thank you, Famar. I think a lot of us are having to re-think our views about telepaths.'

⁜

As the days wore on, the ship started to buzz with news of attacks along other trade routes. There was some discussion about whether there was any point in what they were doing; space was too huge for one ship to make any difference.

'We only have to get lucky once,'

'But how long will that take?'

'No one knows, that is why this is an opened-ended mission,' the retort came.

'How much use is one telepath going to be? Seriously, has anyone thought about it?'

'How stupid are you? Of course they have! Did you not pay attention during the briefing?' The man's colleagues laughed.

David sat at a table nearby and smiled. The attitude on the ship had certainly changed since he had been on board and it gave him hope that they would let him stay when this was over.

⁜

'There have been two more attacks on other routes. The last one had fatalities,' Admiral Yoland told his son during a conference call.

'Do you want us to change our position?'

'No. Neither of the attacks were close to each other. You move position and they could move in. Wherever you are will be a gamble on whether you catch them or not. How is it going with the telepath?'

'Surprisingly well. The crew have really taken to him.'

'Good. The UTA were very unhappy about him coming on board though they would not say why.'

'Then why did he get the place?'

'He really wanted it and the UTA could not offer anyone better. There is a lot of interest in how well a telepath can work on a ship. If this is successful it could bring a lot of changes.'

'I had my doubts, you know I did, but this is working better than I hoped - even if we don't find a rogue ship.'

'Good. Please keep me updated on your progress,' his father said, and the connection was cut.

Chapter 8

DAVID walked into the canteen and saw Jon sitting with his team on a table nearby. He smiled at them and walked over. He had not seen Jon for a few days due to the shifts he had been working.

'So, you are still talking to us then?' Jon asked him. 'I heard a rumour that you were too good for us now you have all those friends in engineering.'

'And here I was thinking that you were avoiding me,' David retorted.

Jon laughed and moved further down the table to make room for him. 'It is good to see you settling into ship life so well.'

'I am. Everyone has been very friendly.'

'I'm surprised you have found it so easy, never having left a planet before. Many people find this kind of travel claustrophobic.'

'Until I had control of my abilities, I was never allowed anywhere. I'm used to being confined. No, I like it here, it is quiet.'

'In these close confines? That is one of the worst things about being on a ship - you can't get away from everyone,' Sali said.

'Unless you are lucky enough to have your own room,' Jon retorted.

'Which is still the size of a cupboard,' David replied.

'But seriously, it drives us nuts so it must be worse for you.'

'No, I have never known it to be so quiet. I'm sleeping

better than I have since I was a child and I'm getting a lot less headaches.' They all looked at him, stunned.

'I'm sorry, David, we don't understand. How can so many people in a small area not be difficult for you?' Jon asked.

'How many people are on this ship?'

'I'm not sure exactly, about a thousand all together.'

'How many live on estates at home? How many estates are next to each other?' David asked. 'There may be a thousand people on the ship but on a planet there are millions more. There is nowhere to go for silence once you leave the training rooms of the UTA.'

'I thought you said you could not read minds unless you wanted to?'

'I can't, but when there are a lot of people it is like being next to a room with a crowd talking. You can't hear what they are saying but that background noise is always there and I can't turn it off,' David said, putting a hand that was shaking slightly to his temple. 'Noise, there is always noise.'

'I don't see why you are so wound up by it, especially if you are saying it is so quiet now,' Sali said.

'Then you are a fool,' David snapped.

'David!' Jon said, shocked.

'I'm sorry,' he said. 'I don't know....' and he lapsed into silence.

'David?' Jon asked, worried by his friend's strange behaviour.

'Just give me a moment.' The whole table sat there and looked at him, waiting. The seconds ticked by and David sat, frozen. No one dared move. Suddenly David took a deep breath. 'Where is the nearest communication unit?' he asked suddenly.

'There is one on the wall,' Jon said, pointing. He was confused because he knew David had used it before, but now his friend seemed panicked and disorientated.

As David stood up, he almost fell over his chair in his desperation to get to the communication unit. Jon got up and followed him, watching as David tried to type in the code for the bridge. When his shaking hands hit the wrong key the second time, Jon did it for him and the connection was made.

'Bridge, are you receiving?' David called, forgetting protocol.

'Bridge is receiving. Who is this?'

'David Wilhelm. You have two ships aft. One is a small cargo vessel but the other one is closing on it and it is hostile, very hostile.'

There was a brief pause and then: 'Report to the navigation station on the bridge, Mr Wilhelm. We are only detecting one vessel.'

'I'm on my way,' David said. He turned and saw Jon standing behind him. A look of understanding passed between them and Jon stepped out of his way.

'Guys, we need to get back to our posts,' Jon shouted. He and the rest of the team headed for their own positions as the ship-wide alert started to sound.

⁂

David ran onto the bridge, then paused briefly as he realised he had forgotten ship protocol again.

'Report to navigation,' the captain ordered. David saw that the main screen was showing the cargo vessel and nothing else. The navigation officer had the same information on the screen in front of her.

'Sir,' she acknowledged. 'I can't get a reading on another vessel. My sensors are saying that there is only the one vessel.'

'There is another vessel out there, trust me,' David said.

'What can you tell me about the second ship? If we are going to open fire, I want to be sure I am doing it because it is cloaked and hostile and not because of a computer malfunction.'

'The ship was not in my range two hours ago. The crew are very hostile and are looking forward to a fight. Their focus is on the cargo vessel - I don't think they are even aware of us. If they are, they don't care.'

'Then let us give them one. Can you can you give co-ordinates accurate enough for firing?' the captain asked.

'It is closing fast and is coming up on 176 eals to the rear of the cargo vessel.'

'Based on that information, it is coming into firing range. Get the weapons ready to fire.'

'Ready sir,' said an ensign who David did not recognise.

'Inputting the co-ordinates now for targeting,' David said.

'Co-ordinates received.'

'Can you fire safely without harming the cargo vessel?' the captain asked.

'Yes sir.'

'Fire one round based on the information given.'

'Firing now.'

David watched the screen as the round left the ship, sped out and hit a target. He saw the explosion. 'Their focus has changed to us,' he warned.

'Damage report?' the captain asked.

'The ship is shedding debris, enough for us to track,' the navigation officer said.

'Confirmed. I can now get a weapons lock. I am also picking up a heat signature. I believe they are getting ready to fire.'

'Fire again.'

Again David saw the shots leave the ship and impact. This time he sensed it was a better hit, and instead of the anger he felt the first time he now felt panic. He pushed his mind out further to try and get more information. All of a sudden he could not breathe. He started to claw at his face as if to remove a mask that was not there. He heard someone calling his name but could not pull his mind back to respond, he was too tied up with what was happening on the other ship.

Pain exploded across his face, the shock making him take a sharp intake of breath - and his connection was broken.

'David.' He opened his eyes to see the captain standing in front of him.

'The hull has been breached and life support is failing fast. They are all suffocating on board.' David gasped, desperate to get air into his lungs.

'Other than debris, I am picking up nothing, I can't give a damage report.' The navigation officer said.

'David, you are the only one who can advise. Do we fire again?'

'No, the crew are dead or dying. To fire again will just cause unnecessary damage.'

'Lieutenant Commander Ramerase, get a crew together and take two shuttles over to the ship. Let us see what we have got.'

'Yes sir,' Ramerase said and started calling out names.

David collapsed and held his head, shaking. He had never felt a mind die before and now he was feeling many of them. He could hear screaming but did not know where it came from. It continued until a he felt a sharp pain to the side of his face and knew no more.

※

'David.' He was being called but his head hurt so much. At first he tried to ignore it and for a moment everything went quiet again but then the shaking started and he was forced to open his eyes, if only to get them to stop. The captain stood above him, looking down, and he realised that he was lying on a sofa. Somewhere in the back of his mind he remembered the feeling of being half carried, half dragged.

'Good, you are awake,' the captain said.

David groaned and slowly tried to pull himself up into a sitting position. He collapsed down as pain shot through his head. 'The other ship?' he asked as he rubbed his temples.

'They have reported back exactly as you said. The hull was breached and life support had failed. They had no escape capsules on board. They were using the space for extra weapons and storage. By the time we docked they had all died,' the captain explained. 'I have called a medic to make sure you are alright.'

'I'm fine. I don't need a medic, they can't do anything for me. I have medication in my room, which is all I need.' David was aware that the captain was calling someone to go and collect it. Once he had finished talking, David asked, 'So what happens now?'

'We will tow the ship back to Starbase Ra and await further orders. I am sorry for punching you.'

David looked at him, confused for a moment, then registered the ache in his jaw and the dried blood on his split lip. He remembered the pain that had helped him cut the mental connection with the dying crew and realised what had happened.

'Don't be, you gave me what I needed,' he replied. As he closed his eyes and rubbed his sore jaw, there was a knock on the door. There was a murmur of voices, the whoosh of a closing door.

'Are these what you need?' the captain asked.

David opened his eyes and saw a small bottle. 'Thank you.' He opened it and swallowed a capsule. After a moment he breathed a sigh of relief as the medication started to work. Carefully he sat up and swung his legs around so he was sitting on the sofa.

'Is there anything else you need?'

'A drink would be good.'

A glass with a rich brown liquid in it was put down on the table next to him. 'I didn't need to be a telepath to know that,' the captain said as he raised his own glass. David picked up his glass and looked at the amber liquid; he had meant water but suddenly this seemed far more appropriate. He lifted it in a return salute before taking a sip. The fiery liquid burned the back of his throat and heated his limbs.

'I hate to ask, David, since you look so rough, but I have to for the safety of this ship and crew. Are there any other hostile vessels out there?'

David put the glass down, leaned back on the sofa and closed his eyes. After a moment he opened them. 'I can still sense the original cargo vessel and your crew on the damaged ship but nothing else.'

'Thank you for checking.'

'Don't thank me, it's what I am here for. Besides it's my safety too. I'll keep checking to make sure.'

'Thank you. When you said the punch was what you needed, what did you mean? What was happening to you?'

'I could feel them all dying, feel their fear and their fight to breathe. I had a hundred minds panicking in my mind. As a result I panicked and could not disconnect from them. The pain from the punch grounded me and gave me the distraction I needed to break the link.'

'This can't be the first time that's happened. Surely you have systems in place to help you.'

'There are, but they involve other telepaths.'

'If there are other telepaths on board, they are

untrained, undeclared and undetected. So without another telepath to help, what's the best thing to do?'

'A significant pain distraction.'

'Like a punch?'

'Like a punch,' David confirmed. 'Cheers, sir,' he said, raising his glass.

'When we're not on the bridge it is Mark.' The captain clinked his glass and they both drank.

Chapter 9

FINALLY, after nearly a month, they approached Starbase Ra with the rogue vessel in tow. It was not the nearest base but it was the largest science station in this sector of space. The specialists had been informed and were meeting them there.

The trip had been surprisingly uneventful. David continued to scan space, looking for threats. Further attacks had been expected so everyone was on edge, ready for action. No one knew for sure if a mayday had gone out, if the vessel was being looked for. Would others try and retrieve it? No one knew how many other ships were out there but, by the spread and time of attacks, there were at least a dozen.

As they started the trip to the starbase, David felt that every movement he made was being assessed. His subconscious reaction to the rogue vessel in the canteen had spread quickly so people read more into his actions than they should have done. At first he was dispirited, thinking that their original mistrust had resurfaced, but though they were alert they were not nervous of him. David realised that they were watching him for an advanced warning of an attack. As the days passed and nothing happened, the crew settled back into their routines.

David did not need to hear the announcement warning the crew of their arrival at Ra; he had been aware of it for the last few hours. He could sense the minds and slowly started increasing his mental boundaries to keep out the noise.

He was still lying on his bunk with his eyes closed when the knock on his door came. 'Come in,' he shouted as he released the door lock. Jon walked in.

'We've docked. I wondered if you wanted me to show you around the base. I know you have never been on one before.'

'How long will we be here for?'

'I don't know. It could be a few hours or a few days. We will stay until we are given permission to leave. Are you alright?' Jon asked when David did not respond immediately.

'I'm fine, I had just got used to the silence on the ship,' he said, as he swung his legs off the bed and stood up.

'Are you alright to come onto the base?'

'It makes no difference if I stay here or go onto the base. I would like to see it though. Who knows if I will ever get the chance again.'

'Why would you not?' Jon asked as they walked down to the air hatch that attached them to the docking bay.

'I was asked to help you get a rogue vessel and we now have one. You know the FWN do not employ telepaths. Why would they let me stay now I have done what I was employed to do?'

'We would not have got the ship without you. They must see that we still need you. It is not as if the new technology will be developed and installed overnight.'

'The politics around this are out of our control. The UTA did not want me to come, so will probably demand my return now I have fulfilled my duties. And the FWN only wanted me because they had no choice. The fact that I want to stay and you want me to stay won't matter.'

'When we were told you were coming on board, nobody was happy about it. A few were even transferred off because they were so vocal about it. The captain thought they would cause trouble on the ship. I had never met a telepath before and I thought you would strip my mind of all my thoughts, but you won me over and you have won the crew over.'

'Thank you. I have enjoyed my time here but I still don't think I will be allowed to remain,' David said as they walked onto the base.

⁜

He had thought that the base would follow the same sterile regulations as the ship and the port on Europa. In some ways he was right: there was the same type of lighting and, as they walked off the ship, the corridors were the same. It all changed, though, when they reached the communal area.

David stopped to take it all in. In front of him was a large open area. Some of the space was taken up by tables and chairs outside what looked like food and drink establishments. He was now being hit with physical noise as well as mental, and also smells that made his mouth water.

'Is the food better here than on the ship?'

'Oh yes. Come with me.' Jon led him to an establishment, where they sat down and looked at the menus before placing their orders.

As he ate, David saw that there were other shops as well, places to buy clothes, weapons, tools, even souvenirs. There were also communication booths; as he watched, he saw several of the *New York* crew go in. 'What is that place?' he asked.

'The communication booths? It is where we can pick up and send any messages to friends and family. It is how we all keep in touch.'

'You can't do it from the ship?'

'No,' Jon said, laughing. 'Urgent messages can be sent

with the authority of the captain and received through the bridge - and if you want to pay a small fortune, you can send them as well. Is there no one you want to talk to?'

'Not that I can think of.' David thought that he should maybe send a message to his father but he did not know what to say other than that everything was going well. He decided against it. 'Do people stay on the starbase?' he asked, after a pause.

'Obviously the people who live and work here do. We can hire rooms here if we want to but we would have to pay for them ourselves. Some do it for some privacy but most of us stay on the ship. When we have finished eating, I will show you the other attractions of this place.'

⁜

'Captain, thank you for joining us,' Commander Xhia said as Mark Yoland walked onto the dry dock where the rogue vessel had been placed. Next to the commander was a senior engineer in the FWN, Val Dempster, who was overseeing the work. The ship had been attached to the starbase's life support and Mark could see people going in and out of it.

'Is the ship of any use?' he asked. Mark had hoped to be docked for only a day or two before getting new orders and moving on. He hated being in one place for too long and they had now been here for a week with no explanation as to the delay.

'It is damaged. The shields failed and the hull breached, killing everyone on board. Medical have removed all the bodies we found. I believe the systems we need are intact but it will take time to work them out. Once we understand them, we need to find out how to counteract them and then install them to our fleet,' Val informed him.

'So it is going to take time for this ship to be of use, if ever.'

'I am confident that we will get there, I just don't know how long it will take.'

'Why are you telling me this? Do you want me to get you another ship?'

'That is not necessary right now - we feel we can get what we need from this one. If we find undetected damage, we may ask you to bring in a second one.'

'So why am I still here?'

'Your reports have been reviewed at FWN headquarters. They are encouraged by how well your crew have accepted a telepath on board,' Commander Xhia said.

'I admit I was dubious at first but David has proved to be an asset. He's gained the trust of those he comes into contact with. His abilities were key to our success.'

'I am relieved to hear that.'

'Why?'

'The FWN are concerned that the attacks will continue. Until Val and her team work out a way to detect them, we are still at as much risk as we were before. Headquarters want you to go back on patrol with David to try and take out any other cloaked ships. Make them think we can hurt them more than we can.'

'Why not capture more and allow other teams to work on them?'

'We only have enough room for the one. The distance you would have to travel with a second ship would not be worth the time or effort, especially since the specialists are all here,' Commander Xhia explained.

'Why was I not contacted directly about these orders?'

'At the moment they are not orders. The admiral of the fleet wanted you to be fully aware of the situation before the request was put to you. They want David back out with you on the *New York* but they can't order him out.

The arrangement was that he help bring in a ship, which he has done. According to the UTA, his task has been completed and they are not under any further obligation to the FWN. They have reluctantly stated that should David wish to remain and assist us, then of course he can.'

'So they want me to convince him to come back out with us,' Mark surmised.

'Yes. They feel that the request would be better coming from you. Should he agree, you will have official orders to go back out and attack any rogue ships you find.'

✠

Mark Yoland was surprised to find David in engineering. While they were on the base, only a skeleton crew was required to maintain the systems. He stood back, listening as they talked about how the engines ran, what could go wrong and how to repair them. He smiled to himself. This was a hopeful sign.

Someone noticed him and the crew came to attention. A few passed worried glances as if they had been caught doing something they should not.

'David, can I have a word with you?' Mark asked.

'Yes, sir.'

'Come with me to the bridge.' Mark turned and walked out with David following. They walked in silence through the corridors onto the bridge and into the captain's office. Mark poured two drinks and handed one to David.

'Is there anything wrong, Mark?' David asked, thinking that this was it, this was when he would be asked to leave. He had been expecting it ever since they docked and had packed his few belongings in preparation. That was why he was in engineering: he was trying to learn as much as he could before it was too late.

'The scientists think that it is going to take them longer

than they thought to develop the technology to detect cloaked ships. FWN headquarters want us to go back out and patrol the areas where the attacks took place and destroy any of the ships that we come across. I would like you to stay on board and help us find them.'

'What do your headquarters think about me staying on board?'

'They want you to, and the UTA have stated they will support your decision either way. You can't be ordered to stay but I would like you to. And from what I've seen of the crew, how they have accepted you and working though their down time, I think they would also welcome your presence.'

'If that was a problem then I'm sorry. The engines had to be off for what they were showing me. They said it was not a problem.'

'How they spend their down time is up to them, just as long as everything is in order when we need to go. Engineers spend years learning the systems; they have a lot more to show you if you remain.'

'I would like to stay very much.'

'I don't know how long we will be out for. I doubt our orders will change until the technology is developed and the scientists don't have a time scale.'

'It does not matter to me how long we are out for. I have no close friends or family who I will miss or who will miss me. I like it on the ship. I like to think I have made friends here and it is quiet.'

'Quiet? There is always noise.'

David laughed, remembering the conversation in the canteen with his friends. 'Different sort of noise. On this ship there are only about a thousand minds to block out instead of hundreds of thousands on a planet. To me it is very quiet.'

'I guess I never thought of it like that.'

'It is amazing, you know,' David said, taking a sip from the glass and feeling the hot liquid burn down his throat. 'My mental range in space is incredible, further than I could ever have believed possible. When I was asked to come I jumped at the chance, it was what I always wanted. But privately I thought they were mad. A few miles in space is very limited but without having to push through thousands of minds to reach my goal, my mind flies. I have never felt so free.'

'So the range you have shown here you can't do on a planet?'

'God no, nowhere near.'

'So if you were to leave the ship in a shuttle, if it was just you and the pilot, would your range increase further?'

'Obviously I have never tried it but in theory, yes.'

'Would you like to try?'

'Most definitely'

'So what do you say,' Mark held out his glass, 'to another mission and new experiments.'

'To another mission and new experiments,' David responded and tapped his glass against the captain's.

Chapter 10

'GOOD morning, sir.' A petite blonde girl in a jumpsuit greeted David as he walked into the shuttle bay. Once David had agreed to stay on board the *New York* they left the Starbase the following day, but it was not until they had cleared the trade routes that the captain had authorised him to go out in a shuttle.

'Good morning. Are you Ensign Winters?'

'Yes, sir. If you're ready, we will get going.'

'Please lead on.'

She tapped a code into the side of the shuttle, the door slid open and a ramp came down. Ensign Winters indicated that he should precede her into the craft. He walked in and looked around, wondering where he should sit; the only time he had ever been in a shuttle was for his brief transfer to the *New York*.

Ensign Winters came in behind him and sealed the hatch. 'You can sit up with me in the co-pilot's seat, if you wish.'

'Thank you. Is there a reason why there is not a second pilot?'

'We don't need one. We won't be out for long and we won't be leaving the range of the *New York*.'

'Fair enough,' David said as he sat down and strapped in, trying to remember how Ensign Teilgar did it on his short trip from Europa to the *New York*.

Ensign Winters sat next to him in the pilot's seat and checked that he had secured himself correctly before strapping herself in. She called the bridge for permission to leave and he felt the engines ignite and the shuttle move off. He felt the minds on the *New York* get further and further away from him until they were a small ball of collective consciousness; he closed his eyes and revelled in the near silence.

'Are you alright?'

'I'm fine, just enjoying the quiet.'

'Why don't you open your mind up and enjoy everything.'

David opened his eyes and looked at her in surprise. 'I can't, I would not be able to stop myself from reading your thoughts.'

'I know. My brother Paul is a telepath. When I'm home I take him up in a shuttle to give him a respite. He has told me what he can do, what it is like for him so I know what I'm saying when I suggest it. I do not have anything to hide - living with a telepath has taught me it's easier to be open about everything. I trust you to keep what you find to yourself.'

'I don't think it would be a good idea,' David said, but he had to admit he was very tempted.

'Fair enough,' she said. 'Just know I volunteered to take you out knowing what I was going to offer you. The offer remains if you change your mind.' David turned and looked at her, not sure what to say. 'There is no hidden agenda,' she continued. 'You would know if there was as soon as you opened your mind - and where would that leave us? I offer it because I know what it means to my brother. I'm used to having my mind read by him and I don't mind. That is all there is to it.'

'I want to,' he admitted, 'but I have not done it since I learnt control. I don't know how far I would reach or the damage I could do.'

'What rating are you?' she asked. When David did not reply, she turned to look at him, confused about his silence. 'Mr Wilhelm? My brother and his friends are fine at this distance and I know I can take it.'

'I have not told anyone else what level I am and until you, no one has asked.'

'So? I don't understand why you don't want to say.'

'You know telepaths are not popular in the FWN. I don't want to cause further tensions.'

'Most of the crew won't have a clue what the ratings mean and I promise I won't say anything to anyone.'

Finally he said, 'I am a level ten.'

'Bloody hell,' she said. For all of her acceptance of telepaths, she glanced at him nervously. 'Paul said there are only a handful at that level and most are insane. He is only a five. Does anyone one else know?'

'Don't worry, I'm one of the few stable tens, otherwise they would not have let me on this ship. I don't know if the captain was told by the UTA, he has not mentioned it to me. I have not told anyone, I did not think it was a good idea on a ship when the FWN is known for not liking or trusting telepaths.'

'I don't blame you,' Ensign Winters said. 'If you want to try opening your mind, I'll ask permission to move further away from the *New York*, or I will teach you fly on your own so you can be totally alone.'

'That would be nice.' She could not fail to hear the yearning in his voice.

'Then let us do what we set out to accomplish today and when we get back I'll ask permission to teach you to fly.'

'Thank you, ensign.'

'Elen. If we are going to be spending a lot of time together, my name is Elen.'

'I'm David.'

✠

'How did it go?' Mark asked him as they sat together in

his office.

'It went well but I don't know how beneficial it was. My range increased when I focused away from the ship but decreased when I focused towards it.'

'How much further could you go?'

David told him and Mark pulled up the various specification. For a few moments he worked on some numbers.

'Well?' David asked.

'With the time it takes for the shuttle to rotate around us, combined with the extra range you have off ship, we gain an extra few clicks,' Mark said. 'According to the report Ensign Winters filed, she recommended that you learn to pilot the shuttle on your own to increase range. Why does she think it would help? What do you both know that I don't?'

'If I'm on my own and away from the ship, I can fully open my mind up. I have never tried it but in theory I could get a considerable extra distance.'

'What do you mean by opening your mind? Why can't you do it here?'

'Because I will strip the knowledge from everyone's mind. I always have to put up barriers around my mind. Ensign Winters and I talked about what would happen if I did not have those barriers in place. I'll be honest: I don't know what will happen but I have to be on my own to try.'

'Do you want to?'

'Yes, very much.'

'Will it harm this ship or any of the crew?'

'No. I would release the barriers slowly. If I was not far enough away, I would keep them in place and ask permission to move further away from the *New York*. I have made friends for the first time - I wouldn't do anything to harm the ship or crew.'

'What about you? The last time you sensed a ship, you got into trouble and I had to punch you to break the connection you had. What if the same thing happens again when you are on your own?'

'I know what to expect now. As soon as I can give you the location, I'll cut the connection and shield against it. Last time was a problem because I didn't know what was going to happen, now I do.'

Mark was silent for a while then said, 'We are out here for the long haul. I would like you to go out in the shuttle at least once a day, twice if possible. While you are up there learn to fly the shuttle if you want to but I want someone to stay with you until we have encountered another rogue vessel. If you can maintain control without intervention, then once I know that you are competent at piloting we can try sending you up on your own. I won't put this ship in danger by having you distracted, but I won't put you in danger by asking too much or pushing too hard. We will review regularly for a balance that works safely. The more rogue ships we can get the better but this is more likely to be a marathon than a sprint. We have the time to get this right.'

'Yes, sir.'

⁜

'Are you ready to take the controls?' Elen asked him. They had been out twice during every shift for the last few weeks and had quickly fallen into a comfortable routine. She took him up and they would do a rotation around the *New York*; anything David sensed was checked and the scans verified with the *New York*. When it was confirmed that there was no threat, Elen started to teach him to pilot and navigate for an hour or two before they completed another rotation around the ship and returned to the docking bay. David then spent several hours in engineering before going back to the docking bay in the evening where the morning routine was repeated.

He was nervous as he reached for the controls for the first time. 'This is just as we practised,' Elen said, trying to reassure him.

'Most people get to do this for the first time on a simulator,' David pointed out nervously.

'That is because they are learning on a planet. You, however, are in the middle of space. Other than the *New York*, there is nothing out here for you to hit. You will be fine.'

'Tell that to the captain when I crash into his ship.'

'Don't worry, you won't hit it.'

'You sound very sure about that.'

'I am. We are a considerable distance away; if you lose control I'll have time to take over and change course. Worst-case scenario and we impact, the shields of the *New York* will destroy us leaving them unscathed,' Elen said cheerfully. 'But the captain would have a nasty report to write, so you had better be careful.'

'That makes me feel so much better.'

'Seriously David we have been through this. You know what to do so just take it slowly,' Elen said. 'I am handing control over to you.' After pushing a few buttons, the panel lit up in front of him. 'Now talk me through what you are doing and why, as you take us slowly around the *New York*.'

Taking a deep breath David moved the shuttle forward.

‡

David handed over the controls to Elen as they approached the *New York*. 'Next time you will dock the shuttle,' she said.

'I look forward to it,' he replied, and meant it. The last

few days he had taken over the controls and was much more confident flying around the *New York*, but this morning was the first time he had flown it out. When he could safely exit and dock the shuttle, he would be allowed out on his own, but he had discussed it with Elen and Mark and they had agreed that no matter how good he was at piloting he would not go out on his own until he had detected a rogue ship and could cope on his own.

Once they were safely docked, he made his farewells and headed for engineering. They were still teaching him but he also had his own work to complete now. He knew that the rest of the crew considered his tasks boring and mundane but they were new to him and gave him a purpose on the ship. He hoped that he would be trusted with more tasks over time and spent several hours reading in his room at night, studying to improve his knowledge.

As the engineering shift ended, he made his way back to the shuttle bay and met up with Elen.

'Are you ready to go?' she asked him.

'You bet,' he replied.

'Then ask permission to leave and, when it is given, slowly take us out,' she said. David followed the drill and flew the shuttle out very slowly. 'As with everything, the more you do it the smoother and faster it becomes. This is only your second time flying out and you are doing fine,' Elen told him.

As David started the rotation around the *New York*, he felt a familiar hostility. 'I need you to take the controls,' he said urgently.

'Why? You're doing fine.'

'There is something out there I don't like the feel of.'

'You are learning to pilot so you can be out on your own. I'm here if you need me but you have to try to deal with this on your own, otherwise there's no point in you going up alone.'

David took a deep breath and directed the shuttle towards the feelings. When they increased to a point where he felt he could gain useful information, he stopped the craft and concentrated. '*New York* receiving from shuttle *Brooklyn*,' he said, hailing the bridge.

'Shuttle *Brooklyn* go ahead.'

'I'm picking up a hostile vessel. Stand by for the co-ordinates.' He typed in the information and passed it over.

'Shuttle *Brooklyn*, please confirm the co-ordinates. We are detecting nothing.'

David checked the information he had sent. 'They're correct. There is only that vessel within my range.'

'Shuttle *Brooklyn*, maintain your position and keep us updated with the vessel's movement.'

David kept a connection with the hostile ship and was aware when the *New York* fired using the information he had given it. Remembering what had happened the last time, he shut his mind off before the missiles hit but he saw his screen light up with the impact.

'Shuttle *Brooklyn* receiving from the *New York*.'

'*New York*, go ahead.'

'The ship has now been disabled and is on our sensors. Please complete a full rotation to ensure there is no other hostile vessel, then return to the ship for a debrief.'

'Received by shuttle *Brooklyn*,' David started moving the shuttle forward around the *New York* but felt nothing, not even the hostile vessel. The *New York* had not just disabled it but had destroyed it.

As they came in for the approach, Elen took over the controls. 'Now is not the time for your first docking,' she said, and David gladly handed them over.

As he walked off the shuttle the captain was waiting

for him. 'Are you alright?' he asked.

'I am, thank you.'

'Will you both join me in the briefing room?' The captain turned and walked out of the door. David and Elen followed him; it had not been a request.

As the door shut behind them, the captain indicated that they should sit down. 'Tell me everything that happened.'

After a quick glance at Elen, David started to explain the actions they had taken.

'You had control over the shuttle until you came into dock?' the captain asked.

'Yes, sir. Ensign Winters was ready to take control the entire time but I was able to maintain the contact and control the shuttle.'

'You had no problems this time?'

'No. I waited until the missiles were en route then cut the connection. We saw the missiles' impact on the shuttle's scans and when I scanned again it was with a great deal of caution. Will I be allowed to take the shuttle out by myself soon?'

'Probably, but you need to be able to dock,' the captain pointed out. 'But good work both of you.'

'Will we be going back to Ra with the new ship?'

'No, we will salvage what we can and destroy the rest. We are to stay out and find as many of these rogues as we can.'

Chapter 11

'SIR, are you Mr Wilhelm?' David was asked by an ensign as he was working in engineering.

'I am. Can I help you with anything?'

'No sir. I mean yes sir, there is a message for you.' The young man handed over a communication chip with a shaking hand. David looked at it in surprise, wondering who it could be from. When The UTA wanted to talk to him, they did so through the bridge; this must be personal, and it would have been very expensive to send.

'It's not going to attack you,' Kate said. She had been taking him through the workings of the environmental controls.

'I'm just surprised. I don't know who would send me any personal messages.'

'Well, plug it in and have a look.' He knew she was brimming with curiosity. When David continued to look at it, she added, 'Unless you want to view it in private. I can finish here if you want to go back to your cabin.'

'I want to finish this before I have to take the shuttle out again.' He put the chip into his pocket and returned to work.

Later, when he could find nothing else to distract him, he sat in his room and plugged in the chip. He did not know who he expected to see; part of him had thought that this was a mistake and the message had been meant for someone else. Then his father's face appeared on the screen.

'Hello David, I hope this message finds you well. I just

wanted to say happy birthday. I know I have missed a few over the years and I am sorry for it, but I hope that if you return to Europa you will visit and I can make it up to you. I contacted the UTA; they said you are doing well and seemed very excited about whatever it is you are doing. I did not have be a telepath to see that. All your friends at the UTA have asked me to send you their best wishes.'

David watched it again and again. It was short and stilted, as if his father did not know what to say. This was not a necessary message; his father had missed a few of his birthdays and, while contacting him at the UTA would have been easy, this would not have been. Even more curiously, it appeared his father had been asking the UTA about him, making sure he was doing well. Next time David was at a starbase, he would try and send a message to make sure his father was okay. Maybe they could finally build some sort of a relationship.

The buzzer went. David paused the message, released the door and Jon came in. 'The gossip is you got a personal message. Is everything alright? I was worried when you did not come for dinner.'

'I'm fine. The message is from my father'

'Is there a problem at home?'

'No, he sent it to wish me happy birthday.'

Jon whistled. 'You must be very close to him for him to spend that sort of money on a birthday message.'

'No, we're not close at all. I stayed with him for a few days before I came on board. Before that I had not seen him since my mother's funeral when I was a child. We've only spoken a few times a year in between.'

'I am sorry. How old were you when she died?'

'Nearly eleven. I was at the UTA learning to control my abilities, so afterwards I just continued to live there.'

'If you barely talk to him, how did you end up staying with him? Did something happen that got you talking again?'

'I got this job and I wanted to see him again before I left, just in case I never returned to Europa. I didn't want to leave things as they were without trying for something more. When I thought I would never leave my home planet, there always seemed to be time and I guess I kept putting it off. When I showed up at his home, I doubted he would let me stay. I even booked a room in a hotel in anticipation of having the door closed in my face. But he let me stay. We were even starting to talk properly when I left.'

'I think the message is his way of saying he wants to keep in touch. Space travel is a great way to lose contact with people you don't want to talk to.'

'I hope so, he is the only family I have. When we get to a base, will you show me how to set up one of those accounts you told me about so I can send a reply?'

'Of course. Now come on, everyone is in the canteen and we need to give you a hard time for not telling us it's your birthday. How old are you anyway?'

'Nineteen, in two days' time. My father was early with his birthday message.'

'You are only nineteen? I assumed you were older. The FWN does not allow anyone under the age of twenty-one on extended tours. The last thing anyone needs is to have someone crack while on board.'

'I guess they needed me more than they were prepared to follow their rules.'

'Maybe it will all change soon. After all, you are still here.'

'They still need me.'

'No, you have done what was needed; you're still here because you are wanted. That is the difference.'

᛭

'Happy birthday, David,' Mark Yoland said two days later, raising his glass in a toast.

'So who told you? Jon?'

'No one. Don't you know by now that I know everything that happens on my ship?'

David laughed and raised his own glass. He had never drunk while he had lived at the UTA, but since coming on board he had developed a taste for the captain's whisky.

'So what do you normally do on your birthday?' the captain asked.

'Not much. I might go out with a few people from the UTA but that would be it.'

'Well, my present to you is permission to take the shuttle out on your own. Ensign Winters reports that you have grown very confident in handling of the shuttle's controls and were calm and capable when you found that last ship - even though docking took a while to master smoothly,' he said jokingly. 'If you want Winters to continue going out with you, she will be at your disposal but she has signed you off as competent for short-range solo piloting.'

'Thank you. It means a lot that you trust me with one of your shuttles.'

'You have worked very hard to earn that trust,' Mark said and paused.

'I hear a "but".'

'It does not matter.'

'I know that I only got this post because you needed me. But I do value honesty because then I know where I stand.'

'I did not want you here,' Mark admitted. 'My father asked it as a favour and I was mad at him, but could not refuse. I was not happy when you started work in engineering but everyone else was fine with it. You started working on how to help us before you needed to. You have located and given accurate co-ordinates on three ships, which is more than the whole of the FWN has been able to achieve. You have won over my crew and educated yourself to a standard where you can take on duties on this ship. You have exceeded your role and taken on others. The FWN have asked for more telepaths because you have been so successful but the UTA won't send any more. Do you know why?' Mark asked. 'No, I am sorry, this is about your birthday, not about the politics between the FWN and UTA.'

'They did not want me to come because I am a level ten telepath. It was a condition of my coming, at my request, that that was not disclosed.' David ignored Mark's suggestion that they move on to other topics.

'I don't understand what that means.'

'Telepathic ratings go from one to twelve, twelve being the highest.'

'So you are a strong telepath but there are others that are higher. I don't understand the problem?' David did not respond. 'David?'

'I don't want you to look at me with horror. I have worked hard to get the crew to trust that I won't strip their minds. My rating level won't change that; if anything, it means I have better control, but I am afraid they won't see it that way.'

'David, you have earned my trust. I don't know what you are worried about but unless you tell me you want to go on a murder spree, I will keep any confidences you want to give. There is no one on this ship that I have to tell.'

'The stronger the rating, the more prone we are to mental instability. The last stable level twelve died a decade ago. There are three stable level elevens and a dozen level tens. The UTA would not send anyone that did not want to come, and you are paying me what a level two would be paid.'

'And a level two cannot do what you can.'

'Nowhere near. They would be no use to you.'

'What would a level ten expect to earn?' Mark asked, as the information started to sink in. David mentioned an amount. 'You wanted to come that much?' Mark said, reeling at what David could earn, more than anyone in the fleet. No wonder they were not paying him what he was worth.

'Yes. I came originally because it is what I wanted. I stayed because your crew made me feel welcome and showed me what I always wanted to learn. The UTA were not happy with my obsession with space and engineering; neither of those are telepathic positions.'

'They let you continue because of your success and having the FWN's approval would boost their standing.'

'More or less. I have no interest in politics around this. I want this to be a success, I want to travel, I want to be able to fix and build my own engines. I still want what I wanted before my telepathic ability surfaced. I want my life, not one that is dictated to me by the UTA.'

'You are welcome on the *New York* for as long as you want to be here and I am the captain. Though I can't afford to pay you any more than we already do.'

David raised his glass in acknowledgement and laughed.

⁜

David took the shuttle out of the docking bay. His palms were sweating because he was so nervous; now there was no fall back, now it was all down to him. He took the shuttle out one click and placed it on a course that orbited the *New York*. He scanned the area of space and felt nothing. He slowly started to open up his mind and felt the crew of the *New York*. He called the bridge and asked permission to move further away, which was granted. Slowly David reached a distance where he could fully open his mind up and for the first time felt truly free to allow his mind to be open and push as far as he could without fear of invading someone else's privacy. He was finally alone with his own mind, his own thoughts and feelings. He had not known such peace since he was ten years old.

Chapter 12

'THE scientists here believe they have discovered a way to detect these rogue vessels. They are requesting that you return to Starbase Ra to have the technology installed immediately,' Commander Xhia informed Captain Yoland.

'Why do they want us? While we have David on board, we are operationally effective. A return to the starbase will leave no one out here that can detect the vessels.'

'This is new technology. Before it is rolled out to other ships in the fleet, they want to know that it works as expected and for that they need David. They need to know that what David senses is what the technology is detecting. I know we can't order him to help us, but the admiral of the fleet is hopeful that he will be willing to stay a little longer.'

'We will head in immediately. I will talk to David and try and impress on him the importance of your request.'

'Thank you.'

Captain Yoland cut the connection and leaned back in his chair. He felt that Commander Xhia was worried that David would refuse to assist at this crucial time and, from what David had told him, he was not surprised by the assumption. How many people would work at an amount so vastly under what they could earn? From their talks, he was fairly sure he knew what David's reaction would be: he would be glad to stay, even if it was only for a little longer.

Chief Engineer Famar Redek would be glad they were

going back in. Two weeks earlier he mentioned that the engines needed some maintenance which could not be done in space, and he had requested permission to take the ship in, but the need for the overhaul was not as necessary as staying out on patrol. Famar had placed another request this morning, along with a detailed report which highlighted his main areas of concern. Now he was glad that he did not have to balance the mission over the efficient running of the ship. The work could easily be done at space Starbase Ra, where they would be heading, and David would be happy. The engineering crew had promised that he could help when they went in.

'Mr Wilhelm receiving,' Mark Yoland said as he hit the communicator on his desk.

'Go ahead, captain.'

'Please join me in the briefing room.'

'Yes, sir.'

David would be happy to help, anything to stay longer on board. But once this new technology was proven, once he was no longer needed, then what? He was not looking forward to this conversation; it was the beginning of the end.

#

The normal high spirits that were common on a space starbase were muted as the *New York* approached Ra. The news had gone around the ship that David might not be with them for much longer. Most of the crew were used to colleagues changing posts, but they were all part of the FWN and friends often went into posts that they wanted and had worked hard to get, so there was always a chance of meeting up again at ports and stations. This was different; they all knew David wanted to stay, but in a short time he might be forced to leave and they would not meet again as this would be the end of space travel for him. The best they could hope for would be occasional messages that they would pick up whenever they left the ship.

They had spent a month on Ra while the new technology was installed and the ship had a complete overhaul, much to the joy of the chief engineer. David went with Jon to set up a communication account and sent a message to his father, thanking him for the birthday message and saying that he was happy and doing well. He did not spend much time on the base before returning to the ship.

The first time was a few days after they arrived. He did not expect anything so soon, but there it was, a message from his father. Smiling, he replied, telling as much as he was allowed to. After that David checked the account regularly but that was the only thing he went onto the base for. He spent the rest of his time working in engineering, learning how to strip and rebuild the systems.

He knew he could go onto the base, that his friends would support him against the prejudice of others, but he remembered the looks and feelings of hostility he had last time, though no one said or did anything. Common sense told him that if he tried he could overcome it, make a good example and possibly pave the way for future telepaths, but his time was getting short and he wanted to learn as much as he could. The engineering crew worked extra shifts to teach him everything he wanted to know. The chief engineer also spent most of his time there, overseeing the work that was taking place. That is where Mark Yoland found him.

'I hear several of your engineering team are not taking advantage of their down time, Famar.'

'I know. I have spoken with them, but they are all of

the same mind. If this technology works, David might not be with us much longer and they want to help him learn as much as he can. I make sure they don't work over the regulations, but this is how they want to spend their spare time.'

'Fair enough. How good is David's work?'

'Very good. He is picking everything up quicker than anyone I have ever known. I would be happy if he was part of my team. The morale here will drop when he leaves us.'

'I know. If I could keep him, I would. Keep me updated on your progress and if you can convince David and your crew to have some R and R on the base, it might benefit them. We obviously won't be leaving until the work is done.'

'Understood, captain.'

※

David settled on his bunk and started to read. The chief engineer had shut down engineering for the night and the crew were going out. They had asked him to join them but he refused, not wanting to cause them trouble on the base.

The buzzer went on his door. Expecting either Jon or one of the engineers, he opened it and was surprised when Elen walked in. He had never seen her looking like this before. Her hair was no longer tied back tightly but hanging loose around her shoulders, and she had exchanged her jumpsuits for a dress. A dress! Where had she got that from? With such limited space, non-regulation clothing was kept to a minimum.

'Elen,' he said stating the obvious then not knowing what to say as he sat up, unable to take his eyes off her.

'I am going out with the engineers tonight. I was wondering if you wanted to escort me.'

'I ...' but the words telling her he was not going would not come out of his mouth.

'Well, come on then, or they will take all the good seats.' She turned and started to walk down the corridor. David jumped up and caught up with her.

As they approached the restaurant, the rest of the crew saw them and shouted their pleasure at their arrival. The evening passed with a lot of laughter; as it drew to a close and those with early shifts started to leave, David got up as well.

'You don't need to leave just yet,' Famar said.

'I wanted to get an early start in the morning.'

'Enjoy tonight and come in when you are ready. There is nothing interesting planned for the morning, I promise.' Those staying longer seconded their boss and David settled back to enjoy what was left of the night.

At the end, as everyone left, he walked back to the ship with Elen. 'Thank you for coming to get me.'

'You are welcome.' They walked in silence until they reached his room. 'I guess I had better go back to my room.'

'Did you mean it the first time we met when you said that you were happy for me to read your mind?'

'Yes, why?'

'I like you. I want to touch you,' he confessed. Elen took a step closer and took his hand and placed it against her face.

'Invite me into your room.'

✳

By the time the *New York* left Ra, David had spoken more to his father than he had in years. In his last message, he said that communication would become difficult again after they left the base and he would send his next message when he could. He did not want his father to think he was not interested in trying to build a relationship.

Once back in space, David felt himself relax as the number of minds reduced. He went back to the routine he had had before: he took the shuttle up at the start of the standard shift, then went to engineering where he finished his tour, before going back out again in the shuttle. He had hoped that it would take a month, maybe more, until he found a cloaked vessel; he wanted more time to learn, more time to spend with Elen.

He knew what she felt for him when they were together; she made no effort to hide it. She gave everything freely but he was aware that he could never reciprocate in the same way. The best he could do was answer all her questions truthfully and hope she knew that. She was the first non-telepath he had been with; he had thought it would be hard but it was not. There was no battle of minds, no trying to protect thoughts and feelings. It was as it was and all he needed to do was accept what she gave. Being raised with a telepath gave her an amazing acceptance of his talent.

Elen had a late shift so David left her sleeping in his cabin when he left to take a shuttle out. They had only left Ra a few days before and were still a considerable distance from where they expected to find a rogue ship. Yet there one was, on the edge of his range, and his heart sank.

'*New York* receiving from shuttle *Brooklyn*,' David called.

'Go ahead, shuttle *Brooklyn*.'

'I am picking up a hostile vessel. Sending you the co-ordinates now.'

'Co-ordinates received. Stand by.' David knew the drill and moved away from the *New York*'s firing line then he closed off his mind and waited for them to fire.

✳

'The co-ordinates you gave us were spot on,' Mark told him later that day, as they sat together over a whisky. 'We checked first with normal sensors but there was nothing, then we looked with the new technology and there it was.' For the FWN it was fantastic news but David saw it as an end. 'They are calling in all ships to have the new technology fitted as quickly as possible.'

'Based on one success?'

'Yes, they were sure it would work. They just wanted you to confirm it, which you did.'

'So they don't want to wait.' David did not expect Mark to answer and continued. 'How long do you think it will take?'

'I don't know, I would guess at least a few months. It will depend on how quickly they can build it and how many ships they chose to install it on. They would like you to stay on while the rest of the fleet is updated to make sure that the system remains effective and to help try and find flaws, but they can't afford to wait.'

'Well, I always knew this would come to end sooner rather than later. The fact it has lasted as long as it has, has been a massive bonus for me. I thought that once the first ship was caught, that would be it. I will stay and help as long as I can.'

'I can talk to my father, see if he can pull some strings and have you stay.'

'The UTA won't let me stay if there is no need and the FWN won't pay me to stay when there is technology that can do the job just as well. And though I don't care for money, I do need some to get by.'

'I feel there should be something I can do to help you. I just don't know what.'

'There isn't. These decisions are being made far above us.'

'You never know. My father is a powerful man with a

lot of connections. You have done him a huge service so he owes you.'

'Thank you, but I don't know if he can help and it could place him in a bad position in the FWN. This is not the right fight. With my abilities, I will be alright,' he said, as Mark refilled their glasses.

⁜

He did not see Elen that night. She didn't finish until he was asleep and went to her own bunk so as not to disturb him. How he wanted to see her but he had no way to contact her on the ship without causing her embarrassment.

He got up early the next day, did his normal rotation with the shuttle then walked into engineering where he was handed a huge pile of work but, as he flicked through it, it was not about a ship the size of the *New York* but a single scout shuttle.

'If you are going to leave us soon, we have to cram as much information as possible into that small head of yours,' Kate told him. 'We have to get you ready for the real world.'

He thought they had worked him hard at Ra but this was a big step up. They kept him too busy to ask questions about the change in his work. Finally, with his head reeling, he made his way to the docking bay.

Elen was waiting for him. 'Evening, David.'

'Elen, what are you doing here?' he asked.

'I heard you might be leaving us soon. I thought I'd take the opportunity to teach you some more manoeuvers.'

'I don't understand. I have been going up on my own for a while now - why do you suddenly have a problem with my piloting skills?'

'I don't, but you have never gone beyond the range of the *New York*. I taught you what you needed to know but there is so much more that you will find interesting.'

'Won't we need the captain's permission to go beyond the ship's range?'

'Who do you think suggested it?'

✳

David stumbled into his quarters. It seemed that everyone had heard that he was likely to be leaving and wanted to teach him as much as possible before he left. Even Bralik had caught up with him and gone through muscle-resistance exercises that could be done in a small space with little or no equipment. The engineering crew were the worst; everyone on board had gone through years of training to get where they were. In a moment of frustration he had pointed this out to them, only to be told, 'There is nothing like practical experience.' They continued to load on the information, until his head ached.

Over the next few weeks, David detected another ship when he was in the shuttle; the *New York* also located it and gained a weapons lock. Then a few days later the call came through from the bridge while he was working in engineering: they had detected a vessel had he? David stopped what he was doing and concentrated hard but there was nothing. He asked how far out it was; when he was told the co-ordinates, he knew the vessel was too far for his range while on board. The technology was now more effective than he was.

A few days later David was called to the captain's briefing room. The orders had come for the *New York* to return to Europa and he knew his time was at an end.

'I am sorry, David,' Mark said, as they sat together.

'You have nothing to be sorry for, I'm just grateful this has lasted as long as it has. Your crew has welcomed me and taught me so much.'

'I am glad you got along well with everyone. If I am honest, I have never seen a crew pull together around someone as they have with you. Have you thought about what you will do next?'

'Not really. I'm sure the UTA will have a nice job lined up for me, either in finance or politics.'

'But what do you want to do?'

'Be on my own in a shuttle.'

'Then why don't you look at becoming a scout?' Mark suggested.

'I was joking when I said I wanted to be on my own on a shuttle,' David retorted. 'It would not be possible.'

'Scouts are an eccentric lot since they are on their own most of the time. But they travel extensively, charting space. One of the hardest things for a new scout is getting the connections they need that will pay them. Those are contacts my father can give you. And Elen and the engineering crew have certainly trained you in skills that you need.'

'The UTA would not allow it.'

'Why not? A lot of scouts' contracts are very well paid, and being away from so many minds is better for you.'

'How do you know that?'

'You told me after you found the first ship that you suffered from headaches from the constant noise. How many have you had since you've been here?' Mark asked. 'You have not restocked your medication and you look better now than when you came on board. Most people on long missions look worse when they finish.'

'You think it is possible?'

'Why do you think I got everyone teaching you the skills of a scout?'

Chapter 13

IT did not take David long to pack up his possessions. Most of his clothing had been supplied by the FWN and now he was leaving he could not take it with him. He picked up his bag and looked around his room. In the time he had spent aboard it had become his home. Now it looked empty, as if he had never been there. How soon before his friends also forgot him and moved on?

His door buzzed. He hit the release and Jon walked in. 'Are you ready?' he asked.

'I think so,' David said, picking up his bag. Jon took it from him and together they walked in silence to the docking bay. The crew had thrown him a leaving party the previous night; the captain had authorised a lot of extra food and drink, stating that they could resupply while in orbit of Europa. There were a lot of tearful farewells. At the end of the night, a lot of promises were made to keep in touch. Elen had spent the night with him and they had said their farewells this morning. Now, as he walked the corridors towards the shuttle bay David did not know what was left to say.

The doors opened as they approached. The captain, chief engineer, Elen and Jon's team, as well as most of the engineering crew, were waiting for him.

Captain Yoland came forward. 'Everyone wanted the opportunity to say their farewells. I hope you don't mind.'

'Not at all,' David replied, catching Elen's eye. He had not expected her to be here.

Everyone came up to him and said good bye; he

could tell they wanted to shake his hand or hug him but could not, making them awkward. Finally he came back to the captain. 'If you ever need any help, any other introductions, just ask,' Mark said.

'Thank you.' David looked at the shuttle as Elen opened the hatch and walked in. 'I guess that is my cue to go.'

'It was a pleasure having you on board.'

'It was a pleasure to be here.' David turned and walked into the shuttle; he saw that Jon was also there, stowing away his bag.

'Do you want to do the honours and pilot us down?' Elen asked.

'I have never docked on a planet before.'

'I know. This will be your chance and I'll be here if you need me.'

David smiled and went to the pilot seat. 'Are you coming down with us?' he asked Jon.

'Yes,' Jon replied, surprising David. He sat down in one of the passenger seats and strapped himself in. David carried out the safety drill and ensured everything was safely locked up, asked permission to leave and, on being given the all clear, flew the shuttle out of the *New York* for the last time.

He could not help comparing it to the first time he was in a shuttle, when he didn't even known how to strap himself in! Now he was flying it. The trip seemed to take moments before David was requesting permission to dock and completing the procedure.

'Neatly done,' Elen said.

'Thank you,' David said. 'Thank you for letting me fly for the last time.'

'It will only be the last time if you let it be,' she replied as she undid her safety harness and stood up.

'You had better not let this be the last time,' Jon said, coming up to him and hugging him. Surprised, David tried to push him away but Jon held him fast for a moment before releasing him.

'You should not have done that.'

'I trust my friends, I would not let any of them go without letting them know how much they mean to me.'

'I know how you feel and I hope we get the chance to meet up again.' He turned to say goodbye to Elen but she had taken his bag and another one and was waiting for him at the exit.

'The captain has given me twenty-four-hour shore leave. Jon can take the shuttle back and pick me up again tomorrow.'

'I have nowhere to go.'

'I have booked us a room on the base.'

After a last goodbye to Jon, David took the bags from Elen and they walked away together.

✴

As David walked out of the shuttle docking bay the next day, having said his final goodbye to Elen, he saw a car waiting for him with a uniformed driver. When Elen told him transport and accommodation had been arranged, he assumed the driver would be from the FWN. This was not what he had expected.

'Good afternoon, sir. Are you Mr David Wilhelm?' David nodded and the driver came forward and took his bag. 'Your father sent me to collect you. He was informed that you would be returning today and would like to ask you to stay with him.'

'Thank you, that's very kind.' He wondered who his father had been in contact with.

The driver placed his bag in the boot while David climbed into the car. The rest of the trip was conducted in silence. David looked out of the window as the car took him home. The trip seemed to take a lot less time than when he left, and it was not long before the car pulled up outside his father's house. He got out and approached the door which was opened by the same housekeeper who had nearly closed it in his face.

'Welcome home. Your father said you might be staying with us for a while. I have given you the same room as before. I hope that is agreeable.'

'Yes, thank you,' David said as he turned towards the driver to take his bag.

'Johnson will take it up to your room,' the woman said. 'Your father will be home for dinner which will be at eight o'clock. Please make yourself at home.' she stood aside to let him in.

Up in his room, David unpacked some clean clothes and took his time to enjoy the hot, high-powered shower in his bathroom. It was something he had missed sorely on board, where water usage was closely monitored. Once he had finished, he took out what he needed for tonight and tomorrow; he would unpack properly once he had spoken to his father and he knew if he was staying or not. He might be welcome tonight but he had no idea what his father's plans were and did not like to presume.

He contacted the UTA to let them know he was back - though since his father knew, they must also have been informed. They wanted him to report the following morning for a full briefing, but that did not stop them keeping him talking for another hour on issues they considered the most important. It was a relief to turn off the communication. He leaned back with a sigh. Before he left, the UTA was his life; now he was not sure how he viewed them. Hopefully tomorrow, when he went back, he might feel more settled in familiar surroundings.

When the dinner hour arrived, David walked into the drawing room. His father was already there. 'What would you like to drink?'

'Do you have a whisky?'

'Several, take your pick,' and he indicated the drinks cabinet behind him.

David chose one before saying, 'Thank you for the car, I didn't expect it.'

'In your last communication you said that you thought your time was drawing to a close. I have friends in the FWN who were able to get me a date for the *New York* returning to Europa and a security pass for Johnson.'

'I'm surprised they allowed Johnson in.'

'I have business there on occasion and he has clearance.' His father paused. 'What do you plan to do now?'

'I'm not sure. I have to go the UTA tomorrow to talk to them about how I found it on the *New York*. I guess I will find out if they have any plans for me.'

'Do you have any plans for yourself?'

'I have one, but I'll need to make some enquires first to see if it is possible.'

'Well, you are welcome to stay here as long as you need.'

'Thank you.'

✳

David returned to his father's house after a long day at the UTA. They had been ecstatic at how well he had done on the *New York*. When the request came in for him to stay longer, their opinions were mixed, which was why he was given the choice to stay or go. The longer he stayed, the more talks opened up between the UTA and FWN; and they were both hopeful about where these would lead. If the FWN accepted telepaths, space travel would become easier for them, opening up more opportunities.

The UTA wanted David to stay with them until decisions

were made about what he would do next but he refused, saying that he could easily travel from his father's when he was needed. A year on a ship with nowhere to go and he was fine; the moment he walked back into the UTA he felt claustrophobic and resented the control they tried to place over him.

'Evening, sir. How was your day today?' Mrs Ransom said, as she opened the door.

'Far too long.'

'Your father is back and in the living room. Dinner will be in half an hour.'

'Thank you.' As David walked in, his father poured him a whisky and handed it to him. 'Now who is the mind reader?'

'I don't need to be, I just know that look. I take it things did not go well with the UTA?'

'It was fine, it just did not feel as if I belonged there like I used to.'

'What did you expect? That everything would be as it was before?'

'I don't know, it had been part of my life for so long, I guess I just thought I could go back to how it was.'

'Once you have moved on you can't go back.'

'Have you?' David wished he had not said it the moment he spoke.

'What do you mean by that?'

'Dinner is served,' Mrs Ransom said and the conversation was dropped.

They sat in uncomfortable silence as they ate. As the dishes were cleared away, David got up to leave the table.

'What did you mean when you asked if I have moved on?' his father asked.

'I saw my old room.'

'Oh. I think we should talk somewhere more comfortable, don't you?' Viktor walked back into the living room, poured two drinks and handed one to David.

'You barely spoke to me for years but my room is exactly as I remember it. Has there been anyone in your life since my mother died? There is no sign in the house that you have met anyone else.'

'She was always there, your mother. I never had to worry or think about her when I was away, she was just there and looked after everything.' Viktor paused. 'Then your abilities emerged and she fell apart. I did not know how to deal with the situation so I just avoided it by staying away on business. Then she was gone.'

'Did you think she killed herself? They told me it was an accident.'

'It was. She had no reason to commit suicide. You were coming home soon and it was the first time she'd been happy since you left. No, I blamed you for her death.'

'Why? I was not there.'

'I know, that is why I blamed you. She gave up without you. She became stressed and careless.'

'I had no control over what happened to me,' David protested. 'I didn't want it, I still don't want it.'

'I know that now, but then....' Viktor paused and David waited in silence. 'I was angry and I needed to blame someone. I was not able to look at my own behaviour so...'

'You blamed me? Is that why you could not even talk to me at the funeral?'

'You remember that?'

'Yes.'

'I am sorry. What I did was wrong, everything I did with your mother was wrong. When she needed me, I was not there. If I'd been a better husband maybe she would have been less distracted.'

'Why did you continue to keep your distance from me once you worked that out?'

'Because I did not know what to say to you. The more time passed, the harder it got. Then suddenly you were on my doorstep. I still did not know what to say but there you were and I thought we might have a second chance.'

'Your housekeeper did not know about me, yet my room is spotless.'

'Even when I blamed you, I could not bear to change anything. After the UTA took you, your mother spent hours in your room and after she died it was the only place I felt close to her - and later to you. Mrs Ransom has only been with me a few years; that area of the house is not her responsibility. I keep your room tidy.' Viktor looked at him sadly. 'I have no excuse for not trying harder.'

'I could have tried too.'

'You were a child and as an adult you did make the attempt. I have no such excuse.'

'I've been an adult for years and I only came here because I didn't know if I would return to Europa. I had nothing to lose.'

'I am glad you took the risk.'

'So am I.' As his father reached for his drink, David said, 'You never did say if there have been other women.'

Viktor choked, 'None of your business,' and David laughed at his embarrassment.

Chapter 14

DAVID had only been back on Europa a few days, yet the noise in his head was making it ache continually again and had brought back the sleepless nights. Reluctantly he had to resort to taking his medication. He would have given anything to be back on the *New York*, or better yet on a shuttle on his own where there was nothing to hear, but he could not see that happening anytime soon. David's biggest fear was going insane or becoming suicidal because of the constant noise in his head, a fear that had intensified since his return.

His father was excited about the job offers put forward by the UTA and was disappointed that David was reluctant to take any of them. Instead David started exploring his options to leave for space again as soon as possible.

Since he had been back, he and his father had had several long talks and gained a much better understanding of each other. Viktor started to accept that his son had to leave again if he was going to maintain his sanity. David found out that while he had been away, Viktor had contacted the UTA and had gained a better understanding of what being telepathic meant. The UTA thought he was stable and would be fine working on a planet.

He had been back for a week when he was asked to attend the FWN to discuss his posting on the *New York*. They sent a car for him in the morning to take him to the meeting; at least it gave him an excuse not to go back to the UTA to give the same answers to the same questions. At least he would get to give the answers to someone new.

When he arrived, he was shown into an office with an elderly man in an Admiral's uniform who looked vaguely familiar.

'David Wilhelm, I am Admiral Yoland. It is a pleasure to finally meet you. My son told me that you were invaluable to him on the *New York*.'

'Thank you, sir. I enjoyed working for Mark and was sorry to leave.'

When they had made themselves comfortable, Yoland continued. 'Mark was also sorry to see you leave. Did you know that he argued to keep you on board but neither the UTA nor the FWN would agree? They couldn't see a role for someone with your skills on board a ship once the technology had been installed and proven successful.'

'He suggested that he would, but I didn't know that he had.'

'Because of you, he has become passionate about the topic of telepaths on board ships. With what you achieved and how well you integrated with his crew, there is now pressure on the senior admirals to allow telepaths to join the FWN. It's a suggestion that I support.'

'I hadn't realised that it was being proposed so soon.'

'When my son sets his mind to something, he does not give up. It will be interesting to see where the future lies,' the admiral said. 'He also told me you became quite a confident shuttle pilot and want to become a solo scout.'

'That is my hope, sir.'

'It's not a career many would choose or can cope with.'

'So I have been told but being on my own does not bother me. I crave the silence that I can't find around other people.'

'If it is something you really want, I will see what I can

do to help.'

'Thank you sir - but why? I have only done what I was hired to do.'

'No, you went beyond that. Having a telepath looking for the rogue ships was my idea. A lot of people did not like it and were waiting for you to fail but you exceeded in the role. You proved beyond doubt that you could fit in and work with the crew. You could say that I owe you.'

'Your help would be appreciated, thank you. But I don't know what you could do.'

'The FWN gives out a lot of contracts to solo scouts. There is often more work than there are people to take it.'

'Are you saying you could get me a scout contract?' The admiral nodded. 'Thank you for the offer, but my understanding is that you don't supply the shuttles and without a shuttle I don't know how much help a contract will be to me. I don't know how long it would take me to pay for one.'

'Is there someone else who could pay for one?'

'No one I would be willing to ask.'

When the contract came through from the FWN the next day for him to scout and map a section of space, David examined it with mixed feelings. Had the admiral listened to him when he said he could not afford a shuttle? This contract was everything that he wanted, but he did not have a shuttle and was years off earning enough money to buy one. Although he was getting along well with his father, asking for so much money so he could take off again was too much.

He put the contract aside; he had a few days to think of a polite way to decline it but at the moment his emotions were too raw. His dream had been handed to him but he did not have the means to fulfil it. He knew that shuttles could be rented until the scouts earned enough to buy their own, but the money he had earned on the *New York* was not even enough for the security.

✳

When David went down to dinner he was thinking that he would take up one of the well-paid positions the UTA wanted him to take. He was going to have to resign himself to years of headaches and work he hated.

'What is wrong?' Viktor asked as David joined him.

'Nothing,' he said, as he walked to the drinks cabinet and poured himself a large drink.

'Don't lie to me. I might not be a telepath but my work means I have to be good at reading body language. I know you are upset - you are more tense now than on your first night here.'

'Admiral Yoland has given me a scout contract.'

'You can't be upset about leaving,' Viktor said. 'You want to go, regardless of the opposition, so what is the problem? You have what you wanted.'

'I have the contract but I can't fulfil it.'

'Why not? I thought you had qualified as a pilot during your time on the *New York*.'

'I don't have a shuttle. Solo scouts either have their own or rent one if they have the deposit and a long-term contract. I do not have either.'

'So without a shuttle, you can't take the contract. What do you plan to do?'

'Turn it down, take one of the contracts the UTA keep pushing at me and save up for my own shuttle. It will take me a few years but hopefully I'll get there in the end and the admiral will still be willing to help me get another contract.'

'When do you have to let them know?'

'A few days. I need to think of the best way to decline the offer.'

✳

The next day David finally made it out to the shops and bought several new changes of clothes so Mrs Ransom did not have to repeatedly wash the same ones every few days. He had just got back home when his father contacted him. 'David, can you please join me?'

'Of course, where are you?'

'My driver knows the location and will be with you shortly.' His father ended the communication abruptly. David was bemused; though he was spending as much time with his father as possible, it was always at home. This was the first time they were meeting somewhere else and David was curious.

The car arrived and David got into it. He had expected to be taken into the city, to a restaurant for lunch, but was surprised as he was driven some distance away into an area where there were a lot warehouses. Finally the car stopped outside one of them and David climbed out. The door was open and he walked through. As his eyes adjusted to the change in light, he saw a shuttle.

'What do you think?' his father said, appearing out of the gloom to stand next to him.

'I don't understand,' David replied.

'You said you needed a shuttle, so what do you think of her? Will she do?'

David walked forward as if in a dream and ran his hand against her hull. 'You have bought her?'

'Not yet. She was recommended to me as a good scout shuttle but I don't know what your requirements are. If you like it, it is yours.'

'Why?' David said turning to look at his father in surprise.

'I know you can work and save for your own but you will be miserable. I never supported you when you were a child, so let me do it now. You have the contract and the connections you need to live the life that you want to live.'

'But the cost ... I can't accept this.' David could not keep the yeaning out of his voice as he looked back at the shuttle.

'I can afford it, trust me,' Viktor said. 'Consider this part repayment for ten years of neglect.'

'Don't say that.'

'It is the truth; it is not because of me that you've turned out so well. You always wanted to travel in space and even with all the obstacles, you are still trying. Let me be the good father for once and give you the means to achieve it.'

'If I go, I will hardly ever see you again.'

'I would prefer to see you on rare occasions and know you are happy than to see you regularly and know you are miserable and I could have done something about it. Just promise to keep in touch whenever you hit a base.'

'Thank you. Can I see her specifications?'

Chapter 15

AFTER the mental relief that solitary deep space travel brought him, the loneliness started to intrude. He had been so desperate to get away from people, had always thought that he would prefer to be alone that he never really considered what true solitude meant.

Before he left Europa, he was given a battery of mandatory tests for both his ability to pilot a shuttle and his metal stability. The latter included intense counselling sessions that examined his ability to be on his own for long periods of time; although he had passed them, he had not appreciated how alone you were on a scout ship in uncharted space. He took the advice of his FWN friends and made sure he had plenty of reading material to keep him busy. He downloaded massive engineering texts as well as programs designed to build and fix the shuttle systems. In the days spent travelling to the relevant section of space, he spent hours studying reports to make sure he was not missing anything before it was too late.

He had been out in uncharted space for weeks before he had to resolve a problem with his engines. He longed to tell someone of his success but there was no one; the best he could hope was to leave a message at a base and pick up the reply the next time he docked.

David started to wonder about the wisdom of his decision to be a solo pilot. Some days as he paced the small living area, he went over and over the exercises Bralik had given him to try and work out his frustration.

Maybe they were right and he needed a lot more time in space to truly understand the isolation. Telepaths did not usually travel in space so there was no base line for him to judge what was normal and what was not. He wondered if, in his intense desire to hear nothing, he had misinterpreted it as an ability to be on his own.

David was twitching with anticipation the first time he headed back to a starbase from uncharted space for a maintenance check. He planned to restock and send a report with his readings to the admiral. It was months since he had spoken to anyone and he had so much to say to Elen, his father and his friends from the *New York*; yet as he approached and started to hear other minds for the first time in ages, he started to build up the walls in his mind. He resented having to do it; he realized he did not know what he wanted. No, he knew what he wanted: he did not want to be a telepath - he wanted a normal life.

The headaches, which had been absent for the months in space, came back as soon as he started to dock. By the time the procedure was finished, David was looking for his medication. As he walked off the shuttle, he was met by someone he assumed was a member of the starbase engineering crew.

'Greetings. You are shown as booked in for a routine maintenance check.'

'That's correct.'

'We've looked over the shuttle's history that you forwarded. I expect it will take two to three days to complete. Assuming there is nothing wrong, of course.'

'Is there anywhere I can stay while I wait?'

'Loads of places. Just ask the base's information panel it will tell you were there are vacancies and prices, it will also give you locations of where to stock up if you need to. Let us know where you're staying so we can contact you when the maintenance is done or if there are any problems.'

'I will do.' Shouldering his bag, David went to find somewhere he could lie down until his headache eased.

It did not take him long. If you did not work on the base, you were a short-term visitor and there were numerous places that catered for transients. His identity was confirmed, he handed over the payment and was given the access code to a room. 'If your shuttle takes longer than the estimated time, we will gladly extend your stay. Just let us know.'

David made his way to his room. It was small, basic but clean and very similar to his cabin on the *New York*. He dropped his bag on the floor, lay down on the bed and closed his eyes.

Thanks to Jon's help when he had been on board the *New York*, David quickly found his way around the starbase. When he woke up, the first thing he did was go to a communication booth and download his full report to the FWN. If anything urgent came up when he was in space, he had a special frequency he could transmit the information on; nothing had, so his information was just general scans. Next he checked his account and was pleased to find several messages from his father and his friends on the *New York*. Hearing them made him smile; it was not so much what they said, it was hearing their voices. His father's news was interesting. Viktor had met someone new and hoped that David would like her.

David spent several hours leaving messages, not knowing when he would have the chance again. He wanted to tell them all his news. He took extra care over his message to his father, reassuring him that he would like the new lady in his life.

The rest of his time on board was spent restocking his shuttle and downloading textbooks. He found a place where he could buy spare parts and additional tools; he had been developing ideas through his reading and was excited at the prospect of building his projects.

The store owner was intrigued by the items he bought. 'What do you want with all of this? You do realize that none of this is compatible to your shuttle. You won't be able to use it for repairs.'

'I know. It is a project I'm hoping to work on.'

'Fair enough.' David signed the paperwork authorizing the transfer of funds and delivery to his shuttle.

On his second night he went to a place that had been recommended for its food and was surprised to walk into a bar. He paused at the entrance and thought about leaving and finding somewhere else then his stomach rumbled, so he found a seat at an empty table. He usually avoided bars; the noise in his head was enough - he did not need noise in his ears as well.

'Hey, you,' a man shouted from a nearby table. David looked at him and saw that he was sitting with several others. 'New scout?'

'How did you know?'

'When you have been out as long as we have, it's obvious,' he was told. 'Every space traveller can pick out a solo. The question is, if you have not done a lot of space travel how did you get a contract?'

David walked over to the table. 'I did some consulting work for the FWN. They were happy with my work and gave me a solo contract.' He deliberately kept his answer brief. 'But how did you know?'

'People only come to a starbase when they have to. If you are on a cargo or FWN ship then the crew stick together. Only solos arrive alone. When you have been out there for a while, you will get to know other solos and make friends with them.'

'Maybe I just don't have any friends,' David suggested.

'Those that are that antisocial stay on their ships

when they can and in their rooms when they can't. They don't come down to the bar.' Everyone laughed. 'You're welcome to join us.'

By the end of the night, he had several more people to add to his communication account. Solos, he learned, were a tight group; they might see each other rarely but they always sought each other out at bases and shared useful information. The other pilots advised him about how to cope with being on his own, even doing something as simple as keeping a diary. 'You might be talking to yourself as you record it but you're still talking and reminding yourself about what you might want to tell people on your return.'

❖

David left the starbase feeling less alone, knowing that there were others out there like him, others he could ask advice from. He had been told that as a solo, he would always be welcome at a solos' table whether he knew them or not. The advice he had received and the project he was planning made him much more hopeful for his second tour.

Chapter 16

OVER the last few years David had built up a reputation as an inventor during his time as a scout. Several of his creations had been taken on by companies and earned him quite a profit. It had been suggested more than once by everyone, except the FWN, that he should stop working as a scout and work on his projects full time but he rejected the idea. Although it had taken him a while, once he had got used to it he enjoyed being on his own most of the time. And he loved the silence.

Whenever he had docked at a base, he sought out other solos. Twice he had been lucky and timed his maintenance and resupply at a starbase where the *New York* was. He met up with old friends - Mark, Jon and Elen in particular.

The last time the *New York* had docked it was for over a week. David delayed his own departure and spent a few days in engineering, amazed at how much he had learnt since he had left; now he outstripped some of the crew in general knowledge. But most importantly, he was able to rent a room with Elen. He had missed her most of all.

'The headaches are paining you more than they used to,' Elen said, as she sat behind him on the bed and rubbed his temples. 'I'm sure they were never this bad when you were on the *New York*.'

'They weren't.'

'Is it because you spend so much time alone? You don't build your barriers as well as you used to?'

'I have been scanning space around the shuttle in the

same way I did on the *New York*. Over time I have been able to push further and now I can feel ships before the sensors pick them up.'

'What does the UTA say about it?'

'I've not told them. I don't talk to them now unless I have to. If they knew, they could order my return and I don't want to go back there.'

'Is this dangerous for you? Could you go out there on your own and collapse?'

'No. I'm just getting stronger and, as a result, everything is getting louder,' David said. 'I really wish you could join me at my father's wedding.' He said, changing the topic.

'I do too, but the *New York* will be too far away.' She paused in her administrations and David opened his eyes and looked at her.

'You want to say something but you are not sure how.'

'My brother Paul, the telepathic brother, has passed his FWN training and will be joining us on the *New York*.'

'When did you find out?' David knew her brother had been training but nothing more. 'Straight onto a deep-space vessel from training? I thought the FWN did not allow it.'

'I picked up the message this afternoon. I am so proud of him, he's the first FWN telepath and it's all thanks to you.' She leaned down and kissed him. 'It apparently caused a lot of debate. As you are the only basis for comparison and had no problems, they decided to risk a deep-space mission and a friendly crew.'

'I hope it works out well for him.'

⁜

A few months after that conversation, David finally returned to Europa for the first time in years to celebrate his father's marriage. He met his new stepmother-to-be only a week before the wedding when she came with his father to collect him from the space dock, but he had been communicating with her whenever he was at a base. Anja was nothing like his mother; she was confident and successful in her own right and more than a match for his father. The moment he had seen them together, he knew that theirs was a true partnership. He was glad that Viktor was finally moving on after his mother's death. They had insisted that he stay with them on the lead up to the wedding and as a result he had been swept up in all the last minute preparations and celebrations.

Anja's wedding dress was made of Lismarian fabric that must have cost a fortune. As she walked towards Viktor, the material had changed from pink to yellow as it reflected her changing emotions. David was intrigued by how the material picked up on the wearer's feelings and reflected them; when he had first heard about it he had looked into it, but the technology was a trade secret. Intrigued he had spent time on his trips trying to replicate it but failed and eventually moved on to other pursuits. Lismarian fabric had been available for the last year or so, but supplies were limited and expensive because supply did not meet demand. Demand kept rising; the clothing was fast becoming a status symbol for the rich.

'You look stunning," David told her after the ceremony, 'my father is a very lucky man.'

'Thank you David,' Anja replied before her attention was called away by other guests.

'Mr Wilhelm, it is a pleasure to finally meet you,' an elderly man said coming up to him as his step mother walked away. 'I am Theron Gallo of Gallo industries.'

'Of course, sir. You bought the designs for my little energy-saving device.'

'Your little device saves me a fortune every year. It is just a shame you would not sell me the patent. I could have made us both a lot of money.'

'I like to retain overall control. You should appreciate that.'

'I do, I do,' Gallo said. 'But tell me ... all of your patents are based on standard materials. Have you ever thought of using the Lismarian materials? You have obviously seen their fabric but they do other things as well, very strong, lightweight materials, brilliant for use in engines.'

'I have heard of them. I tried to get the specifications but the company would not release them unless I agreed to work under contract to them and in a lab they have specified, they would not agree to me working from my shuttle.'

'You could always stop working as a scout and work for me full time, I have an agreement with them. Then you would have access to everything you need. Just think of what we could achieve together.'

'Thank you for the very generous offer, but it is not the first I have had and the answer will be the same: I am not prepared to give up being a shuttle pilot just yet.'

'I could offer you a small fortune.'

'Money does not interest me, I'm afraid. The silence does.'

'I can't give you the same solitude but let me know if you change your mind,' Gallo said and walked away.

Theron Gallo's was not the only job offer David received that night and by the time he went back to his room, his head was killing him. Only a few days more, he thought, before he could leave. But tomorrow he had to visit the FWN.

✳

'It is not the normal type of job a scout would take, David,' Admiral Yoland said when they met in his office. 'I will understand if you don't wish to take it but your specialist skills make you the logical choice for this.'

'What is it you need?'

'There have been reports of ships going outside our charted space. We don't know where they are going or why.'

'Why can't one of your ships investigate?'

'We have tried. It is not a regular occurrence but we believe it has been going on for several months. We have ships patrolling and there is nothing; we withdraw them and the reports start again. We have sent other scouts and ships to search the area but they detect nothing, without knowing their path or approximate timings, the area of space is just too large. And we can't justify such an extensive search when we don't know what, if anything, is going on.'

'You are hoping that I might pick up something using telepathy where your scans have failed.'

'Mark believes that you kept practising after you left him and your range has increased greatly. Is it true that you can now cover a greater area of space than our scans can?'

'It is. Is there anywhere that I can't go in this area?'

'Not that I am aware of. There has been nothing reported that would be a hazard but we have very little information about what is out there. You will need to be careful.'

'Why don't I go out on one of your ships? That way you will have the benefit of both your scanners and my mind.'

'There are many people in the FWN who feel too much money and time has already been spent on this. You would be doing this for me and not under a FWN contract.'

'Why do you care so much about it?'

'The best I can call it is a hunch. There is something about the activity that I don't like, and I don't like the fact that nothing has been found with the resources that we've put in already.'

'Do you suspect new cloaking technology?'

'No. Now we know how it works we have been able to adapt as needed so far, but I do suspect that they do have the capacity to cloak, it would explain why the non FWN fail to pick up any trace of activity.'

'Do you suspect someone in the FWN knows what is going on?'

'I suspect many things and can prove nothing. That is why I am asking for your help; you don't answer to anyone.'

'I take it that if I find anything I report direct to you and no one else?'

'Yes, David. Thank you. Let me know what you sense but make sure you keep a safe distance from those ships.'

'I will do. You gave me the chance to get into space and become what I am. I owe you more than this.'

⁕

'I thought when I finally got you back here you would stay for good. I know you have had some very good job offers,' Viktor Wilhelm said.

'I have, but it is not what I want. And besides, if I stayed I would be in the way of the newlyweds.'

'No, you would not! Please stay so we can get to know each other properly,' Anja said.

'Thank you, but I don't find being around people easy. I am looking forward to going back into space.'

'Surely if you spent more time around people it would become easier? Please stay, you are welcome here.'

'No,' Viktor said. 'If he needs to go, he has to go.'

'I don't understand. I thought you wanted us to all spend time together, to try and be a family,' Anja protested. Viktor and David looked at each other. 'What don't I know?'

'It is nothing to worry about, I promise. I have been asked to do a favour for an old friend. Once it is done, I will be back for a proper visit.'

Chapter 17

AFTER his conversation with Elen several months ago, he started to consider a retest from the UTA to make sure he was gaining in strength and there was nothing more to the worsening headaches. He had found being back on a planet harder than expected, and he was worried what would happen if his suspicions were correct and he had increased a level. The UTA, however, had made it very clear that they were unhappy with his career choice. That was one of the reasons David had avoided going home. He suspected that he was only allowed to live the life he wanted because his father's influence and the political pressure caused after his own successful time on the *New York*. If he had increased in strength, he would be one of the very few sane level elevens and the UTA could argue their need for him to work for them. David preferred to take the chance with his health, and left Europa again shortly after his meeting with Admiral Yoland.

It took David weeks to get to the edge of mapped space where the ships were most often detected. He docked at the last starbase and made sure he had as many supplies as possible and that his shuttle was serviced appropriately because he expected to be out for longer than ever before. The last thing he did before he left was check if he had any messages and send responses to his family and friends. He was careful what he said to those on the *New York*, especially Mark, because he wasn't sure what the admiral had told his son. As far any of the crew were aware, including Elen, he had just taken on another scout mission. The last message he looked at was from the admiral; he had nothing further to report, so David let him know where he was and that he would be in uncharted space the next day.

Admiral Yoland was not able to give him a definite location for where these ships went, only the points they entered and exited this area of space. As the old saying went, it was like looking for a needle in a haystack.

David had been in uncharted space for months and detected nothing except one other scout ship. He knew the pilot and they spent a few hours exchanging news while they were in communication range. Keeping a close eye on his supplies, David knew he should consider going back to charted space soon so he checked the most direct course back and how long it would take. He could stay out for a week, maybe two before he had to turn around and go back.

Thinking there was little to gain in pushing it too close, he decided to do one last check before going back. He checked his sensors first, but there was nothing. Before lying down on his bunk, he opened his mind as far as he could. He always started close and moved out to make sure there was nothing there that the shuttle had not detected. The FWN ships might have the technology to detect cloaked ships but he did not.

At first he thought the results would be the same as always but then he sensed minds right on the edge of his limit. They were too far away for him to detect anything useful, other than the fact there were a lot of minds so it was not another scout. He guessed they were out of the range of any sensors.

David jumped up and set the shuttle in the direction he

had felt the ship. He tried to keep in touch with the minds but he could not maintain the level of concentration he needed and pilot the shuttle at the same time. Frustrated, he put on the autopilot and stretched his mind out again until he found the ship. If he felt it moving in a different direction, he would have to break contact again to reset the direction of the shuttle. He hoped that the other vessel was not a lot faster or he would lose it quickly.

David finally lost the ship after two days. Trying to maintain contact over such a great distance as well as pilot his shuttle was not possible to sustain; the only thing he could do was keep travelling in the last-known direction and hope that he would catch up with it. He searched with no luck for a week afterwards; he was unable to pick it up again and had been travelling further and further into uncharted space. He kept a close eye on his supplies, reducing them to a minimum to make them last, but he knew he had to make his way back to a starbase soon.

He was wondering how far he could push it when he picked up the ship again.

The next day David was able to get closer and closer as the ship changed direction. By evening he no longer had to place the shuttle onto autopilot to fully open his mind; the vessel was finally in his operating range so it must have come to a stop. He was fairly sure there was a planet nearby as he felt other consciousnesses but he did not understand what he felt; he assumed he was just too far away. Worried that he would lose the ship again if he stopped to rest, he continued to travel as fast as his little craft could go.

By morning, the other vessel was coming into sensor range. David held back so his presence was not picked up. He confirmed through the shuttle's sensors that the ship was stationary, in orbit around a planet. To make sure, he checked the star maps and confirmed what he already suspected: the planet had not been mapped; no one had assessed it; no one officially knew it was there. So what was the ship finding of interest? Why had it not filed a report, as required by law, on a newly discovered planet?

David placed the shuttle on autopilot, opened his mind and directed his attention towards the ship. To his surprise, it had several telepaths on board, which meant that if he pushed too hard he might be detected. All he could feel for sure was their intense interest in the planet so he turned his mind towards it. He was intrigued at what he might discover, so he tentatively opened his mind, not knowing what to expect.

He felt millions of minds; he tried to focus, to get a feeling for these people, but the sheer volume made it impossible. The overall feeling he got was one of contentment and everyday life. He could not understand the thoughts, only the general emotions. As far as he could grasp, these were basic people who had nothing to offer the FWN and by law should be left alone to develop on their own. Which raised the question: what was the ship doing here?

The FWN, on being informed of the planet's existence, would formally assess it. If it was inhabited and they could verify what the population was capable of, and if they were very near being able to travel in space, then first contact would be considered. That would be carried out by highly trained FWN ambassadors following strict protocols. If, as David expected, they were nowhere near space travel then the area would be deemed restricted to allow the population to develop naturally. Which meant that this ship should be nowhere near this planet.

David was so engrossed in trying to gain a better sense of the inhabitants that he did not notice that shuttles had left the ship and were heading down to the planet's surface. He was surprised when the minds he was reading went from contentment to fear. He felt their growing panic; he should have cut the connection as the storm of feelings grew but curiosity kept him tied to them.

He could never have guessed what was to come.

The terror.

The pain.

David gripped his head and pulled at his hair, screaming. He could not stop as he felt his skin being ripped off him again and again.

⁂

'Captain, there is another vessel out there.'

'There is nothing on the sensors. Are you sure?'

'Yes, captain. I think it is a solo sitting just out of sensor range. Whoever is watching us is a telepath and his mind is screaming with what is happening on the planet. That's why I can hear him now.'

'Can you give me good enough co-ordinates to bring it down?'

'I believe so captain.'

'Then fire, I don't want the scout reporting to anyone.'

⁂

Even while his mind was reeling, David felt the impact on his shuttle and the spinning motion. The sudden change in movement shocked him but he was too disorientated to understand what was happening. He reached out to turn on the auto pilot and shields but both were already active, he tried to disconnect his mind as he could not make any sense of what was happening because the mental pain was just too great.

David's world continued to spin both mentally and physically until he was thrown sharply forward and he knew no more.

Chapter 18

DAVID became aware of blistering heat and his parched throat. He slowly opened his eyes and saw that he was still in his shuttle, strapped into the pilot seat. The metal of the terminal he was lying on was so hot he could feel it burning his skin. He tried to push himself up but his head exploded with pain. He collapsed back onto the terminal, preferring the heat to the pain of moving and slipped thankfully back into unconsciousness.

Thirsty, was his next thought. So thirsty. He tried moving his jaw in the hope of producing some saliva but there was nothing. He pushed himself up and grabbed his aching head in both his hands, groaning as his surroundings spun around him, then he waited until everything settled and the nausea passed. Once everything started to stabilise he slowly unclipped himself and went to the water dispenser. He poured a full glass and, ignoring everything he knew about the best ways to hydrate, gulped it down as quickly as he could to quench his extreme thirst and ease the pain in his mouth and throat. His stomach revolted almost immediately; soon he was vomiting and he collapsed again.

David did not know how long he lay on the floor of the shuttle before he was able to pull himself up. He reached for the water again and this time he sipped it slowly. He needed to move, to get to the med kit to get the medication which would rid him of his headache and to check if he had other injuries, but his body would not listen to his brain. He felt the dark creeping back. He had to move or he would die where he lay. But no matter how hard he wanted to, he could not get up and the darkness won.

⁜

Disorientated, David opened his eyes and finally took in his surroundings. He was lying on the floor of his shuttle, he remembered that, but now he took in the alarms and flashing lights on the terminals indicating multiple system failures.

What had happened? He remembered the pain in his head and the spinning sensation. Had his autopilot failed?

No, there had been more, so much more. As he concentrated, David remembered he had been looking for ships for Admiral Yoland. He finally found one and was monitoring it. He was curious about the planet and surprised that there were life forms on it and then...

David started to shake with the memories. Then there had been torture and death on a massive scale, and he had not been able to disconnect from it. He had felt them all as they died.

He moved slowly, his head still pounding. He found that he could push himself up from the floor and carefully crawled towards the med kit and took the headache medication. As it took effect he could think more clearly. He grabbed the scanner and checked to see if he had any other injuries; from the results he saw that he was bruised and had minor burns to the side of his face. That confused him for a moment until he remembered feeling the heat from the terminal before he lost consciousness. Had there been a malfunction that made it overheat and burn him?

He staggered over to the terminals. Sitting in front of the pilot's station, he started to make sense of what his shuttle sensors were telling him. He had crashed! He knew that, but how? His shuttle was on autopilot and should have kept him in the same position. He always put the shuttle on autopilot when he opened up his mind; there should not have been a problem.

Slowly David tried to assess what systems were working. It looked like the shields had held until the last moment, so while there appeared to be a lot of damage most of it seemed to be repairable - though it would take considerable time and depend on the remaining systems staying stable. Life support appeared to have failed; luckily he had landed on a planet with an atmosphere that could sustain him. Nothing he looked at explained the burns to his face; it must have been a temporary fault.

Once he was happy that the systems were stable and not about to overload and blow him up, he started to go through the shuttle's readings, hoping to find a reason for the crash. It did not take him long; the ship he had sensed in orbit had opened fire on him. Though it had not been a direct hit, it had clipped the edge of his shields, causing him to spin towards the planet. The planet's gravity had drawn him in and the autopilot had not been able to compensate quickly enough to prevent the crash landing.

Would they come and look for him? Or would they assume as he plummeted towards the planet that he was dead? He tried to open his mind to see if he could sense them, but the pain flared up and stopped him. It would be a few days at least until he could use his abilities again. He checked to see if the ship's sensors could pick up anything, but they did not. He didn't know if that was because there was nothing to find, or if the sensors were failing as well. He hoped it was the former.

Satisfied that there was no immediate risk, David checked to see if there was anything he could find out about the planet he had landed on. As the results came up, his heart sank. There were two suns, and the planet was in close orbit with one of them. With the failed life support, the temperature in the shuttle must have gotten so high that it had heated the terminal to a level that had burnt him. He had thought that he had time to fix his shuttle but, if the readings he was seeing were correct, he would not survive for long if he did not get the life support operating soon. The shuttle was still cool so he assumed that the planet was not in the orbit of both suns. He had no idea how long he would have until the temperatures soared again. Having assured himself that other than the heat the atmosphere was fine for him to breathe, he opened the hatch and walked outside.

There was nothing that he could see, other than miles and miles of flat land and some patches of land where vegetation grew. He saw one sun in the sky, but the brightening on the horizon indicated that the second would soon ascend. David went back into the shuttle to see if he could programme the sensors to map the rise and fall of the two suns; he wanted to see how long both suns were in ascent so he could work out what hours he would be able to survive outside.

Soon the temperature inside the shuttle started to become unbearable. David tried to open the shuttle's hatch to let in more air but instead of a relieving breeze, a wave of scorching heat rolled in. Pain exploded in his face as the heat hit him, aggravating his burnt skin. He fumbled for the controls to shut the hatch as he gasped for breath. It was only then that he looked at the readings outside the shuttle; in his naivety he had not considered how much hotter it could get outside. He felt the metal of the shuttle heating up; knowing it would get hot enough to burn him, he lay down on his bunk, hoping that the mattress and sheets would not be affected by temperature. They had not been damaged earlier.

David had no concept of time as he lay on his bunk, sweating uncontrollably. Several times, as his thirst got stronger, he got himself a drink of water. He didn't want to unless it was necessary. All fluids were recycled, which was what allowed them to last so long, but there was always waste and loss. In this heat he would sweat out anything he drank and he would quickly run out of water unless he could find an alternative supply. Until he knew if that was possible, he would have to be careful how much he drank, and a wash was totally out of the question.

He did not know how long he lay on his bunk but slowly he became aware that the temperature had dropped. Remembering what had happened the last time he opened the hatch, he checked the outside temperature; though it was still very hot, it was similar to the internal readings so he opened it. The fresh air was a relief; the wind was hot but it created a pleasant contrast to the stifling atmosphere in the confined space.

It would be days until he knew the planet's cycle around its two suns. In the meantime he needed to get the life support fixed as quickly as he could. He was no doctor, he did not know how long he could survive in this heat. For all he knew, this might be the planet's winter and the temperature could get higher still. David grabbed his tools and started to pull the systems apart.

He had not finished fixing the life support as the temperatures started to rise again. He continued for as long as he could before he started to get disorientated and sweat dripped into his eyes; it was impossible to work with his hands so damp. He got a drink, lay down on his bunk again and closed his eyes. Sleeping might be impossible but he hoped he would be able to doze, he needed to rest so badly but he could not afford to do it when the temperature was cooler. He set an alarm to make sure he was woken up on a regular basis so he did not miss any valuable working time.

He could last only another few days, unless he managed to get the life support working again. Two days, he decided; if he could not get it up and running in two days then he would go out and look for water and somewhere better to shelter from the heat, like a cave. With determination, he went back to work.

Chapter 19

DAVID'S head did not stop aching. It was no longer because of his mental abilities but because of dehydration. The extreme heat was becoming unbearable, but he was close, so close. He made a few more connections on the circuit board and then ... he heard the life support coming on line, felt the air blowing through the vents and the temperature started to drop.

Breathing a sigh of relief, he moved over to the dispenser and took a long drink of water before grabbing his headache medication in the hope of getting a temporary relief. Finally he felt he could lie down to sleep for the first time since he crash landed.

He woke up panicking because no alarm had woken him before he remembered he had fixed the life support. David had no idea how long he had slept for but it must have been for some time because his mouth was uncomfortably dry. He tried to ignore it at first and tried to go back to sleep, but when that did not happen he sat up and reached for a drink of water. He sighed with relief as it trickled down his throat.

As his thirst eased, he realised that he felt more alert. He checked the time and saw that he had slept through a full cycle. The readings showed that the heat outside was still too great for him to leave the shuttle to find water. He checked the life support system and was pleased to see that it was working well. He set the alarm to go off when the external temperature dropped low enough for him to go outside and turned his attention to the shuttle's other systems while he waited.

The buzzing of the alarm made him jump; he had been so engrossed that he had forgotten all about it. David turned it off and checked the external temperature; it was still hot outside but it was becoming bearable. It was finally time for him to go out and search for water. He wished the sensors on the ship could indicate the best place to look.

Once he started thinking about going outside, he realised that there was little he could take with him which would be of use. Living on the shuttle for so long meant that he had never needed to pack items for a walk in an unknown environment; he did not even have a hat or a bottle to carry water in. He grabbed one of his T-shirts and tied it around his head, covering as much skin as possible, had a long drink of water and headed out.

As David opened the hatch hot, dry air flooded in. Taking a deep breath, he left the shuttle. Walking down the gangway, he felt the intensity of the suns. His feet hit a dry and dusty surface and, looking in front of him, he saw a long stretch of nothing. The land was flat and broken only by the occasional batch of scrub. There was no way there could be water in that direction - there was too little vegetation.

He walked around the shuttle to see if there was another direction he could start with and there, in the distance behind the shuttle, he saw mountains with greenery around them. He had no way of knowing how far away they were but he knew that was his best chance.

He thought he was fine, fine for him anyway. Spending so much time in space made the rare occasions he returned to a planet difficult; the pressure from real gravity was so much greater than on the ships. This planet was easier to cope with than Europa; he guessed it was smaller therefore the gravity was less. It was years since he had had to walk anywhere, other than around a starbase. He had always taken walking for granted, it was something easy that he could just do, but soon he was breathing hard and sweating from more than the heat.

David had set a timer to let him know when the period of bearable temperature was half way though so he could turn back, but he had not taken into account his physical stamina. He ignored the feelings of tiredness and thirst; all he could concentrate on was the greenery ahead of him. He kept pushing on, waiting for the alarm to go. His surroundings became slightly greener and his hopes started to rise. The buzzing brought his attention back from the horizon and he turned it off. *I'm so close,* he thought, *so close to my goal, it's just a little further...* He was sure that he would be able to make it. He kept on staggering forward, so desperate for water which he hoped was just ahead of him.

He did not know how much longer he staggered forward. He was so exhausted and desperate for a drink that he was no longer taking in what was around him. All he knew was to keep going. Then he couldn't go any further and blackness folded in on him.

⁂

David felt something cold splashing on to his face - water was dribbling over his mouth! He opened it and used his tongue to lick the fluid that landed on his lips. When it stopped, he tried to open his eyes but it was so bright he closed them again and slipped back into oblivion.

⁂

His back felt as if it were being ripped apart. He was being moved and none too gently. He tried to move, to stop the rough treatment, but that made his whole body feel as if it were burning up. The heat was unbearable and he ripped at his clothing. He was burning and he could not stop it. He heard someone screaming in pain and did not realise it was himself.

Slowly the burning eased and once again water was dribbled into his mouth. He heard voices but he could not understand them. He tried opening his eyes again and looked around. He was in some sort of structure, rough and badly made, and he could see light coming in through the gaps in the badly constructed ceiling.

He raised his hand and touched his face. He could feel the heat of his skin and bumps that must be blisters. Slowly he pulled himself up into a sitting position and saw that he was lying on a worn, rough woven rug – that was the only word he could think of to describe it, though it was not made of any material he had seen before. His back protested with the movement. Turning around as best he could, he saw his top was covered in dirt and torn in areas and he realised that he must have been dragged here.

He could hear voices but he could not understand what they were saying. That wasn't surprising for if this planet was uncharted, its language would not have been added to any translation device. He extended his mind to see if he could get a sense of the people, if they were a danger to him. He felt their minds; alien as they were, they recognised his mental touch and reacted to it. Everything went quiet. They were telepaths, he realised with a shock, and strong enough to block him out. The FWN had encountered other species during their explorations but none of them had telepaths, a fact that the UTA liked to use in its arguments about human superiority.

David heard a rustling sound and cautiously he turned his head to the entrance. He watched as a small being, humanoid in form, walked in and stopped. He couldn't see it clearly as it was standing in the shadow of the doorway. The creature said something that David did not understand and he shook his head in frustration.

'I'm sorry, I don't understand,' he croaked, his mouth and throat still so dry that he had trouble forming the words. Then he felt a warm, welcoming touch in his mind, reassuring him. He closed his eyes briefly, wallowing in the feeling of safety and reassurance before returning the feelings of thanks for the water and for being taken out of the sun.

The being walked slowly into the room and out of the shadow and David got his first look at this new species.

Stunning, was his first impression. The being's skin was almost translucent and David could see the shadow of its internal organs moving inside, but the most striking thing was the swirling pattern that covered it from head to toe and to the tips of its fingers. He sensed the being was male although he lacked the genitals of a human male. There was something familiar about him but for the moment David could not think what. Then another creature appeared with the same skin patterns – this was definitely female as it had a moving foetus inside its body. Obviously reproduction, however it happened, was not a problem.

The male said something to the female and David felt her exasperation. She handed the bowl she was carrying to him and turned and left the room. As she turned, David saw what appeared to be wings hanging down her back to her waist. Could she fly? He doubted it as the wings looked too small to take her weight.

The feeling of familiarity persisted but his head hurt so much that he could make no sense of it. The male came forward slowly and David realised that he was nervous. He knelt down and offered the bowl to him.

David reached out and tried to take it, but his raw and blistered hands were shaking too much and he couldn't get a stable grip. The creature helped him hold the bowl steady and pushed it gently towards his mouth. It was full of water and David drank greedily. Handing back the bowl once it was empty, David mentally expressed his gratitude. Then, as if the water had helped to focus his mind, he realised why the creature looked familiar: he had seen the patterning on its skin before - on his stepmother's wedding dress. How was that possible? Had the design been copied by the people who had been in orbit? But David's mind was so clouded that he struggled to think properly.

Chapter 20

DAVID had moments of clarity when the male stood over him and poured water into his mouth and he gasped at it, as if it were his last. As the burning pain in his face and hands became unbearable, he felt another mind easing it away, and something else that he could not grasp... Then with relief he lapsed into unconsciousness.

Opening his eyes, David saw the rough ceiling above him. It seemed strangely familiar; whatever material it was made of was loosely woven and left holes for the sunlight to stream through, except for directly above him where it had been patched with pieces of cloth. Moving cautiously, he realised he was no longer hurting so badly. He felt the edge of the roughly woven rug beneath him and then he encountered dry dirt. He slowly tried to push himself up but collapsed again, feeling weak and frustrated as he tried to remember what had happened. How he had got here? Then the flashes came into his mind of the strange alien hovering over him and giving him water. Had he been hallucinating? Did he have a fever from the severe sunburn? He had so many questions.

His hands were still red and blistered but as he flexed his fingers there was no pain and the blisters seemed less inflamed. His face also seemed to be healing; he hoped that there would be no scarring or long-term problems. He tried to push himself up again slowly and this time he succeeded. The room was empty; there were also large open windows but he was lying in the shade.

He heard a noise and looked towards the sound. There

was an opening, a crude doorway covered with another rug. It moved and in walked the alien male. David had not been dreaming: he was confronting his first non-human. He remembered that there were strict protocols that needed to be followed but he could not remember them.

'Hello,' he said. The alien looked at him and said something in a language David did not recognise. 'I don't understand you. I'm sorry.'

David felt another mind in his. He remembered it from before easing his pain. The mind was not asking him anything directly but showed him images of food and drink and a feeling of a question. David replied with a positive thought; they might not understand each other's words but, being telepathically compatible, he realised they could communicate with pictures and emotions.

The male, understanding him, left and returned after a moment with water and a bowl which contained something that looked like soup. David took them gratefully, his stomach cramping with hunger. How long was it since he had last eaten? Slowly he sipped the soup, knowing that if he drank it too quickly he would make himself sick. As he drank, the male watched him, David could feel his curiosity and his uncertainty.

Once he had finished, the male took the bowl and mentally questioned if he wanted more. David projected an image of water and was given another cup of water. It was surprisingly cold, considering the heat of the planet. Where did they store it for it to be so cold? It did not taste stale, it was fresh in a way that water on a ship could never be. It was the best thing he could ever remember tasting. In answer to his thought, an image appeared in his head of snow-capped mountains and water running off them.

'It came from a stream?' David asked, surprised, then

realised his question was pointless; it would not have been understood.

The male expressed curiosity so David returned the image of running water and said 'stream'.

'Stream,' the male repeated.

David pictured himself and pointed at his chest, 'David.'

'David,' the male repeated then pointed at himself and said, 'Hannoki.'

Maybe they could learn each other's language this way. Hannoki sat next to David, making it clear he wanted to learn more about him and, as David had, recognising that there was a way they could learn to understand each other better.

※

David's head ached with concentration from maintaining communication with the alien mind but it was not until the temperature started to rise that his mind started to wander. The basic structure shielded him from the suns' rays but did nothing to reduce the incredible heat. He thought it was bad on the shuttle, but it was nothing compared to this.

As the temperature rose he started to lose concentration, and then lost it all together. David remembered Hannoki's confusion as he struggled with the heat, a heat that did not bother the alien in the least. As he collapsed back onto the mat, his hands and face starting to burn again, he remembered from the ship's reading that this was going to get a lot worse over the next few hours. How had he survived it when he was racked by the fever? He hoped for the same oblivion to release him from the coming pain. However, the extreme heat did not come as expected; it was still unbearably hot but something else was shielding him. David did not have the strength to think about it and lapsed into unconsciousness.

When he came round, David knew that the heat had been considerably less than the outside temperature. What was keeping him from cooking alive? What had stopped his blood from boiling? The thin walls and ceiling of the building were surely not capable of it. Opening his eyes, he saw Hannoki sitting next to him, apparently concentrating. David touched Hannoki's mind with his own and was surprised by what he felt. Hannoki was creating a barrier around him, protecting him from the heat. David relaxed back onto the mat, relieved at the respite, even though he did not understand how it was possible.

As he became more aware of his surroundings, David felt Hannoki's tiredness. The temperature outside had become bearable again. Whatever Hannoki had done for him over the last few hours had not been easy for him. As David pushed himself up into a sitting position, the barrier Hannoki had been holding in place dropped. David felt a rush of hot air that made him gasp in surprise. He felt Hannoki gather his mind to put the barrier back into place, but David reassured him that he could cope with the heat and he felt Hannoki relax and a sense of relief as he slumped slightly.

David sent his thanks. In response Hannoki expressed his confusion over his inability to cope with the heat. In his mind David saw Hannoki standing outside under the full force of the two suns with his face turned towards them and his wings spread out. He was feeding off the suns' rays, David realised; that was how he got most of his energy. He did not know how many of the suns' cycles Hannoki had stayed inside with him, protecting him, which meant that he had not been able feed as he normally would. How long could he continue like this? No wonder he was so tired.

These people lived on a world with two suns; their biology had adapted to make the most of it. But David was something else to them.

What could he let them know? David knew there were extensive protocols around this, but if he did not get back to his shuttle then he could not survive without Hannoki's help. David remembered the ship in orbit over the planet and the extreme pain the creatures had felt. If he said he came down in a shuttle, would Hannoki think he was connected to whatever pain the ship had inflicted?

The images of the orbiting ship came into his head combined with thoughts of confusion. Shocked, David realised that Hannoki must have picked up on the images in his mind; he was so used to being a powerful telepath that he was not accustomed to anyone reading his mind so easily – or without his consent. He realised that if he wanted Hannoki's help and trust, he needed to try and explain everything.

David showed Hannoki how he had been alone in the shuttle, his curiosity at what the ship he saw was doing, the extreme pain and rapid descent of the shuttle and the crash that followed.

David felt Hannoki's confusion. In return, he was sent images of dead, skinned bodies with their wings cut off, left to rot under the suns. The horror of what he saw made David vomit the limited contents of his stomach. He had thought the Lismarian fabrics must have been copied by someone who had seen these people but with what he was being shown, another horrific possibility occurred to him. Maybe the fabric was not copied but was the skin of these people. But why take the wings? Then he remembered that many large companies were using other Lismarian products, products for which he had never been able to get the specifications.

People were wearing skins - his stepmother was wearing a skin for her wedding! Humans had not eaten meat for generations and the wearing of skins in any form had been illegal for even longer. How was this possible? Anything that was imported was strictly checked to ensure nothing was being brought in that would affect the ecosystem... David's mind reeled with it all, then a calming influence came over him so that he was able to rationalise his thoughts. Taking deep breaths he controlled himself.

'I am sorry, I am so, so sorry,' he said, crying, not sure if he was apologising for his behaviour which was upsetting Hannoki, or if it was for the actions of his kind. David managed to project his feelings of regret, which were returned by Hannoki as he realised that David had no idea what was happening on his planet.

David knew he had to report back to Admiral Yoland as soon as possible, but for that he needed to get back to his shuttle and fix his systems.

Chapter 21

HANNOKI came into the room and handed David some cloth, similar to what he had been lying on, but larger and thinner. David turned it around in his hands, then images came of the burning heat as he had staggered away from his shuttle. Hannoki indicated that David should put the cloth over his head and wrap it round himself, like a cloak. David did so, making sure he covered as much of his exposed skin as possible.

He stood up and followed Hannoki through the doorway into the room beyond. It was the same shape and size, with stools and a table and more mats on the floor. There did not appear to be any other rooms so had Hannoki and his family sleeping here while they looked after him? Following Hannoki outside, David looked around and saw that the mountains were a lot closer and the ground much more fertile. Looking into the sky, he recognised that the suns were descending to their lowest point.

'Where are we going?' David asked, turning to look at Hannoki. He saw that the alien was covering himself with a similar piece of cloth; did he expect to get cold once the suns went down? Or was there another reason? David asked Hannoki mentally, and Hannoki replied with an image of his shuttle. When had Hannoki been there? Before or after David had collapsed? There were so many questions but for the moment he could not think of a way to frame them so that Hannoki would understand.

As he walked away from Hannoki's home, David turned around and saw it properly for the first time. It was a small, crudely-built structure and it was not the only one; there were several others nearby and more in the distance. The land around them looked as if it was being farmed. David had assumed that Hannoki was isolated but it looked like he was part of a farming community. Did the people know about him?

A noise that sounded a lot like a laugh came from Hannoki and David saw an image of other aliens but without the extensive markings. They were crowding into Hannoki's home, wanting to look at the strange, mad being. Great! David thought. That was not the best first impression!

Hannoki took David back to where he had collapsed. There was a clear imprint of his body and the footprints made by his booted feet. Together they followed the footprint trail back to the shuttle. As they walked David tried ask further questions about the skinned bodies; he wanted to know if Hannoki understood why they were being attacked but, without words, he was reliant on projecting images which caused Hannoki a lot of emotional pain.

David was frustrated but he hoped that with time he would learn enough of the language to ask the questions he really needed answers for. With this in mind, he used the walk back to his shuttle to improve his vocabulary by projecting simple images, like a bowl or rug, and naming them, Hannoki repeated the word and then taught David the word in his language. Once they were both happy, Hannoki projected an image and the process was reversed.

David had not realised how far he had walked before he collapsed. The suns were going down and they were walking during the coolest part of the day but he was starting to struggle with his illness caused by the sunburn, dehydration and his lack of fitness. Both suns were on the rise again when the shuttle finally came into sight.

Hannoki stopped when he saw it and his overriding emotion was fear and guilt. The images that went through David's head answered a lot of his questions over what had been happening, though how old Hannoki's memory was he did not know.

Hannoki had been working a little distance from home on a crop he was harvesting when he had seen changes in the sky. Remembering the stories that this was a bad sign. He and the aliens around him had ducked into the vegetation and watched as the ship came through the atmosphere and landed. Humans, David recognised, in protective suits for hostile environments had come off and walked towards a group of people, who were standing watching, in shock. Hannoki was about to come out from his hiding place when the men from the ship started grabbing those who were closest and pulling them to the floor. They cut the wings from their backs and started to strip the skin from their bodies while they screamed in pain.

Hannoki wanted to stop them, to help his friends, but the pain that ripped through him crippled him for hours. The others who had been hiding with him dragged him away. When he was capable of thought again, he was lying some distance away from home. He flew home in panic to reassure himself that his family was safe, then he returned to the field and saw his friends' bodies rotting in the sun. The shuttle was gone.

With tears running down his face, David tried to project his sorrow, horror and regret. He sank to the ground and started shaking until he felt Hannoki's cool hand on his forehead and the impression of regret for sharing his memories. David took a deep breath.

'Thank you, is there any more?' he said before reinforcing the question mentally. Hannoki hesitated at the request but, at a further push from David, he revealed the rest.

Hannoki approached the bodies; he couldn't identify them because their hair, skin and wings had been removed. He did not known what to do or who to go to; all he could think was that they could not be left out in the sun. He dragged the bodies into a pile and started to dig; once he had a grave large enough, some sanity started to return. He started to contact the families of people he had seen before the attack. None of those who arrived could know if their loved ones were there or rotting elsewhere, but this was the first burial that was announced so they came to pay their respects. There were more people missing than found. Hannoki had felt similar pain at different times as others were attacked at distant locations. David realised that these attacks had been going on for some time.

When David crash landed, Hannoki did not know if he had come to attack them, the shuttle looked the same but David did not, he had waited to see what would happen but nothing did. Then he had found him collapsed and not knowing what else to do, had brought him home. While David was sick, Hannoki picked up on the pain he had felt before the crash, his fevered nightmares of skinned bodies, and had decided to learn more before deciding if David was an enemy.

David did the only thing he could think of to reassure Hannoki and took his hand. He opened his mind fully; though Hannoki would not understand the words, he hoped that the images, thoughts and feelings would convince him that David wanted to help, that he was horrified by what was happening. If he could get his shuttle working again, he could get them help; what was happening would stop and they would be safe again.

Feeling Hannoki's mind go through his amazed and energized him. He suspected that Hannoki was stronger than him, stronger than any human, but until he had been invited to invade David's mind he had no idea how much stronger he was. The power made David's blood hum, but also gave him hope. Hannoki was sane, so were powerful telepaths driven insane by expectation? Lack of training? Or was the human mind just not developed enough to cope?

Hannoki went through all of David's memories; David could feel his fascination over a people, planet and culture so different to his own. He was relieved that, though he had not tried to prevent it, Hannoki had not seen memories of his father's wedding. Until he knew if his suspicions were correct about where the material for the dress had come from, he did not want Hannoki to know what was happening to the skins.

Finally Hannoki withdrew his mind and David immediately missed the connection. Taking a deep breath he started to push himself off the ground. A strong cool hand came under his arm and Hannoki helped him rise. David became aware of how hot it was and turned towards the shuttle, Hannoki supporting him as he went.

The shuttle was hot to the touch as he typed in the release code for the door; it slid open and a rush of cool air came out and David sighed with relief. The life support was still working. He turned and saw Hannoki standing outside. He indicated that he could enter but Hannoki just stayed where he was, then took a step backwards and projected an image of him returning when the suns had gone down. David expressed his worry over the distance Hannoki would be travelling but the alien laughed before removing his cloak and holding it in a tight ball in front

of him. He turned and David saw his wings, the wings
he thought would never take the weight of their bodies.
They opened up and he realised that, when spread, the
wings were in two layers and twice the size as when they
were folded. Clearly Hannoki had a much quicker way
of travelling.

David closed the shuttle door. He checked his medical
supplies but found nothing that would help sunburn.
He took something that would relieve the pain. Finally
he was able to lie down and rest without the feeling of
burning up.

Chapter 22

DAVID almost didn't believe it when he heard the engines finally come on line. It was not with their normal smooth hum but with a grinding noise that made him wince, though eventually the tone evened out and held steady. He held his breath as he listened, thinking that at any moment they would fail, that his repairs had not been sufficient and he would have to start again.

Slowly he let out his breath as the sound remained stable and started to check the readings to see how well they were functioning. Satisfied that they were working as well as could be expected, he turned the engines off; he had limited fuel left and could not risk burning it unnecessarily if he wanted to break out of the planet's atmosphere.

He checked the outside temperature; it was too hot for him to go outside. Before he risked taking off, he needed to check everything again to make sure there were no signs of stress or leaks. He would have to wait for the outside temperature and the engines to cool off first.

A banging on the door distracted him. Without checking who it was, he released the lock, There was only one person who would come: Hannoki. He came regularly, but David did not know if it was every day or not because he had completely lost track of time.

Hannoki walked on board the shuttle and put down the container he was carrying. 'Good evening, David,' he said.

'Good evening Hannoki.' David got up and poured the

contents into the shuttle's water storage. 'Thank you, the water is very welcome.'

'The ground was burnt outside.'

'I managed to get the engines working. They get very hot but I have not been outside yet to look.'

'It is still too hot for you, unless you want me to shield you.'

'Thank you but no. I have several tests I can run in here before I need to check outside. The engines need to cool down before I examine them. It will be several hours before they are cool enough for me to work on them outside.'

David had taken up Hannoki's offer of a kinetic shield several times; this had allowed him to move around outside the shuttle during the time he had been here and had helped him to complete the repairs. David had tried asking how Hannoki could offer this protection but did not get an exact answer, only that Hannoki and some of his friends had this power but most of the other aliens hadn't. He did not think that Hannoki was being deliberately obstructive; it was either something Hannoki could do but couldn't explain or they had not learnt enough of each other's languages to describe the process.

'Will you be going soon?' Hannoki asked, breaking David's train of thought.

'I don't know. I need to run a lot more tests first to see if the engines are working properly.'

'You have time now for more talking or do you need to finish work?'

'I always have time when you come here, Hannoki.' They settled down together. David was amazed how quickly his friend had picked up a new language and had recorded their conversations so he could store the words he learnt into the translator database. He was not good at retaining them, not like he was with numbers, which is why Hannoki talked to him in English.

Hannoki's visits always brought relief from his work and he always arrived with water, after David's first attempt to collect water himself had nearly killed him. He had been resting, trying to build up his strength before he went out again on another search, when Hannoki arrived with a heavy, ceramic container that was full of water. Since then Hannoki had brought more than enough to keep him going - but now food was becoming a problem. Hannoki occasionally brought something edible but David got the impression that they did not have much to eat because of the planet's temperature. He wondered how much food could be spared. With his supplies already limited when he crashed, David had to be very careful about how much he ate. He was always hungry and none of his clothing fitted him properly – they were starting to hang off his body. He would not survive forever without food and no one knew where he had crashed, so no one would be looking for him.

At first Hannoki had not wanted to come on board the shuttle but David could not leave the hatch open for long because the strain on the damaged systems was too much. He sent reassurance to him that there was nothing on board that could hurt him. When he first came on board, Hannoki had panicked and fled, but he returned. David knew Hannoki was still not happy coming inside but had accepted that it was necessary if he wanted to learn more about this new arrival on his planet.

Several times David wished that he had an environmental suit so he could work outside on the shuttle without Hannoki's help and he could explore the planet to find his own food and water. But there had been no need for one to get to the life pod and he was not meant to land on planets. And with a survival suit, he might never have met Hannoki. He would have looked like one of the men who were killing the aliens; he would have been their enemy rather than a curiosity.

'It is cooler now if you want to look outside,' Hannoki said suddenly. David did not know how much time had passed since Hannoki arrived and, locked inside the shuttle he had no idea what the outside temperature was.

'That would be good,' David said. After quickly checking to see if Hannoki was correct, he released the shuttle's hatch. He picked up the few tools he would need. Once outside, he saw what Hannoki meant by the burnt ground: beneath the engines were twin lines in the soil that had turned black.

'What caused?' Hannoki asked him.

Not having a clue how he was going to explain it with their limited vocabulary, David showed him the image of the engines firing and the flames and heat coming from them. He felt Hannoki's astonishment. David was fast discovering that there was no technology on this planet; they had simple tools and containers, the cups and bowls were all crude ceramics, probably made and cooked in the heat of the two suns.

An image appeared in David's head of something bright streaking though the air, followed by the pain he felt when his people were killed. David could sense Hannoki's question: would his shuttle make the same tracks in the sky?

'Yes, it will look the same.'

Chapter 23

DAVID knew the shuttle was finally as fixed as it could be and it was time for him to go. He checked the outside temperature and guessed it would be a while before Hannoki came, so he started to clear everything away in readiness for his departure.

How long had he spent on the planet? The ship's clock had been damaged in the crash and, with no idea of the time, David couldn't reset it. It was imperative that he leave now while he still had some fuel. Also, he could not remember the last time he was not hungry and he had started to feel dizzy and listless. There were lumps and discoloured patches on his skin that had started to itch and bleed where he had been exposed to the sun. He did not know what they meant, but he knew they were not normal.

With everything ready, he sat back and waited for Hannoki. They had been spending more and more time together and Hannoki and had started to bring his eldest son, Milkoy, with him. Knowing that time was limited, they were all keen to learn as much about each other as possible.

It was not long before the knock came at the door. David opened it and Hannoki walked in with his container of water. He looked around the shuttle and saw that everything had been stowed away. 'You are going?'

'Yes, I did the last tests today and everything is ready,' David explained as simply as he could.

'When?'

'I was just waiting to say goodbye to you.'

'Will you be back?'

'I hope so, if my people will let me.'

'I hope you will return.'

'So do I, and I plan to do everything I can to find out who is attacking your people.'

'Thank you.' They looked at each other, and neither knew what to say.

'I could not have survived here without you. Thank you,' David said.

'I liked to help, liked to talk to you.'

'Me too.'

'Do you have time to come back to say goodbye to Petrra and Milkoy?'

'Yes, I would like to say goodbye to them.'

The last time he met Petrra she was pregnant and did not trust him, David wondered how she would receive him now and what she thought of her husband and son visiting him as often as they did. He knew from Hannoki that she had had the baby and they had talked a great deal about it.

As they approached the cabin, Petrra walked out holding the baby in her arms. She smiled and waved David inside where he saw Milkoy and another child. David had not met her before but knew her name was Mesrra; she clung nervously to her brother's leg. The children both had the same patterning as their parents.

Mats had been placed in a circle on the floor and David sat down between Hannoki and Milkoy as Petrra served a thin, lumpy soup. David noticed that he was given much more than everyone else. He ate the food gratefully and tried to talk in their language, which made Mesrra laugh. Finally Hannoki took pity on him, spoke to him in English and translated for his family.

David stayed until Hannoki told him that the suns

would soon start to rise. With regret he stood up and said his farewells then Hannoki walked back with him to his shuttle. As David opened the hatch he realised that, now he was going, he did not know what to say to his friend.

'Can I watch you leave?' Hannoki asked, breaking the silence.

'You can't be close when I take off, it would not be safe.'

'I understand. Did you want the water?' He said pointing at the container that was still on the floor.

'Please. I don't know how long it will take me to get home.' David emptied the water into the shuttle's systems, before handing the contained back to Hannoki. 'I do hope to see you again.'

'So do I.' Hannoki grabbed David's arm and then turned and left.

Once David was happy that his friend was a safe distance away, he started the shuttle's engines. He had not been able to do a trial take-off because he was severely limited on fuel. He still was not sure he had enough to make it to the nearest starbase.

Taking a deep breath, David took off. As the shuttle accelerated, everything started to shake and for a moment he thought the shields would fail and the shuttle would break apart. But then, suddenly, he broke out of the atmosphere and it stabilised. Releasing his breath, he checked the shuttle's systems; although there were no failures, as he had expected he did not have enough fuel or power to get him to the nearest base. His best hope was to broadcast an emergency signal and hope it got picked up. If he had to, he could always put himself into cryo sleep in the escape pod and set the beacon.

David always knew there was no guarantee that he would get back safely, but he could not have survived for much longer on the planet. He had to play the best odds.

He cut back on anything that was not essential, reducing his life support as far as he could, and set the shuttle on the most direct course. He continually scanned with his mind for any vessels that might be in the area but he was afraid that, until he got near to known space, the only ships he would encounter would be the ones killing Hannoki's people. He did not expect anyone from the FWN to be looking for him; this was not exactly an approved mission and scouts often went missing - it was one of the risks of the job.

He slept when he could, knowing that he used less air when he was unconscious. The cold made it difficult and the reduced oxygen was making it hard for him to concentrate. After a while his mind started to drift and he began to lose track of time. Part of him thought that now was the time to set the mayday beacon and climb into the emergency pod, but he kept thinking just a little longer.

He checked the sensors again but could not read them. He rubbed his eyes to help focus them but it did not help. He leaned back, thinking that he just needed to rest for a moment. How long he sat in the pilot's seat he had no idea; he even started to imagine things.

'Mr Wilhelm? Sir, can you hear us?' the voice whispered in his head. When he did not respond, when he thought he was going mad and tried to block it, there was a more forceful, *'David, David.'* Something was familiar about the voice and he tried to reach for it. He had just touched what he realised was a collective mind before he knew no more.

⁜

He was warm and comfortable and, for the first time since he crashed, he was not hungry and thirsty. He opened his eyes and saw that he was on a bed in a white, well-lit room. He was no longer on his shuttle or in Hannoki's cabin, but he had no idea where he was. He tried to push himself up and immediately someone was with him, gently pushing back down.

'Mr Wilhelm, I am Dr Rogers. How are you feeling?'

'What happened? Where am I?'

'You are safe, you are on the *New York*.'

'I'm still dreaming,' he said and drifted back into unconsciousness.

'So you're awake at last,' a familiar voice said the next time David opened his eyes. He turned his head and saw Jon sitting next to him.

'I really am on the *New York*? I thought I was dreaming.'

'The doctor said you seemed out of it when you last woke up. You gave us all a scare.'

'I don't understand. How did I get here? I don't remember setting the beacon.' He tried to sit up but could not, and realised that he was attached to various machines. 'What's wrong with me? Am I alright?'

'I can't answer anything on the medical side but I'll get the doctor to come and talk to you. As for the rest, the captain wanted to know as soon as you were awake so let me call him and he will explain things better than me.' Jon stood up and moved away. David lay back and closed his eyes. He could not believe he had been found, and by the *New York* of all possible ships.

'Mr Wilhelm, do you remember me?' David opened his eyes at the new voice and turned his head towards the speaker.

'You're Dr Rogers. Am I alright?'

'You will be. You were suffering from mild hypothermia because of the life support settings, and you were severely dehydrated and malnourished, all of which are easily remedied,' the doctor explained. 'More seriously, you have developed skin cancer. It is a condition that was common in our past. We can treat it easily enough but you will have to stay here in the medical bay until we can transfer you to a proper treatment facility.'

'Cancer? I didn't think people got it anymore.'

'Most causes were genetic and could be stopped before it developed; other forms were a result of the environment. Once the causes of the disease were found, they were eradicated. There are still cases but they are not common. Skin cancer like yours is caused by high levels of UV radiation. If you were on a shuttle, I have no idea how you developed it. We'll have to run more tests to see if something in your genetics was missed.'

'I got sick because of sunlight?'

'If you were exposed to high levels, yes,' the doctor confirmed.

'I know that expression on your face, David. I don't need to be a telepath to know that you recognise why you got sick' Captain Yoland said, as he walked up to the bed and into David's line of vision. 'It is good to see you awake finally.'

'Mark, it is very good to see you but I still don't understand how I got here.'

'I will explain in a moment, but that look on your face at the mention of sunlight making you ill means something to you. Where have you been? A lot of your shuttle's readings have been corrupted by system failures and those that we have been able to download make no sense.'

'I had to protect the core systems.'

'I was not criticising David, just stating a fact.'

'I crashed on a planet that had two suns. The heat was extreme.'

'How long were you there for?' the doctor asked.

'I don't know, I lost all sense of time. I can't even guess the date.' David started to rub his temples in frustration.

'When I crashed, nearly everything failed. I got the things that I needed running but the central clock was not one of them.'

'David, it is fine. When you are feeling stronger, we can help you piece some of this together. I can tell you that from your last transmission to when we found you, you were missing for eight months.'

'I didn't think it had been so long,' David said.

'Dad was worried when you failed to report in at a starbase,' Mark said, sitting down next to the bed. 'He contacted me and arranged for us to patrol the area.'

'How did you find me? I said to Jon that I did not think that I had set the beacon. The last thing I remember was that I needed to do that and get into the emergency pod. I know it sounds strange, but I think someone was calling me.'

'Someone was, or rather two people: Paul Winters and George Hendrick.'

'Elen's brother? I remember her saying he was going to be posted to the *New York*. Only a handful of telepaths have graduated the FWN. I'm surprised you have two already.'

'George was supposed to go to the *Las Vegas* but we got him transferred because he is the strongest telepath that the UTA has allowed to join the FWN. And he's a good friend of Paul's. We thought we would need his strength to find you.'

'Did they find my mind before your scans found my shuttle?'

'Yes. To be honest, with no beacon and so little power left, I don't know if we would have found you in time without their help.'

'Thank you for coming for me,' David said as he started to drift off again.

'I am just sorry it took so long,' Mark said. 'I know you

need to rest and when you are stronger we must talk more, but is there anything I need to know now?'

'If we are still in unmapped space, there could be hostile ships that have been involved in horrific activities.'

'What things?'

'The stuff of nightmares,' David said and he lapsed back into unconsciousness.

✳

When he woke again David felt better than he had done in a long while.

'Good morning,' Elen said. 'How are you feeling?'

'Good morning,' David responded as he turned his head and saw her sitting there. 'I hear I have your brother to thank for finding me.'

'He was more than happy to help.'

'When I heard him calling me, I thought I was going mad. I'm so glad I was not,' David said. Then, as memories started to resurface, 'Do you know what state my shuttle is in? The captain said that a lot of the systems had failed. Do you know if they were able to download anything?'

'I have had a look at it, I'm amazed you were able to get the thing to fly again. You have done what the engineers called "some interesting repairs". I think Chief Engineer Redek decided to wait until you could work on it before they tried to download, just in case they got it wrong and deleted vital information. There is a lot of curiosity over what happened to you. Anything you want to tell me?'

'Sorry, Elen, but until I've spoken to the captain I don't feel that I can discuss it.'

Elen laughed, 'Didn't think you would but it doesn't hurt to ask.'

'Do you how much longer until we reach the starbase?'

'We are not going to a starbase,' Mark Yoland said. He had walked in unnoticed, 'Ensign, would you leave us?'

Elen stood immediately on hearing the captain's voice. She squeezed his hand and promised to come back when her duties allowed.

'Dr Rogers spoke with the starbase's medical bay about your condition,' Mark said. 'They don't believe they can give you the medical treatment you need in the long term and at present you are responding well to the short-term medication. They agree that the best thing for you is to return back to Europa as quickly as possible. I can get the doctor for you, he can go through it all better than I can.'

'No, he said before that I would be fine. I guess there will be plenty of time for the finer details later,' David said. 'I really need to talk to your father though.'

'He's keen for an update as soon as you are well enough.'

'I'm well enough now.'

'Alright, just let me talk to Dr Rogers. The call will have to be made from my office for the secure link.'

Mark left and David pushed himself up into a sitting position. He was surprised by the effort it took; he had not realised he was so weak. Mark returned a few moments later with the doctor.

'Captain Yoland tells me you feel strong enough to leave in order to give a report. Let me run a quick test. If the results are satisfactory you can go, but you must come straight back here. If at any time you feel nauseous or dizzy, you return immediately, regardless of whether you have finished your report or not. Have I made myself clear?'

'Yes, doctor,' David said.

'Alright then.'

A nurse approached with a hover chair. 'I can walk,' David protested.

'I don't care, you go in the chair or you don't go at all.'

With a sigh of frustration, David swung his legs out of the bed and climbed into the chair. He was shown briefly how to use it and warned not to exert himself by trying to walk. 'I feel like an invalid in this thing,' he complained as he slowly manoeuvred it out of the medical bay.

'I hate to be the one to break it to you, but for now you are,' Mark retorted.

As they made their way to the captain's office, they passed several people in the corridors. Many of them paused to say hello and ask how he was. He acknowledged them before moving on. Once in Mark's office, he opened the link to the admiral.

'It is good to see you alive, David. I was getting very worried about you.'

'Thank you, sir, and thank you for asking the *New York* to look for me, I would not have made it back otherwise.'

'Mark has told me that when you were found you warned him there could be hostile ships in the area, I take it you found out what is going on.'

'Yes, sir,' David said, and started to explain everything that had happened to him since they had last spoken.

Chapter 24

DAVID returned to the medical bay with a feeling of relief. Mark, who had been present during the conversation between David and his father, was very quiet as he walked back with him. He did not ask any questions but David could feel his shock and disgust and knew he was preoccupied and mentally processing everything he had learnt.

It had become clear as he had started to explain what had happened that neither the admiral nor Captain Yoland expected anything so horrific. They both had had numerous questions that left David feeling drained. He had not expected it to be so hard to talk about his experiences but he found that as he did, he remembered the pain and missed Hannoki.

'I am sorry, David. If I'd had any idea, I would never have sent you alone,' the admiral apologised. 'I suspected that they were using the area of space for illegal trading, or trying to find planets they could stake a claim to ahead of official surveys, but not this!'

'It is alright, admiral. As you said when you asked me, you did not know who else to send because the rest of the FWN were not interested as they did not consider it important.'

'Which raises many more questions. Why were these skins allowed to be sold? Why were no questions asked about the suppliers?' the admiral asked. 'I need to think over what you have told me and make a few enquires. Can you forward me a copy of any reports and readings you made?'

'I was told the shuttle's systems were failing when I was found. I don't know what can be retrieved. I don't know if anything has been downloaded yet by the engineering crew.'

'My crew have tried to retrieve the information but so many systems were damaged when the shuttle crashed and you made some inventive repairs. They don't want to risk a rebuild and download without talking to you in case they lose information.'

'I will talk to them straight way.'

'No. When the doctor clears you to work on the shuttle will be soon enough,' the admiral said. 'The enquiries I need to make here will take a few days and you look ready to collapse again. We have some time to get the full report.'

'Another attack could happen at any time. We need to do what we can now.'

'I know, David, but you need to trust me to do this properly.'

⁕

'When can I get up again?' David asked the doctor the next day, 'I need to get to work on the shuttle as soon as possible.'

'I appreciate that your work is important and I have promised the captain I will let you start as soon as I consider you well enough. In your current state you won't get much work done before you collapse and your recovery will be delayed. Please believe me when I say that if you rest now, you will work better and longer and reduce the risk of your health deteriorating.'

'You don't understand, any delay could cost lives, I can cope with bad health.'

'I understand your frustration, believe me I do, you

think you can do a few hours today and tomorrow and the next, the engineers will start to know what to do and soon you will have whatever it is that the captain thinks is so important. What I am saying is if you do a few hours today you will be too sick tomorrow and the next. If you rest now I promise you the work will be done quicker and with less chance of mistakes being made,' Dr Rogers pointed out. When he saw the determined look on David's face he continued before he had the chance to argue with him, 'I, like everyone, did not like telepaths when they first started on board, but when I began to accept them I learnt in some ways they make the best patients because I can't lie to them.'

'I don't understand, I just need you to let me out of here.'

'That you don't understand just reinforces what I am saying. You are still too unwell to think straight.'

'I don't have time for this,' David said, and started to swing his legs over the side of the bed. Dr Rogers grabbed hold of his arm. 'Don't touch me,' David snapped. He tried to pull away but did not have the strength to do so.

'I know it makes it hard for you not to read my mind but that is the point I was trying to make. I can't lie to you. If you can't listen to what I am saying, then see what will happen.'

Angrily David took the doctor's challenge as permission to read his mind. He got the surface thoughts that the doctor wanted him to read easily enough, but could not get any more before his head started to explode in pain. Dr Rogers let go of his arm and David sagged onto the bed, grasping his head. The doctor gently helped him back onto the bed and covered him with a sheet.

'I can't do anything,' David said as the doctor gave him pain medication and, David suspected, a sedative.

'You will, you just need to give it time,' was the last

thing he heard as he drifted off into unconsciousness.

David was sitting in the shuttle with several of the engineering crew, explaining what he had done to rebuild the systems. Panels had been removed and wires trailed everywhere connecting the shuttle to the *New York* for power. The team had been limited to the chief engineer, Kate Jenson, and a handful of others that David had worked with regularly when he was on board. No one new was allowed to work on the shuttle.

After a few days' rest, a compromise had been reached. He was allowed to advise for a few hours a day and if anyone on the engineering team was concerned about his welfare, he had to return to the medical bay. David was frustrated by the restrictions and they made the work slower but he knew enough not to complain. Each day he was sent back to the medical bay and, after a brief argument, he would collapse thankfully into bed. After a few days of this, Dr Rogers threatened to impose twenty-four hour bed rest before letting him work again. As a result, David was careful for a day or two and returned to the medical bay before he was forced to do so before reverting to staying as long as he was physically able. He knew people were not happy with him but he did not care; he cared about his shuttle and the information that was stored on it.

Finally David checked the work, then re-checked it.

'What do you think?' Famar asked him. He had already gone through everything himself and could not see anything else they could do.

'It is as good as it is going to get. I think it is time we updated the captain.'

'I think we are finally ready to start to download,' the

captain was told. He went straight to the shuttle bay and sat with Famar and David listening to his chief engineer's briefing. 'We have isolated the files so we can transfer the information in small sections to protect as much of it as we can should the systems overload.'

'Do you think that is likely? What risk is there to the *New York* if there's an overload?'

'There should be no risk to the *New York*. Our systems are well protected. There is a risk of the shuttle systems overloading but we have reduced it as much as possible. There is nothing further we can do to repair the shuttle and any attempt to rebuild the computers with what we have on the *New York* could remove everything stored on them. Our only other option is to wait until we get to a starbase or port and have their engineers try.'

'No, I want to include as few people as possible. I don't want questions about where the shuttle has been and what happened to it. If this is successful, are the restrictions I requested in place?'

'Yes captain. Only you and David will have direct access to all the reports. Anyone else will have to go though you to view them.'

'Then let's start. I want to know what we have before we reach Europa. How long will it take?'

'To reduce the risk of the shuttle's systems overloading, we will download as slowly as possible. How long depends on how much is stored and still retrievable.'

'At the slowest rate of download, I would estimate it will take about seventy-two hours,' David said. 'Once the first few files have been completed, we can try to speed up the process,

'Is there anything else you need to do here?' the captain asked David.

'That depends on whether Famar can oversee the downloading in case anything happens.'

'I was not planning on leaving,' Famar retorted.

'Then can you join me in my briefing room before going back to the medical bay?'

'Of course.' David stood up and followed the captain off the shuttle. He did not like leaving it; it had been his home for so long and he knew that once they had arrived at Europa it would be destroyed because the damage was too great to fix. If he ever went out again as a scout, it would be in a new shuttle. At the moment he did not know what the future held for him; he could only imagine what his father was going to say when they next spoke. He knew Mark had sent a message to Viktor to let him know his son had had been found alive.

'It is never easy, you know,' Mark said as they walked down the corridor. David looked at him in surprise. 'I know the look. That shuttle is your pride and joy and seeing her as she is now is painful because you know you will never get her back.'

'I didn't think I was being that obvious.'

'You're not. I just know you and I know people who have lost ships.'

'She was the nearest thing to a home I ever had,'

'Now that is just sad,' Mark said, as they walked through into his rooms, 'and maybe a little self-pitying. It is a large part of your life but it is not all your life. You have us here on the *New York*, and Elen, your father and stepmother and, who knows, there may be more family out there just waiting to meet you. You have other homes, other places where you are welcome.' Mark took a seat and waited for David to settle himself before continuing. 'You are choosing to bury yourself with your shuttle but there are other people in your life.'

'Is this part of captain's training?'

'No, just experience from nearly a lifetime in space. I am not a specialist but I know how to recognise trauma.

It may not feel like it to you but until this, you only experienced the good side of space travel. There are a lot of negatives to it.'

'I'm fine. If I was not, then Dr Rogers would have spoken to me but he has not so there is no problem.'

'Dr Rogers has *tried* to talk to you. He says you are highly resistant. He considered confining you to the medical bay but thought maybe you would listen to me where you would not listen to him. The crash on the planet and exposure to the suns has left you ill. It will take time for you to get better but you will. But you need to deal with the mental impact of the crash as well as the physical. You, of all people, understand mental health and its impact.'

'I'm not insane.'

'I never said you were. I think your fear of being mentally unstable is stopping you from asking for help. What you are going through would cause post-traumatic stress for a lot of people; being a telepath will make it worse because you feel everything on a mental level as well. My advice is to get help. No one will think less of you for it.'

'Dr Rogers can help me?'

'All doctors in the FWN have psychiatric training, but it's not his speciality. He may suggest you talk to either Dr Dickinson or...'

'Dr Galride? Dr Rogers tried to introduce me. I will talk to them, I promise.'

'Thank you, David.'

As David stood up to leave, he remembered something else Mark had said. 'What did you mean by other family members I need to meet?'

'I should not have said that. You need to talk to your father. Now go back to the medical bay and talk to the doctor.'

Chapter 25

AS soon as the *New York* entered Europa's orbit, David was to be transported out of the medical bay and into a shuttle. He would be flown straight to the planet surface to a medical facility. He did not like the idea; he was sick and tired of being ill, and hated the medical bay where he was continually checked on and tested. The worst thing was the lack of privacy; he was used to having his own room, somewhere he would not be disturbed. He had not had that since coming onto the *New York*, and he did not know how long he would have to stay in the Europa facility.

'My father has contacted yours,' Mark reported before David left the *New York*. 'He told him as much as he can about what has happened. He is going to meet you at the medical facility. I don't need to remind you that you can't discuss what has - and is - happening.'

'You just did,' David pointed out. 'I know what I can and can't say, Mark. You don't have to worry.'

David was met at the shuttle docking bay by medical staff who wanted him to put him into a wheel chair. 'How far away is the medical centre?' he asked.

'It is on the other side of the port, but the ambulance is just outside.'

'Then I'm more than capable of walking there.'

'Sir, that is not the correct protocol.'

'As I'm not FWN, I don't have to follow your protocol. I will walk to the ambulance.' He shuffled past them, down the corridor and outside to the waiting vehicle.

During the trip he submitted to various tests and answered questions about his health. When the vehicle stopped and the doors opened, the staff did not try to get him into the chair again.

As he climbed out he saw a man waiting for him. 'Welcome, Mr Wilhelm. I am Dr Delgar and I will be in charge of your treatment here. If you come with me, I will show you your room and go through these results with you.' He indicated a file he had just been handed. 'We'll see if there is anything else we need to cover.'

David followed the doctor down various corridors until he stopped at a door. David went inside and saw just the one bed; he was relieved that finally he would have some privacy. For the next hour he and the doctor went through an edited version of what had happened, confirmed the treatment he had had on the *New York*, his test results and what would happen next.

As Dr Delgar finally turned to go he said, 'Your father is here. Do you want to see him?'

'Of course. When did he get here?'

'Just before you but we had to go through your admittance procedure first. I will have him sent to your room.'

David did not have to wait long before there was a knock on his door and his father stood in the doorway.

'I was not sure if you were able to take visitors when I first got here,' his father said. 'They told me you had developed cancer.'

'I'll be fine. The medical staff on the *New York* were able to halt the progress of the disease and alleviate the symptoms. Now I'm here, they should be able to treat me properly and I can be released.'

'I was really worried when I did not hear from you. I did not know who to contact other than Admiral Yoland. All I got for weeks was that he was looking into it, until finally you were found - but sick. He would not tell me anything more. What happened to you? Where have you been to get skin cancer when you live on a shuttle?'

'I'm sorry Father, but you must know that I can't talk about what happened. Please don't ask me any questions.'

'I know we have not always got along, but I do love and worry about you. I know about secrets so I won't ask you any more questions, but if there is anything you can tell me to satisfy my curiosity I will be all ears.'

'Sorry, for the moment you are going to have to be patient.'

'Fair enough. Why don't I catch you up on how Anja and I have been doing?' Surprisingly, Viktor looked slightly nervous.

'That would be nice. How is she?'

'She is very well, as is your baby sister.'

'She has had a baby?' David smiled at the news. 'What is she called? Do you have any pictures?'

'She is called Catina and of course I have pictures.' His father pulled out his phone and scrolled through numerous photographs. 'I can bring her to meet you.'

'I would like that, how old is she?'

'Three months.'

'So how pregnant was Anja at your wedding?'

'At our age we thought it best not to wait on ceremony.'

※

Finally David was being released. He had been frustrated by the restrictions the doctor placed on him on the *New York*, and he thought things had improved on Europa when he was given his own room, but he soon learnt that was not the case. He was only allowed out of his room for medical treatments and there had been several arguments over the use of a wheelchair. The only thing that kept him sane was the visits from his father, stepmother and baby sister.

He would have to come back once a week for further treatment and was on a course of medication until the test results came back clear, but he was sure that in a few months everything would be fine and he could not wait until he had his life back.

As he walked out of the medical centre, he saw his father waiting for him with his car. 'Are you ready to come home?' his father asked. David knew that he was asking more than if he was just staying for a while until he was better and the thought of having somewhere and someone to come back to sounded good.

'Yes, I am,' he replied. He handed his bag to the driver and climbed into the car. 'So how are my baby sister and her mother?'

'They are doing very well and waiting for you to arrive home.' For the rest of the short drive they talked about family. David was happy for his father but part of him found it painful; as a child, he had never felt that his father wanted him. Viktor was trying to make up for it now. David didn't know whether they would ever talk about it but for now he was content to build a relationship.

It was not long before the car pulled up outside the house. As David climbed out of the car, his stepmother opened the door holding his sister in her arms.

'Anja,' he said as he kissed her cheek in welcome, before looking down at the small bundle in her arms. 'She grows bigger every time I see her.'

'I know, I can't believe how quick she is growing,' Anja said, laughing. 'How are you feeling?'

'So much better for getting out of that place and being home.'

'Good. Come on in,' she said and walked into the house.

✳

'I have not replaced your mother, you know,' his father told him that evening, as they sat together drinking whisky after dinner.

'I know. Anja is very different to how I remember my mother. You have moved on and I'm happy for you.'

'I know our relationship has never been an easy one but I really want you to be part of our lives. I want you to know your sister.'

David laughed, 'And you visiting me every day at the medical centre and inviting me to stay until I recover didn't show me that? Mother has been dead for years. It was time for you to move on and I'm very happy for you. I'm looking forward to seeing my baby sister grow up. As for us, I think we are doing alright now.'

'Thank you. I look forward to having the chance to get you know you properly. The short visits and long-distance communication only ever gave me a taste of the man you have grown into. I hope we will get to know each other again and you will let me make up for my past neglect. My life now has taught me how badly I behaved towards you in the past.'

✲

David spent the next few months getting to know his family. He fell into a relaxed relationship with his father and stepmother, but he fell head over heels in love with his half-sister and spent as much time playing with her as possible. When she slept during the day, David worked on a machine that was capable of absorbing power and expelling it with amplified force. His father had given him rooms in the house he could use as a workshop and, with their joint connections, he was able to get all the materials he needed, except Lismarian materials which Theron Gallo refused to give him access to unless he signed a contract with them. Theron tried hard to convince David to work for him and give up his travels. David had not wanted to work with him or the materials, he just wanted confirm if they came from Hannoki's people.

He was determined to create something that would help Hannoki and his people. He decided the best course of action was to allow a variable on the power absorption; he would build it with his best guess but would bring in parts and tools to allow for alterations. He knew that when - if - he got back to Hannoki's planet, it would take a lot to get it working probably.

In some ways he spent those months in limbo; knowing that he could not go anywhere until he was medically cleared meant that he did not worry about it. He had no shuttle and until he was given a certificate to fly again, he could not buy one.

Everything that he had recorded on the shuttle's logs had been downloaded successfully onto the *New York*. At his request he had been given a copy, and the originals were sent to Admiral Yoland. What the admiral made of them David did not know; he heard nothing from the FWN and when he had tried to enquire he was put off and never given the chance to talk to the admiral.

As his course of treatment was coming to an end, a new wave of Lismarian clothing came into the shops. David increased his requests to talk to the admiral but he was never put through and he worried about the silence.

His father picked up on his repeated calls to the FWN from the phone bills. 'What is wrong?' he asked. 'You can't be thinking of leaving us again so soon. You are not well enough yet to consider it.'

'I need to leave again, but not yet. I'm worried about the admiral. He was working on what I had found and I can't believe that he is refusing my requests to talk to him.'

'When was the last time you spoke to him?'

'On the *New York*, just before we docked at Europa. He said he would come and see me and I have heard nothing from him since.'

'Have you tried to see him at his office?'

'I was not granted permission to enter the base and I can't talk to the admiral to get the permission.'

'What are you going to do?'

'I have sent a message to the *New York* to see if the captain can help, but there will be a delay before I get a response. I can only wait for now, but it is very annoying.'

'If the FWN is dealing with it, why are you so worried? The admiral is a busy man. When they have something to tell you they will.'

The advice sounded sensible, but David could not believe he had gone through so much to be discarded. He knew these people, but he could not explain any of this to his father. 'I hate being sick, I need to get back out there. I need to get back out into space.'

'I wish you could tell me what this is all about.'

'So do I. I really need a clear perspective but I can't tell you what I know. If I can't get hold of the admiral, I need to get back into space as soon as possible.'

'If it is that important to you then I will help as much as I can with trying to contact the admiral and with the shuttle. Though Anja will kill me if she thinks I'm putting you in danger.'

'I would find a way without you.'

'I know. That is why I want to help you.'

Chapter 26

A message was delivered to David at his father's address. The sender was Captain Mark Yoland on the *New York*, the date a week previously. He assumed it had gone through a lot of hands and been viewed by many others as there were no restrictions shown on the message. David took it to his room and played it.

David, unfortunately I have some bad news for you. My father has passed away. I wanted to make sure you knew as you became so close to him and the FWN would only inform the next of kin. He was found at his home address when he failed to return to work. They are trying to determine the cause of death but early indications are of suicide. Obviously this message will take time to get to you so I don't know whether more will be known by the time you receive it. I have asked Lieutenant Jarvis to answer any questions you have due to the obvious time delay and cost of communicating with me.

That was all there was. David sat there, shocked; in all his attempts to contact the admiral the FWN had never told him he was dead, why? He could not remember reading anything in the news but he did an internet search to see if there was anything he might have missed. There was nothing. Why had no one announced the death? Someone as influential as the admiral should have had an obituary posted.

The message from Mark was a week old; how long had it taken the FWN to inform him? Mark had not given the date when his father had died; had Mark sent this message the same day? The variables David thought of made him realise that he had no idea how long the admiral had been dead. He watched the recording again and again.

Before joining the *New York*, David had been very bad at reading body language and detecting tone of voice because he always spent his time with the same people, telepaths he trusted and had grown up with. On the *New York* he was very guarded with his skills to avoid any accusations of illegal mind reading, so he had to learn other ways to read people; he had to pick up mannerisms and tone. These skills had held him in good stead over the years and they helped him judge who to trust and who to avoid. Now those skills were telling him that Mark thought something was wrong; he was worried about the cause of his father's death and, being on a spaceship, he couldn't do anything about it.

The FWN might not want David to know about it - but why not? It was well known that the admiral had got him onto the *New York* then helped establish him as a scout pilot; it was obvious that he would want to know about the death. Did Mark think the FWN was keeping it a secret? By telling him, was Mark indicating his lack of trust in the organisation, except for Lieutenant Jarvis? He guessed it was the best place to start and placed a call.

In the end it was not one call but several before he got hold of Lieutenant Jarvis. 'Mr Wilhelm. Captain Yoland told me that I could expect a call from you. How can I help you?'

'All the captain told me was that his father was dead and to contact you for further answers. The message took a week to arrive so I know very little about what happened or if there will be a memorial ceremony.'

'I'm sorry, sir, but I can't discuss this over the phone. If you let me know when you are available to come to our base, I will be more than happy to meet with you here.'

'Thank you.' David gave the dates he was available. He expected Jarvis to make excuses and put him off so he was surprised when a date and time were confirmed for the next day.

⁜

The lieutenant must have warned security on the base because when David arrived and confirmed his identity, he was given directions. As the car stopped and David climbed out, an ensign came out to meet him and lead him to Lieutenant Jarvis.

'Thank you for coming,' he said as David walked into his office. He shut the door behind them, closing out any listening ears. 'I'm afraid I could not come to you. It has been very busy here since the admiral passed away.'

'Of course. I understand. Thank you for taking the time to see me.'

'I have put together a report for you including everything you are authorised to see. The reason I wanted you to come here is that my superiors do not want this information taken away and ask that you do not discuss it.'

'Why all the secrecy?'

'You will understand when you read the report. But, as I said, the FWN require that you do not disclose what is in the file.'

'As always the FWN has my complete discretion.'

Jarvis pushed the file across the table towards him. 'You will have to read this here I'm afraid.'

'I understand.' David picked it up started to read.

'David, David can you hear me?' He looked up and stared at the lieutenant. *'Admiral Yoland said if I projected my thoughts to you, you could hear me.'* David nodded

slightly. '*Pretend to read the report while you listen to my thoughts.*' David nodded again and turned a page. '*I don't know what you have been told but the official report will say that the admiral committed suicide. However, certain evidence is being withheld. What it is I do not know.*'

'*How do you know there is anything missing?*' David implanted the question.

'*When the admiral reported what you had found out the response was not what he expected. He thought there would be outrage and immediate action but instead he was put off. I know he was angry and frustrated and was pushing for a military deployment. Shortly before he died, he had a big argument with the other admirals. He had no reason to kill himself. He was not done fighting.*'

'*Can you give me the names of the admirals who would not act on the information?*'

'*They are all listed in the report. If there are others, I do not know who they are.*'

'*Does Captain Yoland know this?*'

'*Not all of it. He contacted me wanting information but I could not give him it over the communication link. He got the hint and sent you to me to get it. I don't know what you can do but at least you can tell the captain when you see him next. This report says that the security systems were checked and recordings viewed after the admiral died and there was nothing, but all of that is easily forged. I know this all sounds like I'm paranoid, but what I know is that the admiral was not suicidal. I worked for him for years as his staff officer, and since he has died any talk about going to your planet has stopped. I don't know who I can trust within the FWN - other than the admiral's son who is not here.*'

'*How many people were told what happened?*'

'*As far as I am aware just myself and the admirals.*'

'*I will see if I can find out anything.*' David said closing the report and handed it back. 'Thank you for your time, lieutenant. The poor admiral - no wonder he was avoiding me. He must have feared that I would discover what he planned to do.'

'His death took us all by surprise.'

∦

David went back to his father's house with his head spinning. The report contained all the names that he needed to try and find some answers. What worried him most was the apparent unwillingness of the other admirals to defend the people, something that should have been at the top of their priorities. What was going on?

The car pulled up outside his father's home. As he entered, David made his excuses to his father and stepmother and went straight to his room, reassuring them that he was alright.

Not sure where to start, he called up and requested a meeting with the admirals that were named in the report, starting with Admiral Mathers. He was not hopeful of any positive response but he had to try. A few days later, they had all refused a meeting.

∦

When the final refusal came through, David was livid. He paced his room, trying to determine what to do next. Who he could go to? His knowledge of the FWN hierarchy was limited; the only person he could ask was Mark and he did not think that was advisable. He sat down at his computer; maybe if he continued to send requests they might finally consent.

When he saw the time, he realised how hungry he was. He shut down the computer and went to dinner; maybe a break would give him a better perspective. Since receiving the message from Mark he had been a virtual recluse.

'David, I'm so glad you have joined us,' Anja said, smiling, as his father poured him, a whisky.

'I'm sorry, I have been a bad guest for the last few days.'

'That's alright. You seem to have a lot to deal with.' The conversation turned to how his little sister was doing until dinner was announced.

'What is wrong David?' Viktor asked as his wife got up to check on their daughter. 'I thought you were coping with what happened to you.'

'I was, when I thought something was being done. Now I don't think anyone wants to know.'

'Do you want to talk about it?'

'I would love to, but I can't discuss work I do for the FWN.'

'If they do not want to act on what you found out, why did they employ you to start with?'

'Admiral Yoland asked me to do the work as a favour to him.'

'But was the FWN paying the bills, or was the admiral? If it's not the FWN, are you still tied by the same restrictions?' When David did not reply his father continued. 'I could read through your contract to find out. I would be happy to give it to one of my lawyers.'

'I don't have one,' David suddenly realised. 'I did have a contract but it expired and instead of renewing it I took work from independent companies. Then the admiral asked me to check something out for him, but there was no new contract. He was worried about the activity and did not think anyone was taking it seriously.'

'Then you can say what you want. The FWN probably won't take it well, and I would advise you to think about the repercussions before you start telling people what happened, but I will do anything I can to help you, if you let me.'

'Do you have any plans for this evening?' David asked.
'Nothing that can't wait.' They stood up and went into Viktor's study.

Chapter 27

DAVID talked with his father long into the night. As he had described the people and how they were skinned, Viktor paled. 'You can't tell Anja, she can't know she got married in the skin of a murdered being,' he pleaded, shaken by what he had heard.

'It worries me what people will think when the truth comes out. It is not just the skins, they take the wings too, though I don't know for sure what happens to them.'

'What are they like?'

'Thin, lightweight and strong. It is hard to examine them when they are attached to a person's back and they don't like them being touched.'

'How long ago were the first attacks? How many of these people have been killed?'

David told him the approximate time and numbers. 'But this is based on what Hannoki told me. There may have been attacks on another part of the planet that he does not know about. Do you suspect something?'

'It might be nothing but I was approached a while ago by a broker asking me to invest in a new product. I don't remember a lot about it because I dismissed the offer as being too good to be true. Since then, several companies have been doing very well, and I almost regretted my decision – until now.'

'Theron talked about Lismarian products, but I can't get hold of any to examine. Do you think the wings have gone into industry?'

'It is an idea. The skins being turned into clothing

would generate a profit; if the wings are also used then the profits will be very high. Some of these companies could be linked to the FWN, which is why they don't want to act.'

'The FWN have a new engine coming out soon. I read about it. It is more powerful and efficient and it is rumoured to change space travel as we know it.'

'Have you seen the plans?'

'No, they were classified,' David said. 'Oh God, if this is true, where do I go from here?'

'Find out everything you can.'

'How? No one is going to admit any wrongdoing to me.'

'You are a telepath, aren't you? Read their minds.'

'I am not allowed to unless certain exceptions apply. I have told you that.'

'Thousands of dead beings is not reason enough? How many more will be killed if you don't stop it?'

'They are not human.'

'Does the law define that they have to be? Do you care about the law?'

'No, it does not,' David said. 'And no I don't. But how do I get close to these people?'

'I could hold a party.'

※

David moved among his father's guests, Viktor had invited the executives of several companies who were suddenly doing very well; he had hinted that he wanted his son to stop working as a scout pilot and to settle down and develop his designs. David was renowned for his independence and refusal to align himself to a company so this change in direction was causing a lot of curiosity. It was known that he had been back on Europa for some time and rumoured that he had been unwell, but nothing more.

'So what are you working on at the moment?' he was asked time and again. 'What can you offer us?' and 'Why are you interested now?' This was the easiest question to answer.

'I became very ill on my last tour. Because of the delay in medical treatment, the doctors have implied that it is unlikely I will be cleared for scout duties again. The weeks I spent in the medical facility made me realise that, though I had been doing what I enjoy, I caused a great deal of worry and pain to my family. It also made me realise that if I died, I wanted to leave a name behind that will be remembered.' He knew that anyone checking on him would discover that he had been in the FWN medical bay, though not what for. It was a plausible explanation for his sudden change of mind and, as a result, he got a lot of interest in some of his designs.

David mentioned various ideas but stressed that he struggled to find materials that would be lightweight and strong enough to take the strain. Three of the people he spoke to hinted that if he signed an exclusive deal with them, they might be able to help.

'How are you doing?' his father asked as David moved away from Pedro Diaz, the chief executive of Exilon.

'I have found three possible suspects. Can you make excuses for me in about half an hour?'

'Of course. If anyone asks, I will say that you are feeling unwell. After all, you have been telling everyone you have spent weeks in the FWN medical bay. Will you be coming back to the party?'

'I don't know. I plan to, but I'm going to do something I have never done before.'

'I'll just say you are not well and play it by ear.'

David spoke to several other people before quietly walking out of the room, making a point of rubbing his temples as if his head were hurting. He made his way upstairs and into his bedroom. He locked the door to make sure he would not be disturbed and lay down on his bed. He was so nervous; this was the first time he was going to read a person's mind without their knowledge and consent. It went against everything he had been taught, but he had to find out if these people knew what was happening to Hannoki's planet. As his father had said, no matter how bad this felt, it did not breach the rules of the UTA; though he was supposed to inform the UTA if he committed one of these breaches, he did not even trust them.

David searched for the three minds he had identified. When he found them, he slowly and carefully picked his way through their minds, getting as much information as possible before withdrawing. Then he returned to the party, where he plastered a smile on his face.

⁜

'Did you find out anything?' Viktor asked as they sat in his study the next day.

'I only did a cursory mind search. People can be trained to identify a deep search and another telepath can also detect when one has been completed. Petro Diaz and Theron Gallo are definitely involved and possibly Yelda Gustof, but I could not get anything to confirm his involvement.'

'It's not much,'

'I know, but I raised the topic of Lismarian clothing with several of the ladies when I knew those three were near enough to hear and then withdrew to monitor their thoughts. They know where the clothing comes from. Theron even thought it was it was a nice little side business.'

'Yelda is a massive defence contractor and Petro has big contracts with various governments for infrastructure buildings. His company has built schools, medical facilities and a starbase or two.'

'So it is everywhere, not just in the clothes worn but in our buildings and defence. No wonder Admiral Yoland could not convince anyone to investigate what he had found out.'

'No one is going to want to hear this.'

'No, everyone we could go to might well be aware of it and condoning it.'

'What are you going to do?'

'Captain Yoland suspects his father's death was not suicide. Lieutenant Jarvis was able to feed me information and may be able to get a message to Mark, but he does not have any authority, I think if I force the issue with the FWN I will end up like the admiral.'

'I can't believe anyone would get the upper hand on you,' his father laughed.

'Maybe not me, I would know they were coming - but what about you? Your wife and daughter? They could get to you all, they could get to anyone I cared for,' David said. 'I want to go back to the planet. They have a few tricks which, with some help, they might be able to use to defend themselves. If they can do that, maybe the companies will back away from them.'

'With the money that these companies are making, they are not going to back down easily.'

'I know but, without knowing what to do here, it is the only thing I can think of. If I push too hard and ask too many questions they will watch me and stop me from leaving. If I do nothing here, I could do something on the planet. How much good it will do I don't know, but it will be something.'

'You will need a new shuttle,' his father pointed out.

'Hopefully I can get one easily enough once I am medically cleared to fly.'

'And a reason to go out without contracts?

'I do a lot of experiments which need zero gravity. They benefit the FWN and other companies that do long-distance space travel. I can say I am going out on solo trips to see if I can work as a scout again while I complete the projects I started before the crash. If I don't ask questions, let them think that I accept the admiral's suicide, let them think that I believe the FWN are doing what they should be doing, maybe I can get back and help them from the planet.'

'They must be suspicious. You went to their headquarters asking questions.'

'Limited, curious questions as a result of Mark's message,' David pointed out. 'I did not ask any unreasonable questions, nothing that would cause concern to anyone listening. The rest was a telepathic conversation; for that to have been overheard without me realising would be highly unlikely.'

'Would it have been possible?'

'Yes, but there are only about six people alive who could have listened into that conversation without me knowing it. Even if they did, it would have raised doubts and nothing more. I listened to what the lieutenant said and mentioned nothing about what I knew.'

—

David listened to the admiral's memorial. He did not have a place inside the crematorium but it was being broadcast outside for those who wanted to be part of it. He recognised a few faces from his visits to the FWN but no one he felt he could talk to, so he stood alone and watched and listened.

As the invited guests walked out, he saw Lieutenant Jarvis. 'Thank you for letting me know the time and date. I appreciate the chance to pay my respects.'

'You're welcome,' Jarvis said. 'There is a surprisingly large turnout, bearing in mind the circumstances of his death.'

'Regardless of the problems he must have had, he was a good man,' David said. 'I couldn't get in contact with Mark. I take it he is not here.'

'No, his duties didn't make it possible for him to get back in time and it was decided that the ceremony could not wait for months until he returned. I'm sorry I have to go.' Jarvis walked off. David did not need to be a telepath to tell that his presence had worried the lieutenant and he wondered what pressure he was being put under at work.

For the first time he was glad of the FWN's distrust of the UTA; for the moment, it put a block on them employing a telepath for nefarious purposes. He did not stay for much longer before returning home; he had learnt what he needed to.

'How did it go?' his father asked him.

'I need that shuttle,' David said.

⚜

Hello Mark. I went to your father's memorial ceremony and was sad you couldn't make it. You would have been proud. My father and I have reached a compromise; he is understandably unhappy with me for wanting to leave again but knows I find it hard to stay around so many people. I have now been medically cleared and I have bought another shuttle and will work on my own projects for a while. I hope to rendezvous soon so I can pass on my condolences in person.

David handed the message to the FWN as he prepared to leave. He only hoped that Mark would get the message about what he planned to do.

Chapter 28

DAVID landed back on the planet, almost in the exact same spot he had left from all those months ago. He checked the outside temperature and realised it was too hot to leave the shuttle. He had packed a climate suit this time but he was reluctant to use it until he had spoken to Hannoki. In the suit David knew he would look like those who attacked Hannoki's people. He sat back and thought over recent events.

After he explained what had happened to his father all those weeks ago, they had talked about what they could do. With his father's money and connections, David was able to get everything that he needed without having to answer any questions. His idea was to create a machine that could increase Hannoki's natural abilities, but his main problem was that he was not sure how they worked; he knew the suns were involved but not how the biological process worked. David began researching everything to do with photosynthesis and though it helped him to understand the process he could find no explanation of how that energy was then expelled. He did not know if the energy they got from the sun was directly linked, for example; did they get stronger with the more sunlight they took in or did their strength remain the same regardless and the sunlight was just for food. He wished they had learnt enough of each other's language that Hannoki could have explained it to him; the best he could do was to build what he knew and bring extra tools and parts to adapt it if he needed to.

His father bought him a new, bigger shuttle that could take the machine and tools he needed. It was not the type of shuttle scouts normally used; it did not have the fuel or life-support capacity but it was capable of getting him to the planet and back with a safety buffer in case he needed to divert or hold back for a while.

Ever since David left the medical bay he had kept an eye on the shops that sold the Lismarian fabrics. He was relieved when it started to sell out and online suppliers indicated that their stocks were low. Low stock! Had someone in the FWN finally listened and put a stop to the trade? But a few days before he planned to leave, he heard excited ladies gossiping about Lismarian products coming back into the shops. It was all he could do to stop himself going to the shops and examining the skins to reassure himself they weren't Hannoki's and his family's.

He left Europa feeling fear rather than excitement and now he was here, waiting painfully to find out if his friend was alive.

As soon as the readings came into a tolerable range, David left his shuttle. This time he was better prepared, with clothing specially created for high temperatures, a wide-brimmed hat and tablets and creams to protect him from the UV radiation. He had been warned that they would only protect him; they could not stop the radiation poisoning, and the cancer could easily return.

As he left the shuttle everything looked as he remembered it. He started towards Hannoki's home; he had always walked there with Hannoki and now he was not sure how much attention he had paid to the route. There were no distinctive landmarks; he just knew he needed to head towards the mountains.

David tried calling out to Hannoki with his mind but the difference in how their minds worked made it a lot harder than contacting a human. Unless Hannoki wanted to be heard, David could not read his or any of his people's minds; he just had to hope that Hannoki was listening for him. As he walked, he scanned the area, hoping for an indication that his friend was alright. Then suddenly, he saw what he was looking for and he sighed with relief.

A dark spot in the sky was moving quickly towards him and growing larger. David remembered the first time he had seen it; he had been working outside when the shape appeared and he had been worried because he had not seen any birds before - and this was one very large bird. It was several minutes until he realised that it was Hannoki.

David was surprised when he saw him fly because the fine film of his wings did not look big or strong enough to hold him. However, when Hannoki unfolded them and they were fully extended, they were triple-jointed and double-layered; they could lift the alien effortlessly into the sky.

David stopped and waited for Hannoki to join him. Soon the dark spot became a definite figure that landed gracefully in front of him and folded its wings so they were impossibly small against his back.

'It is very good to see you Hannoki. Are your family alright?'

'They are, thank you. There has been another attack since you left but it was not near here.'

'I was so worried about you.'

'You told your people what is happening here?'

'I did and, they are trying to find those responsible for the attacks. I don't know how long it will take so I have brought something with me that might help you.'

'What could help?'

'It is a machine. If it works, it could enhance your shielding abilities. But because I don't know how you do what you do, I'm not sure how effective it will be.'

'A machine like your shuttle?'

'My shuttle is a different sort of machine but yes. Do you want to see it, to see if it works?'

'Yes, I want to see anything that could help.' Together they turned and walked back to the shuttle. 'You are in the same place as before. Why did you not come nearer?' Hannoki asked.

'I didn't know what had happened since I left and I didn't want to cause upset by coming too close.'

'My friends know you, they would not have been upset. If you can move closer than you would be welcome, and you will save me the flight out here.'

David smiled at the last bit; he had never thought about how inconvenient it must be for Hannoki to come to him every day.

'If you are sure it will not cause your family problems, I will fly closer, but please let your people know before I do because everything nearby will become hot and the engines will throw up a lot of dust. It will be unpleasant if they are close by when I land.'

'I will let them know. Can I see the machine?'

David led him on board and showed him what he had built. 'I could only work according to what we know about photosynthesis,' he said. When he saw Hannoki's confused expression, he clarified. 'Photosynthesis is name we give when something takes energy from sunlight. I hope this will work but if not, I've allowed for changes to improve it.'

'How should it work? What should it do?'

'If it works, these conductors,' David pointed to parts of the machine, 'will channel and amplify the energy you put into the machine so you can create a bigger and stronger shield.'

'How big will the shield be?'

'I don't know. This is all theory at the moment. Until we try it, I won't have the answers that you want.'

Chapter 29

'I need to stop now,' Hannoki said, as the second of the suns started to go down.

'Are you alright?' David asked. They had been making such good progress and this was the short part of the day that he found bearable.

'I am fine, but with the suns down I will have nothing left to pull on.'

David paused for a moment, thinking. 'I know that you got some of your energy from the suns and I have seen how you stretch out in front of them. But just how reliant are you on it?'

'I could not live without it. We still need some food and water but we can go longer without those than we can without sunlight.'

'I had no idea you were so dependent on them.'

'You can't feel the energy of the suns all around you?' When David shook his head, Hannoki continued. 'We use the energy for many things. We all use it to survive and for day to-day energy. As I said, we still need food but we don't have to eat every day. When I do other things like create a shield, I consciously draw more energy in and then form it into what I want before pushing it out.'

'You said not everyone is as strong as you. How do you know who is?'

'By our markings. The stronger you are, the more you have. It is thought that it is through these,' Hannoki ran his hand down his arms, 'that we take in the suns' power.'

'How much can you take in?'

'I don't know, I have never reached that point.'

'Have you ever tried from up there?' David asked, pointing at the mountain.

'No, but why would that make a difference?'

'There would be less atmosphere to stop the suns' rays.' Hannoki looked at him, not understanding. 'Trust me, you'll feel a difference. Can you fly up there? Or do you want to come up in the shuttle?'

'I have never tried. My friend did it once and he is not as strong as I am so I should be able to do it without any trouble. But I can't try until the suns come up. Do you think your shuttle can get you there?'

'It will get me up there easily but I need a place to land.'

'It might take you a while to find one.'

'If I can't find one, I should be able to create one. But unless you are in the shuttle with me, it would not be a good idea if you followed me up.'

Hannoki looked at the shuttle. 'I am sorry, going into the shuttle when I know I can leave as soon as I want is hard enough. I don't want to be trapped in it. I will wait for you to come back and tell me what you saw.'

⁜

David went up in the shuttle. As he got to the peak he manoeuvred into position so he could hover over the mountain and take scans of the area, looking to see if there was anywhere suitable to land. From a distance it looked like a handful of jagged peaks; now he was amazed at the extent to which the mountains stretched and the height they reached.

He landed carefully and checked the external readings then double-checked them, not quite believing the difference between the surface and here. He scanned the atmosphere and realised that the ozone layer was very thin. David doubted he could leave the shuttle without his environmental suit and he had no idea how this would affect Hannoki. Putting on his suit, he walked outside and looked around him.

The mountain he had landed on was the highest peak and the air was so clear he could see for miles. Slowly he turned around and what he saw took his breath away; he had never seen anything so magnificent. There were rolling peaks as far as the eye could see. Everything near the mountains was green, fed no doubt by water running off the range. The sunlight might be extreme but the temperature was lower. On any other planet these mountains would be topped permanently with snow; he knew the planet must get some because he remembered the first time he landed the peaks were white. He wondered how long the snow stayed for and if it was the only water or if there was a large amount of rainfall which would account for the surrounding greenery. Was this the only place that got regular rain or were there other mountains on the planet? As he looked over towards the area Hannoki lived, the peaks fell away sharply. The rich green growth thinned into a vast expanse of dry land.

David stood there taking in the view until he saw the first sun coming up and he had to put his visor down to protect his eyes. When the second sun started to rise, he knew he should go back down otherwise Hannoki would worry about him. With regret he went back to his shuttle and, taking off his suit, flew the shuttle off the mountain range.

Hannoki was waiting for him as he landed back near his farm. 'What did you see? Were you able to land?' he asked as David opened the hatch.

'It was spectacular, I have never seen anything so breath-taking in my life,' David said. 'I could see for miles.'

Hannoki smiled, 'I would like to see it. Do you think

that it would be of benefit for me to try and fly there?'

'I'm not sure,' David admitted, brought back to the reason he went there. 'It was colder and the atmosphere was weak, making the suns' rays much stronger. I don't know if the conditions would cause you problems or not.'

'I would not know until I tried. If you came up as well, could you help me down if I needed it?'

'You want me to fly you?' David asked.

'Only if you have to,' Hannoki confessed. 'If there are problems you could get me back quicker than I could fly back down.'

'I would not leave you up there. But if I leave the shuttle this clothing won't be enough. I would have to wear the environmental suit I brought with me.'

'It is different? I thought you were managing better now.'

'I am, but the difference is enough to cause me serious problems.'

'Would it be better if you wore it here? Last time you were here, your skin looked different.' David thought about how sunburnt and blistered he was by the time Hannoki found him; his skin had never had the chance to heal until he was found by the *New York*.

'It would be better if I wore the suit when both the suns were out.'

'Then why have you not used it?'

'It will make me look like the people who are killing you.'

'You think I would confuse you for one of them?'

'No, but I didn't want to upset you, your family or friends.'

'I know it is your people who are attacking us but do not make yourself sick because you are worried about how we might feel.'

'Alright then, thank you,' David said, surprised at

Hannoki's easy acceptance. 'When do you want to go up?'

'The suns are out, we could go now.'

'OK. I will need to show you where I can land.'

'Why can't I just follow you up?'

'The heat from the engines would be too much.'

'I remember seeing you take off, I don't want to get close and I can't fly as fast as your shuttle. I was just going to follow the white lines that it left behind.'

He was talking about the condensation trail, David thought, mildly surprised that he was creating one on a planet this hot. 'That would work,' he said, thinking it was a lot simpler than anything else he had in mind.

'Then I will see you up there?'

'See you there.' David walked back in to the shuttle, closed the hatch and started up the engines.

⁜

'I will join you outside shortly,' David said. When he walked outside, he saw Hannoki standing there with his arms outstretched and his wings spread wide, exposing as much of his body as he could. 'Are you alright?'

'It is wonderful, I have never been so, so ... full? I can't think of the right work to describe how this feels but it is very, very good.'

'Would you be stronger up here?'

'Yes, very much so.' David saw a slight shimmer on Hannoki's skin; it had taken on yellow hue. 'I feel as if I can do anything up here.'

'At least now we know where you will be most effective,' David pointed out.

'I am keen to try to see if I can get your machine to work up here.'

'Then let us unload it and try.'

Chapter 30

HANNOKI left the peak first. David waited until he thought he would be nearly home before starting his engines. He had never tried to track Hannoki on the sensors and now was not the time to try, though if they were going to do this on a regular basis it might be worth it as it would reduce the chance of him accidently hurting his friend.

David landed near the farm and, as he walked out of the shuttle, he was met by Hannoki and his two sons.

'I can't believe how big your children have grown,' David said, as the youngest came running up to him and grabbed his leg. The last time he had seen him he was a baby in arms, but he remembered that Hannoki had told him their children grew a lot quicker. David was surprised at the trust in the small clinging boy; looking up he saw Hannoki and Milkoy laughing at his stunned expression.

'He is just learning how to read people with touch. It will be a while before he fully develops his telepathic ability, so for now he touches everyone he sees.'

'Fair enough. How much will he be able to read from me?'

'I am not sure. He reads feelings and strong thoughts from us, but how much he will get from you I have no idea. From his frustration and his death grip on your leg, I don't think he is getting anything.'

'That is a relief. I know a lot that is not suitable for him and I can't shield that. What is he called?'

'Kelac.'

'Hello, Kelac,' David said to the top of the boy's head then turned and looked at Milkoy. 'How are you?' he asked in their language.

'I am well, thank you,' Milkoy replied in David's own language, taking him by surprise, Milkoy had not spoken it before.

'I hoped you would return and you are very bad at learning my language, so I have been teaching my family,' Hannoki explained, and David laughed.

David asked Hannoki to talk to his friends and neighbours to make sure they were happy for his shuttle to be so close and to warn them what he looked like in the environmental suit. They thought it was a strange request; most of them had seen David when he visited Hannoki before and, as they were as reliant on telepathic communication as they were verbal, they could tell the difference between David and the raiders.

Hannoki spent several hours a day experimenting with the machine. Sometimes Milkoy came and watched. David took readings and spent the hours when both suns were in the sky making alterations; the problem he was having was maintaining the energy output, Hannoki could not control the enlarged shield and it collapsed time and again.

David suddenly started to feel irritable, but put it down to being confined for so long in the shuttle and his inability to work out what he was doing wrong with the machine. Then he heard banging on the hatch and opened it to see Hannoki, his skin tinged red and his face distressed.

'What has happened? Are your family alright?'

'They are fine but another attack will happen soon. We are worried because we don't know where they will go.'

'How do you know?'

'Can't you feel it? Can't you feel them coming?' David realised that there might be more to his feelings of irritability. He let Hannoki in, then settled into the pilot's chair, cursing himself for not thinking about doing routine mental scanning as he had while he was on the *New York*.

'I have not checked, give me a moment.' David sent his mind up to scan the space above the planet and there it was, a rogue ship in orbit. He could feel the hostility coming from it. 'You are right, but I don't know where they plan to land. I can feel they are getting ready but nothing more. You could sense them without looking for them?'

'I can sense them because they are focused towards the planet. I don't need to look for them, I just feel them when they are near. It gives me bad dreams or mental flashes if I am awake.'

'From your previous experience, do you know how long we have until they come down to the planet?'

'It can vary, but I don't think it will be long.'

'Then I better try and get this ready.' David looked at the machine and cursed silently; he had removed several parts and it would take time to replace them. To make matters worse, he had been stripping components from the shuttle so he could not take Hannoki and his family and friends away from the danger unless he could put everything back quickly.

David kept part of his mind open hoping to be forewarned of an attack but he could pick up nothing definite from this distance. As his anxiety grew, he kept having to wipe the sweat off his hands as he tried to get the shuttle operational.

David felt it as the shuttles left the main ship. 'Hannoki, they are coming!'

'I know, can you feel where they are going to land?'

'No, I can see images from their sensor readings but they mean nothing to me,'

'Can you show me? Is it something I would be able to interpret?'

'I don't know,' David said, opening up his mind to Hannoki so he could see everything that David could.

'They are coming down near here.'

'Are you sure?'

'Yes, I recognise the mountains as the ones you see here.'

'God, I need to get this back together,' David said. He blocked out everything in his need to concentrate; he could not believe that everything he had gone through to come here could all be for nothing.

He could hear the shuttle engines as they broke through the atmosphere and he knew he would not be ready. If only he had had another few days and Hannoki's family could have been protected. He opened up the weapons locker and took out the handgun stored there and hid it in the back of his trousers. Walking out of the shuttle, he saw Hannoki standing nearby with his wife and children and several others who lived on the same farm, looking up at the sky at the first sign of disturbance.

'Can you fly away from here?' David asked.

'Petrra, Milkoy and I could but the other children's wings are not developed enough and Mesrra is too heavy for us to carry. Most of our neighbours can't fly well enough to escape them.'

'Then take your family and the others and go into the shuttle. Lock the door and don't come out until you sense they have all gone.'

'What about you?'

'They do not want me, but I might be able to stop them looking for you. If they come here, they will see the shuttle and expect to see me. Hopefully they will not look any further.'

'How do you know they will not kill you?'

'They would have no reason to. The engines are off line so, as far as they are aware, I am stranded here. If they think I can't leave then I am no threat to them.' David pushed them all into the shuttle. 'Trust me, I will be fine,' he said, clearing his mind of worry and trying to communicate a feeling of calm reassurance in the hope that Hannoki would not ask any further questions.

David watched with relief as Hannoki picked up his youngest son and led Mesrra and Milkoy into the shuttle without any argument. Once the others had followed him in, he closed the door.

David watched as not one shuttle broke through the atmosphere but five. He took a deep breath to control his nerves as they came closer and he felt the hot air move around him as they passed low over him. There was no avoiding it now; they knew that he was here and all he had to do was wait for them to come.

He did not have to wait for long. Three of the shuttles flew over but two landed close enough that David could see the hatch of the nearest one open and several people walk out. They all wore environmental suits and carried weapons. They headed straight towards him as the people on the other shuttle headed towards the huts.

Three of them came up to him and another two circled the shuttle, checking it. 'What are you doing here?' David was asked.

'I am a scout for the FWN. My engines started to fail and I crashed here.'

'Here? At one of the few settlements in the area?'

'I had no choice where I landed. Luckily there was no one here otherwise it would have been a serious breach of FWN law.'

'Strange point of view. The local people could have

helped you.'

'Or if they were hostile, they could have killed me,' David pointed out. 'My records show this is not a charted planet and I am not allowed any contact with non-Federated members. Are you scouts here to chart it?'

'No,' the man said, laughing. 'We are after other things. Have you met any of the indigenous people?'

'There is no one here but me.'

'There are others here. Our sensors picked up multiple heat signatures,' one of the others said.

'I have been here for a few weeks. If you picked up anything, it was my attempts to restart my engines.'

'What do you take me for? A fool? I know the difference between heat signatures and an engine burn. Where are the people?' the man ordered.

'I told you I don't know what you are talking about,' David said. As he spoke, he saw the others coming out of the huts with nothing.

David's throat was grabbed and he was lifted off the ground. He had forgotten that a lot of environmental suits gave strength to their wearers as he tried to claw at the metal-clad hand that held him.

'Where are they?' the man demanded as his hand squeezed David's throat. David remembered the gun he had hidden in the back of his trousers; he tried to grab for it, but someone pulled it from his fingers and he was searched to make sure he had no more weapons.

'Not very clever of you.'

'Fuck you,' he managed to whisper.

'No, fuck you. There is only one place they could have hidden so quickly and, once we have forced entry onto your shuttle, we will slaughter them all. The only choice you have is whether you choose to live long enough to watch or not. Are you going to give me the codes to your shuttle?' David just stared at him, 'Falrick, how long to get through the shuttle's door?' his assailant demanded.

'We don't have the equipment here, we would need to go back to the ship.'

'I don't have time for this. Tell me the code.'

'Go to hell,' David gasped.

'Stubborn fool. Trip,' he shouted. As one of the suited males walked forward, he continued, 'Strip his mind for me, I want that code.'

'With pleasure, boss.'

David felt another mind trying to read his and he started to laugh, but it only came out as a choking sound.

'I can't get anything from him; he is a telepath and a much stronger one than me.'

'Damn it. What have you read from us?' the boss asked.

David smiled; not reading a person's mind was so ingrained in his training that he hadn't even tried but anything he could learn now would be of benefit, and he didn't think the rules still applied. He started to read as much as he could as quickly as he could; he kept smiling at them, even as the hand around his throat tightened.

David was thrown to the floor and gasped for air, his concentration momentarily broken by his inability to breathe properly and the pain in his side from the kick that followed. He blocked out the pain and continued to strip their minds. He estimated that the telepath they had with them was a level five who would not be able to detect what he was doing or prevent him.

All the occupants of the shuttles started to circle around and watch. There was no one here for them to skin so they had nothing else to do other than watch in amusement as David was kicked yet again. Having gained everything from their minds, David realised there was nothing he could do to stop them; they were going to kill him any minute then force open the shuttle's doors and kill everyone inside.

The boss pulled out a gun and pointed it at David's head. David took a deep breath as he stared at his soon-to-be killer. He could not fight his way out; there was nothing he could do but hope to die quickly and with dignity.

'Get on with it and kill him,' one of the others said.

The next thing David knew, he was covered in blood and organs. Bone and metal fragments cut his skin as the man with the gun was blown apart in front of him. David fell back as shouting started all around him. He saw the others go for weapons but one after another the suited figures collapsed in a bloody mess until no one was left standing.

Stunned, David turned and saw Hannoki and his wife walk out of the shuttle with their hands glowing. As the last of the suited figures ran for his shuttle, light came from Hannoki's hand and the figure fell to the ground in bits.

How had Hannoki done this? Why had no one done it before? This level of retaliation would have stopped any attack long ago. David tried to pull himself up off the floor as Hannoki walked towards him but the world spun and he collapsed into darkness.

Chapter 31

OPENING his eyes slowly, it took David a few minutes to realise he was lying on his bed in his shuttle. His head was pounding; thankfully the only light was coming from the pilot station. He winced as he swallowed because his throat was so dry that it hurt. He pulled himself up and reached for a drink of water. It didn't ease his discomfort as much as he hoped but it did help him to concentrate on the patchy memories swirling around his mind. They were fragmented and impossible to believe - until he stood up, turned on the lights and saw the dried blood covering his clothing and hands.

His stomach churned in disgust and it was all he could do not to be sick. He staggered to the medical cabinet and took something for the pain in his head and to settle his stomach. After stripping off his clothes, he started to scrub at his arms and face. He felt the sting of open wounds and watched as the water turned red.

David picked up a medical scanner and ran it over his body; there was bruising to his throat, which explained why it hurt so much, and minor cuts to his face, chest and arms but nothing that would account for the amount of blood he had just washed off. He started to shake as he realised that his impossible memories might somehow be real.

He looked around and saw that everything was where it should be. Whatever had happened had not been in the shuttle. He checked the computer readings and saw that the outside temperature was at its peak; he also picked up the other shuttles but no human life signs.

'*Hannoki?*' David called out in desperation, not knowing what had happened to him.

'*I am here, we are all fine.*'

'*Did everyone make it?*'

'*Everyone here, but I could feel deaths some distance away.*'

'*I'm sorry*' then David continued after a pause, '*I don't know if I remember everything correctly. How did I get on the shuttle?*'

'*There is a lot to explain. When I am finished here, I will come back and tell you what has happened. Just know for now that you are safe.*' Hannoki closed off his mind, leaving David with a lot of questions.

While he waited for his friend to return, he looked at the shuttle's systems. He needed to get it flight ready again, but he could not stop thinking about what had happened. How had he ended up safe in his bunk when there had been so many men from the ship against Hannoki and his people who were all unarmed and did not know how to fight? David remembered shouts and flashes of light; shock and fear from the humans flooded his mind, clouding everything else.

It was not long before he gave up working and went back to his bunk. He did not know how long he lay there before he heard the banging on the door. Just to be safe, David checked with his mind who was out there. When he recognised Hannoki, he opened the door and waited for him to walk in.

'How are you feeling?' Hannoki asked. 'We could not wake you and I did not know what to do other than get you out of the sun.'

'You did the right thing, thank you,' David said. 'I can't seem to get what happened straight in my head. I thought I saw you make them all explode but that is not possible, is it?'

'I did not think it was possible either. I have never had to try to do anything like that before,' Hannoki admitted. 'I knew what was happening outside, I knew they were going to kill you and then come after us. I went out thinking that I could shield you to try and give you a chance, but when I went outside the sight of them made me angry. I intended to push the one holding you back but instead he went...' Hannoki did not seem to know how to continue.

'He blew up,' David finished for him.

'Yes, then the others came towards us and I continued. Pettra and Milkoy started as well, and then the invaders were all dead.'

'So you have worked out how you can defend yourself. If you keep doing this I don't think anyone will keep attacking you.'

'I don't think everyone can do it. Not many of us can create a shield and the other thing was even harder to do.'

'Is there a way to work out who can or can't?'

Hannoki held out his arm and traced the patterning with his other hand. 'The more of these marks we have, the more we can do.'

'I don't understand? How does it work?'

'I am not sure. I have told you before that we feed off the suns and the more marks we have, the more we can take in. Petrra and I have a lot of marks compared to our neighbours; we can work harder and longer and we need very little to eat. My parents taught me a few other things like how to shield, but it looks like we can do much more.'

'I have only seen the extensive patterning on your family. How many others have it?'

'I know of another family. They are not as strong as us but close. How many more I do not know. We rarely leave our communities.'

'If there are others who can do what you can, you can start to organise yourselves, defend yourselves.'

'If there are others then they would have defended themselves, but they have not stopped the invaders.'

'How do you know any of them have tried? You did not know what you could do until today and this is not the first attack you have witnessed. This time it was not your people being attacked, so you were not overcome with their pain. You had time to think, you had a plan though your anger and fear. That changed the outcome. I know others with a detailed pattern like you have been killed,' he said, thinking of his stepmother's wedding dress. 'You need to find those who are strong enough and let them know what they are capable of. See what you can do together.'

'What about the machine you have been working on?'

'It is something for you to use to defend your family and neighbours. But after seeing what you can you for yourselves, I think maybe it could be put to better use. I need to know how many more of you can do the same as you but the question I really want answering is if you can pass energy between yourselves.'

Hannoki's skin took on a pink tinge and David remembered that the skin changed colour depending on what the wearer was feeling. It was the first time he had seen this colour. David had no idea what he had said to trigger the reaction, 'Are you alright?'

'I am fine.'

'Did I say something wrong?' David asked. Hannoki went pinker then stood up and started to pace, covering his face with his hands.

'Hannoki' Petrra called from outside the shuttle.

'Come in, Petrra' David called. He watched as she saw her husband and laughed. Hannoki went even pinker.

'I don't understand,' David said. 'What's going on?'

'She is laughing at me. She thinks it funny that I am not hiding my feelings well.'

'What does pink mean?' Hannoki might be showing his emotions on his skin, but his mind had slammed shut.

'Embarrassment,' Pettra said. 'What were the two of you talking about?'

'I asked if it was possible to share energy, to pass it from one person to another.' Petrra laughed again.

'What am I not getting?'

'We pass energy between each other when we mate. It is an intimate act.'

'So not something you would experiment with.'

'Not really, no. Though there are different ways to pass energy between each other, it is not the accepted thing to do,' Petrra replied.

'Do you really think we could defend ourselves?' Hannoki asked.

'I think you have no idea how strong you are or what you are capable of. You need to find out, both as individuals and as a group. That gives me another idea for the machine. We would not want to work on my idea here, we would want to go back to the peak. But first we need to get rid of the bodies and the shuttles. When they don't return to the main ship, someone will come looking for them.'

'We have got rid of the bodies already but we could not move the shuttles.'

'I will see if I can move them. It will depend on their security settings. How did you dispose of the bodies?'

'Burnt them. There is nothing left but ash. Is that a problem?'

'No, it just means there is nothing left to find.'

✳

'Captain, three of the shuttles have reported in, but I have not heard from the other two.'

'They should have reported in by now. Have you tried calling them?'

'Yes, captain. I cannot raise them on the communications and I'm no longer picking them up on our sensors.'

'What do you mean you can't pick them up? Are the sensors faulty?'

'Our sensors are operating correctly. One shuttle might have failed but I can't understand why there are two that I can't pick up. They are just not there anymore.'

'Sir,' another ensign interrupted. 'There were several energy readings a short while ago from the position where they were last reported. It may have caused a failure with anyone near it.'

'These people have no power,' the captain said. 'What caused energy readings? Why did you not bring this to my attention sooner?'

'These people have no technological capability. There are no other ships in orbit so we are alone here and I did not consider it important.'

'That was not your decision to make. Could it have been one of the shuttles exploding for some reason?'

'No, these were a lot of small, short bursts. They barely registered on my scans. It could have been something happening naturally on the planet.'

'Have the others check the area before returning here. Have them report direct to me.'

'Yes sir.'

⁂

'Hannoki, stop,' David said as he saw the shimmer appear again around him. He was fast learning that this occurred when he pulled in a lot of extra energy.

They had gone back to the mountain peak after David

had moved the shuttles. It was easier than he expected as no security had been set onto the controls; presumably the invaders had not considered Hannoki's people or himself a threat. David took the shuttles into the forest at the base of the mountain peak and shut them down so they could not be seen or traced easily. He knew others would come looking and he hoped that when they found no sign of them, they would assume the missing shuttles had gone elsewhere.

They had only just got to the peak when David turned to Hannoki and looked at him in surprise. 'Don't you feel it? The other shuttles are coming; they are looking for their missing people.'

Hannoki paused and David knew by the look on his face that he was concentrating. Then the shimmer stopped. 'We need to go back down now.'

'No, they are only searching. If I move the shuttle now, it will appear on their sensors. They will know it is here and they will target it. If you need to go back, then fly down but I can't move the shuttle until they leave.'

'Are my family at risk?'

'I don't think so. They're only looking for their people. Tell your family and friends to hide and hopefully the people from the ship will think there is no one here and that is why their friends moved on.'

'Why am I not picking any of this up? Last time I knew before you did.'

'Last time everyone's thoughts were focused towards you and your family and now they are not - that must be the difference. Maybe they have to be thinking about you for you to know about it.'

'So if it is not directed at us, they won't hurt my family?'

'All I can say is that it is not their plan at the moment. They are trying to find the men that you killed. You disposed of their bodies and I moved their shuttles away from any farms. Hopefully they will not be interested in looking at your family, and my shuttle should not be detected up here. The main concern is how much the others reported back before they were killed.'

'I have to go back down. I am sorry,' Hannoki said as he ran off the side of the mountain with his wings outspread.

David watched him go, knowing he could not physically do anything to help his friend. Instead he opened up his mind and monitored the minds of those on the searching shuttles so that if there was any indication that they would attack he could warn Hannoki. There was nothing.

He mentally watched them as they found the shuttles and landed next to them and check the empty crafts. Hannoki and his people had stripped the bodies before burning them and the suits were buried elsewhere. He felt the searchers confusion when they did not find anything they could explain. He heard the conversation they had with the ship in orbit, a ship he had not even thought to scan until that moment. David cursed himself for not thinking about it earlier; he'd been too preoccupied with what was happening on the planet. He waited until the men left the planet to return to the ship before settling down and concentrating on the ship and its objectives.

'*They are leaving the planet,*' David told Hannoki. '*I will come down shortly, I just need to clarify a few things first.*'

'*Good. Everyone saw the shuttles pass and they were scared. Are you alright?*'

'*I am fine. I will be back soon.*'

⁜

The captain listened to the report from his other units. They had found the shuttles empty and abandoned in a forested area. They were only found when they started to scan for metal; it was obvious there had been an attempt to hide them. There was no trace of their companions and no locals lived nearby.

The captain told the telepaths on the teams to scan the area to see if they could detect anything and in particular to try and contact the missing telepath. They came back with nothing; they could only feel the local population but not knowing their language were reliant on their emotions. The indigenous people were shocked and scared, which was exactly what would be expected after an attack. There was no aggression from them.

The missing teams could have gone rogue, the captain thought. Maybe they left the shuttles because they knew they could be tracked easily. Maybe they planned to return to them later. The problem was, these shuttles were designed for short-range transport; unlike the scouts, they would have no way to get back to a starbase on the fuel that they carried, only to another ship in orbit.

'Scan the area. Are there any other ships in orbit?'

'No, Captain, we are alone.'

If they had double crossed him, they would need to wait until another ship collected them, which they would not do while they were in orbit.

'Tell them to bring the shuttles back on board and then move out of orbit. But keep us in sensor range of the planet,' he ordered.

'Yes, Captain.'

'Also monitor for any more energy bursts. I want as much information about them as possible.'

'Sir, they barely registered on our sensors. I don't know how much information we will get, especially if we move further away from the planet.'

'Could these bursts have occurred before but been missed?'

'It would be possible.'

'Then go through all our previous readings, see if there

is anything similar. I want to know the result either way. Tell the team leaders to come to the bridge once they have returned.'

※

He slammed the desk in frustration when he received the message that there would be a delay because of unforeseen circumstances in the delivery of the cargo. What unforeseen circumstances? That planet was a dustball where the wheel was the height of advancement. The message was vague; they would have said if there were technical failures. Someone must be interfering, he thought, and the list of people was very, very small.

He hit the communicator on his desk. 'I want to know what the *New York* is doing - and that telepath David Wilhelm.'

'Yes sir.'

He knew that finding the *New York* would be easy; it was the FWN flagship, its missions would be documented and its position well monitored. But that annoying telepath? That was another matter. He had the finances, and his father had the connections, to go where he wanted and, once outside standard space routes, he could go where he wished without being monitored. As a registered scout, Wilhelm had permission to leave charted space when he wished, unless his authority got cancelled first. He cursed himself over such a basic oversight.

'Also check on David Wilhelm's scout authorities. If they are still current I want them cancelled.'

'At once, sir.'

The report that came through showed that the *New York* was in dry dock for maintenance on its life-support systems. David Wilhelm was in uncharted space and had been for some time, which meant he could be anywhere. David had announced his desire to develop his experiments in zero gravity, so why did he need to travel to uncharted space. What was he up to?

The man sent a message back to his suppliers, telling them to look out for Wilhelm. They should be able to detect his shuttle easily; if they found him they should find out what he knew then dispose of him and his shuttle.

He did not know what David could do - or what he hoped to do. Scouts, like most spacefarers, sent messages from whatever starbase they went to and had accounts where they could retrieve messages sent by family members. He wondered if there was anything in those messages which would be of use to him; the only problem was that any request for them would be recorded, as the storage systems were publically owned and run. He could, however, see any communication between David and Admiral Yoland or the *New York* without raising too many questions.

In the meantime, he retrieved Captain Yoland's report about finding David. He suspected it had been edited to Admiral Yoland's specifications; he was sure David remembered everything that happened to him but, as a level ten telepath, he could shut out any attempt to read his mind. David's health problems could only have been gained from a planet with high levels of UV radiation, which 'Lismar' certainly had.

David had also spent hours talking with Admiral Yoland over secure networks, who had then started asking uncomfortable questions and putting in orders to go to the planet before his death, orders which had then been cancelled. The admiral had certainly known a lot about what was going on and David must have been his only source of intelligence. The man cursed, wishing he knew who else had been told, and how much David had disclosed to his friend Mark. It could not have been anything much otherwise Mark would not be sitting quietly in a dry dock.

✠

The captain of the rogue ship received the orders to find a scout shuttle and pilot, interrogate him before disposing of him. Rough and ready means would be needed as none of his telepaths could hope to break a level ten; most of them were self-taught and not known to the UTA. He had no problem with his orders but was surprised that there might be a scout shuttle on the planet, let alone a high level telepath.

The vessel's specifications had been forwarded to help with the search. The captain laughed: other than his own craft, how many shuttles would be on this dustball planet? Initially he scanned the area where the abandoned shuttles had been found, then he had the area extended to cover the entire planet.

It did not take long to find David's shuttle because it was sitting by the farm where his missing men were supposed to have gone. If the telepath was involved in his men's disappearance, torturing him for information would not only be a duty it would be a pleasure.

'Get the men to suit up and get down to the planet. I want the shuttle and pilot and I want him alive.'

'Yes sir. How many of the men do you want to go?'

'All of them. We don't know what happened to the others so I am taking no risks. Make sure they go prepared.'

'Yes sir,' the reply came and the orders went out. 'Sir, sensor readings show that the shuttle engines have started. It looks like it is getting ready to take off.'

'If and when it moves, I want to know where it goes and so we can get it when it lands.'

Chapter 32

'ARE you ready to go back up the mountain?' David asked, as he checked that the machine was safely tied into the shuttle.

'I am, I will see you up there.' Hannoki took off and started to fly and David laughed at his friend's eagerness.

Once David was happy everything was stowed correctly, he started the engines and decided to see if he could pick his friend up on his scanners. There he was, a little dot moving up the mountain at considerable speed. David smiled at the small blinking light and waited until it was nearly at the peak before taking off; he was careful to keep Hannoki well in front until he landed. As soon as David landed and turned off the engines, he opened the hatch and Hannoki walked up the ramp.

'How was the flight up?' David asked as he put on his suit.

'Brilliant, as always. I can't believe it took me so long to try it.'

'Are you ready to help me unload this thing and give it a go?' David asked. Together they started to manoeuvre the machine off the shuttle.

Once it was on the plateau and turned on, David said, 'I was thinking about what happened when those men attacked and it gave me another idea on how to use this. The machine can't sustain the level of power you are putting into it to hold a shield, which is why it kept collapsing. I don't yet know how to adapt it to make it work, but what if you put the energy into it and release it in the explosion like you did before? That might work.'

'If I do that, I won't be protecting my family any more. I would be killing people.'

'Killing them before they kill you is still protecting your family and friends - just in a more aggressive and effective way. If you had created a shield to protect me, they would have waited until it went down. When I thought a shield was the only way you could defend yourself, I thought it would work as they would move to easier targets. This way you are not pushing them to another farm, you are getting rid of them. Trust me, they can only lose so many people and shuttles before they cannot afford to come here anymore.'

'So if this works, we might be able to stop them from coming back.'

'It would be likely, if their losses were high enough.'

'Alright, let's give this a go.'

'Just remember, I don't know how much power the machine can take and you are more powerful up here, so start slow.'

'I know,' Hannoki said as he sat down. He had only just started drawing in the energy when David felt it.

'Hannoki, do you feel them?' David asked. He paused what he was doing and looked up; when he could not see anything, he mentally scanned the sky.

'I thought they had left,' Hannoki said.

'No, they must have withdrawn out of my range and waited. But they are not after your people this time, they are after me. Hannoki, you need to leave now.'

'What will they do to you? What do they want with you?'

'I am not sure, I just know their orders are to bring me in alive and to be careful. They are scared because they don't know what happened to their colleagues.'

'Do they think you killed them?'

'I think that is what they are assuming. They know you

are not capable of defending yourselves. I don't think they know much more, they are just following orders.' David was finding it hard to isolate individual thoughts from such a distance when they were moving so fast. 'Hannoki, please go while you can.'

'No, I can help you.'

'There are a lot more of them this time and before you had Petrra and Milkoy to help you.'

'They made it easier but I did not need them. Anyway, up here I am stronger and I have the machine.'

'It is not ready; you have not even tried to hit anything yet.'

'Then now seems like a good time. Up here I can't hurt my friends and family in trying.' As he spoke, the shuttles could be seen breaking the atmosphere.

'Please, Hannoki, just go.'

'No. They take you and then what? They will keep coming back for us, only we won't have you to help us. Now is the perfect time to see what I can do with your machine.'

Before David had the chance to say any more, Hannoki started to pull in energy again and feed it into the machine. As the first of the shuttles neared, Hannoki fired for the first time. He clipped a wing on one of the shuttles, causing it to veer to the side suddenly and crash into another shuttle. They both went down.

'Petrra, we are under attack up on the mountain. I have made some of them crash. Can you or Milkoy get to them make sure they are dead?'

'Of course, though from what I can see, they are coming down some distance away. Why are they attacking you and not us?'

'They have discovered David is here and they want him.'

'Keep him safe. Milkoy and I will do our best here.'

Reassured that his family would be able to stop those

that crashed on the ground, Hannoki let off another blast and took down another shuttle but his third shot missed as the remaining shuttles started to anticipate the trajectory and moved out of the way.

David did a quick scan of the shuttles' capabilities and was relieved to see they carried no external weaponry. He guessed the ship carried minimal shuttles and cargo to reduce weight – and why arm yourself against people who cannot fight back?

Checking the readouts on the machine, he saw that the levels were spiking more with each blast. For some reason there was an unstable element; at the moment it was within acceptable levels, but how much longer that would last he did not know.

'David, they keep moving, I can't hit them and they are getting close.'

'Can you get two shots off close to each other?'

'Yes, that is what I am doing but I am not hitting anything.'

'Fire one shot towards the shuttles. As it approaches them, sense the direction they plan to go and send the second to meet them there.'

'I don't understand the words they are thinking.'

'Then do exactly as I say, but I won't be able to monitor the machine's readings so I won't be able to tell you when it won't be safe anymore.'

'Just tell me where to aim,' Hannoki said, as he let loose another shot.

David was already reaching out his mind and saw where the pilot intended to move. He gave Hannoki the mental image, another shot went off and another shuttle went down, and then they repeated the tactic.

The remaining shuttles began to turn and pull up. 'They are leaving, they are returning to the ship,' David shouted.

'They will be back,' Hannoki said as he continued to fire on the departing shuttles. They were now relying on speed to get them away instead of flying tactics.

David stopped reading the pilots' minds and checked the machine. 'Hannoki, you have to stop now,' he said, as he saw the machine was about to overload.

'There are only two more left. I can get them so they won't ever hurt us again.'

'If you don't stop now, the machine will overload. It could explode.'

'I will be fine.' Another blast went off and Hannoki started to draw in more energy to put into the machine, which was starting to spark.

'Hannoki, you must stop now before it is too late.'

'No,' Hannoki shouted and he left off another blast. The next thing David knew, he was spinning away from his friend and came to a stop by hitting his own shuttle. Heat and dust smashed into him and he thanked God he was wearing an environmental suit otherwise the explosion of the machine would have killed him.

Frantically David tried to get to his feet but he kept stumbling. His first thought was to get to his friend but, as he scrambled forward, the smoke started to choke him, checking the suit he saw a tear. He did not get far before he realised there was nothing he could do to save Hannoki, so he turned and crawled to the entrance to the shuttle. Once inside, he closed the door and ripped off the suit and now it was clear it had ripped in several places as he had several cuts and burns. He grabbed the burn medication and applied it to his damaged skin with shaking hands. Once he'd treated all the burns and cuts, he checked what was happening outside. His heart sank; other than debris from the machine there was nothing. His sensors confirmed what his eyes had seen: there were no life signs.

'*Hannoki*' he mentally shouted. '*Hannoki!*' He searched frantically but found nothing.

'*Petrra,*' he called, knowing that his mate would be aware if Hannoki was still alive. He could not find her mind either.

'*David, David are you there?*'

'*Milkoy, I can't get hold of your mother. Is she alright?*'

'*No, she called my father's name then collapsed, dead.*'

'*Oh God, what happened to her? Did one of the shuttle crew get hold of her?*' Had others landed on the planet while they were being attacked?

'*No, I think she died because father died. What happened up there?*'

'*I am coming down. I will see you in a few minutes.*'

⁑

'Sir, the energy spikes have started again, but they are of a much higher intensity than before.'

'What is causing them?'

'I don't know. The signature is nothing the sensors recognise. We are getting an incoming communication from the shuttles.'

'Put it onto loudspeaker.'

'*Ranger* from Shuttle 2, we are under attack. We have already lost two shuttles and are taking evasive action.'

'Where is the attack coming from? What form is it taking?' The captain demanded.

'Shots are coming from that mountain peak where the scout is. Each one is powerful enough to destroy a shuttle, sir. I have never seen anything like it.'

'Keep on course and bring me back whoever and whatever is doing this.'

'We are on approach.' There was a pause. 'We are losing shuttles again. Wherever we move, there is a shot waiting for us. It is like they know what we are going to do before we do it.'

'It is the bloody telepath. Use the telepaths you have on board to try and block him out.'

'They are trying, but it is making no difference.' The captain cursed, he was not used to being up against telepaths in space. 'Captain, we can't land on the peak. The plateau is big enough for another shuttle but it will be a slow landing. We'll be taken out long before we touch down.'

'Return to the ship, I want a full report.'

'Bloody hell, there are only two of them,' then the communication cut out.

'Shuttle 2, Shuttle 2 are you receiving?' Nothing came back, apart from static,

'Sir I think they have all gone,' the comms officer said.

'What do you mean all?'

'All the shuttles. I am not reading any of our shuttles.'

Chapter 33

LANDING the shuttle next to Milkoy, David opened the hatch and walked out to meet him – then did a double take, Milkoy's skin had taken on a grey tinge.

'What happened on the mountain David? What happened to my father?'

'Can we talk out of the suns? They are too hot for me at the moment.' David felt the suns' power on his burns and knew that until they healed he would be even more limited.

'I thought you had clothing, a suit you could wear.'

'The suit was destroyed on the mountain and until these heal,' he held out his damaged arms, 'they will keep burning and get worse in the suns.'

'Then come into the cabin.' David followed Milkoy into his home. It was still very hot inside but he dared not suggest to Milkoy that they talk in his shuttle; the youngster had been through a lot already and David was about to give him worse news. 'I don't know how much your father told you while he was up on the peak, I can't hear your mental communication unless you let me.'

'He just said that shuttles were coming and we should look for any survivors from those that crashed.'

'It would have been unlikely that anyone survived.'

'You lived when your shuttle crashed,' Milkoy pointed out. David did not feel it was appropriate to point out that the differences between his shuttle and these ones. Scout shuttles had strong shields to protect for attack and space debris, short range ship to surface shuttles did not require them.

'They didn't leave as I thought. They came back to find me and though I told him to go, your father would not leave me. He knew that if they got hold of me, they would probably kill me. He used the machine to destroy the shuttles and he was determined to get them all. It was too much for the machine and it overloaded and exploded, killing him.'

'My father got them all?'

'As far as I could tell, yes, he got all the shuttles from the ship.'

'Then he did it. My people are safe now. They won't come back.'

David closed his eyes as he realised that Milkoy thought that it was just this one small group of people attacking them. Now he had to tell him that though one ship had failed, another would come, and another, until Milkoy and his people caused so much damage that it was no longer profitable to plunder the planet. The fight was far from finished.

'No, Milkoy, they will probably still return, though not for some time. They will need to get more shuttles and crew but until they think the risk is less than the gain, they will continue to return. This is the first time they have been challenged. I think they will try again but next time they will be better armed.'

'So my father gave his life for nothing!'

'No, because of your father they run scared, and we might be lucky. They don't know what happened but they know I am here so they will assume that I brought weapons to the planet. They probably think that if they can get rid of me then their problem will be resolved.'

'So where do we go from here? You said the machine was destroyed so if they come back what hope do we have?'

'I can build another one. I brought a lot of spare parts. The shuttle recorded all the readings from the machine so I can look at them and find a way to make it work better.'

'How long will it take?'

'A few days to build the same machine again. I don't know how long to assess and learn from the readings and to make adjustments to stop the overload, and I won't know until I have a chance to look at the readings.'

'So they could get here before you have rebuilt it?'

'I should be able to tell quickly whether it is something I can or can't build. I know roughly how long it will take for that ship to get to a location where it can replace its missing shuttles and crew. Even if a different ship is due, they will be reluctant to engage until they can improve their defences.'

'I don't understand what you are trying to say.'

'I know what I can do and I know the time scales. I will work to the best option.'

'What do you want me to do in the meantime?'

'What you were doing before. Look for others that are strong like you.'

'OK, I can do that.' Then, as if rational thought had started to come through, he added, 'I need to bury my mother first. Is there anything left of my father? We bury couples together.'

'I don't know. My suit was damaged in the explosion and the conditions on the mountain are too hostile for me without it. I tried to get close to see but I could not. I am sorry. I know he was dead, but I don't know what was there.'

'I have to make sure there is nothing to bring back down. I know he flew up there. How did he find it?'

'Exhilarating, he found it exhilarating.' Milkoy stood up to leave. 'How did your mother die?' David asked before he left.

'She died because my father did.'

'I don't understand.'

'When we mate, we are joined closely together. When one dies, the other does as well.'

David shut his eyes, struggling with the pain of loss. It was bad enough that Hannoki had made his choice, but to take Petrra with him as well…

'She knew, she knew what he wanted to do.' David opened his eyes and saw Milkoy had come to stand next to him. 'I don't know everything that passed between them but I do know she said goodbye just before she died. Father would have asked her before he sacrificed himself. The choice was theirs to make.'

'Thank you.'

⁜

When Milkoy flew up the mountain, he was able to understand his father's joy. The air currents twisted and turned him around but also gave him a lift he had never experienced before. But his pleasure was short lived as he landed on the plateau and saw the result of the explosion. Carefully he walked passed the shards of twisted metal, every now and then bending to move a piece to see if anything lay beneath it, but there was nothing. There was nothing left of his father to bury with his mother. With a heavy heart, he turned and flew back down to where his siblings and David were waiting for him.

'Did you find anything? Do you need me to fly up there to bring anything down?' David asked him.

'There is nothing left to find. Mother will have to be buried alone.'

'There must be something left unless your bodies disintegrate easily in fire.'

'I don't know. We very rarely light fires because they cause so much damage. Occasionally the heat from the suns will cause the crop to catch light but we always put it out quickly.'

'Is there any reason why I can't take your mother up the mountain and she can be burned there so your parent's ashes are together? If we die on our planet, we burn our dead. We call it cremation.'

'No, the fire risk...' Milkoy started to say.

'Not on the mountain, there is nothing up there to fuel a fire.'

Milkoy paused as if having to adjust his thinking. 'She would like that, to go the same way as her mate.'

※

Later that day David stood in the shade of his shuttle while Milkoy, his brother and sister and several of their friends and family stood around the burning body of Petrra on the mountain top. Some had flown up, like Milkoy, though none had found it as easy as him. David had transported the others in the shuttle, though they were anxious the entire trip.

David had wanted to come up before to clear the debris but Milkoy asked him not to; he wanted his family and friends to see what had happened, had wanted his parents to be remembered for their sacrifice. So he had collected a few branches from the forest that surrounded the mountains, sure that they would be needed to help the body burn, but they were not. Petrra burnt easily and, as he watched the body disintegrate quickly and cleanly, he could understand why there had been nothing left of Hannoki.

David stood at the back, watching. He wanted to be here to mourn the passing but he also knew he and his people were directly responsible for their deaths and the guilt lay heavily on his shoulders. Once the fire had stopped, he watched as the others embraced, sharing their grief.

David stayed where he was until Milkoy came up to him and drew him in, followed by his brother and sister and then others he did not know. He tensed with the first embrace out of habit, but he could only communicate with these people on a mental level when they allowed it so he did not feel anything else at their touch, and he was glad that he could hold his friends.

Chapter 34

DAVID returned to the peak once he had taken the mourners back to their farms and the suns had gone down. With the higher altitude, he was careful to make sure he covered his skin in the lotions he had brought and covered up as best he could.

The air was cold as he walked off the shuttle and he had to remember that just because it was not hot he could not stay out for long. He did not try and see what was salvageable or not; he just loaded everything onto the shuttle. He did not want to leave anything behind, littering the area; he would go through it all once he was back at the settlement. Anything he could not use he would store on the shuttle until he could dispose of it off planet.

Before he left, he mentally scanned the skies above him, making sure that there was nothing there. Though he could not read the local people as he could his own, they still hindered his ability; instead of working around the noise of other minds, it was like pushing through a metal wall. There was nothing now, but he had no idea how far he could reach so did not know if the ship had gone or withdrawn to wait for reinforcements. Maybe they had left as they still had some cargo to get rid of. He would have to come up here regularly to make sure; if Milkoy was like his father, he would only sense them when the threat was aimed at them directly.

David returned reluctantly to the farm. For the first time he regretted he that could not feel their emotions and he did not know what they thought of him. He stayed in his shuttle and went through the remains of the machine to see if there was anything left that he could use. There was not much, but he had not really expected anything different. He stored the rest away until he had somewhere to dispose of it.

Before starting to build the new machine, he reviewed all the readings, the continual spiking of energy that had destabilised it, caused it to overload and then explode. David's heart sank as he realised that all indicators showed that the unstable element was the power Hannoki had put into it. He had enough parts to build another machine but would he be able to resolve the problem with the overload when he knew so little about the capability of these people? He could make the machine stop and shut down when it went critical but that could leave him vulnerable to attack.

Someone rapped on the shuttle's hatch, making him jump. Confused as to who it could be with Hannoki dead and Milkoy away, David opened it. With relief, he saw Hannoki's daughter, Mesrra, standing there with water.

'Father used to bring you this. Do you need it?' She asked the tentative question in his own language.

David smiled. Milkoy had helped him fill the shuttle's water storage before he left so he knew he would be fine for a considerable time, but he was touched that they continued to think of him. 'Yes thank you,' he said and walked out to get the jug the child was carrying.

He took it into the shuttle and emptied it before returning it to Mesrra, who then ran away. David closed the hatch and returned to his work. She came several more times with the jug of water, each time getting braver until she eventually walked onto the shuttle. David wondered if she was using the water as an excuse to learn more about him and the shuttle. He was tempted to teach her, but he did not know Milkoy's views, and while he was away the children were being looked after by an aunt who kept her distance.

The first he knew that Milkoy had returned was when he opened the hatch when there was knocking on the door. He assumed it was Mesrra but when he looked up he saw someone who, for a moment, he thought was a stranger. Then he recognised the facial features of his friend but the patterning on his skin was different. David felt the reassuring touch of Milkoy's mind in his own.

'When did you get back?' David asked, as Milkoy walked onto the shuttle.

'Before the second sun set yesterday.'

'Did you find others who were strong?'

'Several others, and they know more and will go and talk to them. I came home to be with my family and to work with you.' He looked towards where David was working.

'It is nearly done. I have made some changes so the machine will stop working instead of exploding when the input starts to get too much.'

'That is good to know.'

'I am sorry,' David said, his face red with embarrassment. 'That was a careless comment.'

'Your skin changes colour too,' Milkoy said in surprise. His hand reached out and stopped just short of David's face.

'It is called blushing. It happens when we are embarrassed.'

'What other colours do you go?'

'Pale when we are ill, red from sunburn - but you have seen me like that before.'

'That was different, that was caused by damage from the suns.'

'I saw that you were grey when your father died. I

thought it was just shock.'

'It was grief. We are trained from when we are infants to control our emotions. To allow them to show in the colour of our skin is normally considered rude, but it is allowed in the case of extreme emotion like recent loss.'

'What other colours will your skin change to?'

'Lots, depending on the emotion. Red, blue, green, yellow, to name a few.' David thought about what he had heard about the Lismarian clothing, that it could change colour depending on the mood of the wearer. He had dismissed it at the time. Suddenly uncomfortable with the topic of conversation, he went back to the machine.

'I should be finished rebuilding the machine in a few days, if you want to try it.'

'If the invaders could come back, then yes, I want to try. I want to protect my people but I don't want to kill my mate.'

'Your father and I had not even started to experiment when the attack happened and it went to full capacity. As I said, I have built in an override that should make the machine stop working. I will monitor what is happening. If in doubt, stop when I tell you to.'

'Let me know when you are ready for me to start practising. I need to see to the farm, it has not been properly looked after for a while. Do you need any water? You said before I left that you would be fine for some time.'

'No, your sister brought me some.'

Milkoy laughed, 'She has always been interested in you. She must have seen either father or I bring you water and thought it was a reason to meet you.'

'I did not teach her anything. I thought if you wanted her to know, you would have started.'

'I would not have minded if you did, but it was nice of you to think of that. I am sure she was disappointed.'

'I will let you know when the machine is ready,' David said. As Milkoy walked off the shuttle, he called after him. 'You said just now you did not want to kill your mate. I did not realise you had one.'

'I did not when I left here. Why do you think I look different now?'

'It surprised me but I was not sure if it was a question I should ask.'

'When we mate for the first time, we join together. Please don't ask how it works as I don't know. Our patterns merge. My mate Karra now has the same pattern as me, as will any children we have until they mate. It does not work this way with you?'

'No we stay the same.'

'Then how do you tell who is family?'

'Sometimes with great difficulty.'

'I find you very strange,' Milkoy said. He departed from the shuttle leaving behind a very stunned David.

⁜

David flew the shuttle back up to the peak. He had told Milkoy the machine was ready to try but he had wanted to finish something first. David saw no reason that he could not head out first; it meant that he did not have to worry about keeping track of where he was.

The suns were up when David landed; they had to be because Milkoy was at his weakest when they were down. David protected himself as best he could without an environmental suit and unloaded the machine quickly before retreating back into the shuttle. At least he did not have to be outside to monitor the readings.

It was not long before Milkoy arrived and knocked on the shuttle's hatch. 'I am ready; tell me what I need to do.'

'Your father drew in energy and pushed it into the machine, which increases its strength. Then he pulled it out and aimed it where it needed to go. He never had a chance to explain how he did it, he seemed to do it more by instinct than anything else. I know very little about your kind so I can't help you work it out.'

'All right. I guess the only thing I can do is give it a try.'

'Start off with a small amount of power and we will see where we go from there.'

*

'I don't understand,' David said, after they had tried over a period of days. After each attempt, David reviewed and tried to make the relevant changes. 'The readings are the same as they were with your father but no matter what alterations I make, I can't change the outcome. It is as if the energy going in is unstable but I don't understand why, because when you do things without the machine there never seems to be a problem.'

'Maybe it is because it is just me. Maybe we need Karra as well.'

'I don't understand how that would help, other than increasing the power and the stability problems.'

'No, we are better when we are together. When we mate we become one, we feel what the other feels, die when the other dies. Maybe the power in unstable because it is incomplete. If Karra and I work together, maybe we can get it to work.'

'Have you spoken to her about this? What does she think?'

'She thinks it is a good idea. She knows the risks of me using the machine and if it is better for us to try this together, then she is more than willing. If it fails, she will die either way.'

'Is she going to fly up the mountain with you tomorrow or does she want a lift?'

'She wants to try and fly up with me. Sorry.'

David smiled at Milkoy's attempt at banter. 'Alright. I will make a few alterations so two people can use the machine. I will let you know once they are complete.'

⁜

David had the shuttle hatch open and was sitting in its shade when they arrived. Karra stumbled slightly on landing and Milkoy grabbed hold of her, laughing, 'I have felt nothing like that since our mating flight,' she said, then they saw him and went quiet.

'Hi. Are you ready to start?' David shouted, pretending he had not heard the comment. They were immediately in control of their emotions and walked towards him. 'Hello Karra thank you for helping us.' David had only met her once when Milkoy brought her to the shuttle to introduce her. She was the daughter of the powerful family that Hannoki had known and had sent Milkoy to talk to. He had been surprised that she understood him, but Milkoy said that everything was shared, including knowledge.

'What is Milkoy's risk is mine. We think it will be safer with the two of us.'

'Do you understand what you need to do?'

'Of course, Milkoy has explained it all to me,' she replied. 'Are you ready to start?'

⁞

'Well, David, is there any difference?' Milkoy asked after several hours of practice with his mate on the machine.

'A massive one. The energy is stable when you work together so the machine's power is not spiking.'

'So it won't stop working or overload if we keep using it?'

'Based on these tests, that seems unlikely. But how much more power can you put into it? You were both putting in less than Hannoki was during the attack. To know how the machine will react during a battle, we have to use it as if we were under attack, namely quick, repeated, high-powered blasts.'

'How did my father do that?'

'I don't know. He never really explained how he was able to do anything.'

'Can I try and see the memory?' When David did not reply Milkoy continued, 'I am sorry if what I suggested was wrong.'

'No, it is fine. I was just surprised you would want to see the events leading to your father's death.'

'I have wanted to see them,' Milkoy admitted. 'We would share these memories among ourselves so they will live on in our families. But your mind is closed and, as far as I know, you have never offered a mental sharing.'

'Very few of my kind can read others' minds like me. They would consider any attempt by me to read them as an invasion of their privacy. Though I grew up among others like me, none of them were as strong as I am. I was always taught that a person's memories were their own and not to be looked at unless permission is given. It never occurred to me you would want to know. I am sorry. I have no objection to sharing my memories of your father with you, or any memories I have when I left here that relate to what is happening.'

'How many of those memories did you share with my father?'

'Most of them. I let him see everything he wanted to.'

'I assumed you and my father shared memories, especially at the start when you were both learning each other's language, but I never knew how much.'

'We did. We started with small, isolated images to help with communication. Later we shared more,' David explained. 'I am willing to share any memories with you that you want to see. I am bringing what happened to your father to the front of my mind.'

Then he felt Milkoy's mind in his and he had to suppress a wave of grief. Hannoki was the only telepath he had ever known who could strip his mind bare. David was not concerned over the damage Milkoy could do because he trusted him, but the similarity between the two minds reminded him of Hannoki and he missed him.

'*Me too,*' Milkoy's voice said in his head. '*If you are so unused to this why did you let him? Let me?*'

'*I wanted him to trust me completely and this seemed the best way. And I trust you.*'

'*They are trading our skins as clothes and you suspect our wings are used for other things. I don't understand why,*' Milkoy said in horror, and David could feel him picking through the memories Hannoki had missed.

'*That is what my friends are trying to find out but it will take time. That is why I am here, to help you defend yourselves in the meantime.*'

'*I know, I could see that.*' David felt Milkoy's mind withdraw. 'I think I know what my father was doing, I think we should give it a go.'

'Are you going to explain it to Karra?'

'No, she always knows everything that I do.'

'Then let's give it a go.'

This time the blasts that Milkoy and Karra released were stronger and quicker, but the machine was still not spiking. 'You are both doing great,' David said. 'Can you put any more power into it?'

In response, the input increased suddenly. 'Let us know how we are doing and how much more we can input,' Milkoy called.

Slowly they increased the power beyond the amount Hannoki had put in, then the machine started to show signs of strain. 'Stop, please stop,' David shouted and they did.

'What is wrong David?'

'The amount of power you are putting in is greater than the machine can take. I will have to improve its capability but I don't know if it will make any difference.'

'What do you mean?'

'The power you are generating is more than enough to bring down a shuttle. The problem you have is if they come down out of your range. I am assuming that you can only hit them if you can see or sense them.'

'Of course. How else would we know where to aim?'

'What happens if you know they are coming and can't aim?' David asked. He bent down and drew a circle on the ground. 'This is your planet,' he made an indentation, 'this is you and this is the area where you can target shuttles coming down. This large area here,' he said, marking the diagram, 'is unprotected. It does not matter how much power you put into the machine; it will not matter because you can't get the necessary angle.'

'So there is nothing we can do for everyone on the other side of the planet. If your people discover that, they won't stop coming.'

'The others you have found who are strong - would you be able to pass the energy to them so they could direct it out?'

'They would not be able to absorb it, it would be too much for them. But I don't know if they could deflect it to where it would need to go. We would need to try.'

'I think we will need to talk to everyone about what they can - or are willing – to do.'

Chapter 35

THEY returned to Milkoy's home as the suns started to set. David landed near the cabin as he always did now and settled down to go over the readings. The primary results had been the best yet but he was keen to do a full analysis and compare how well the machine worked with both Milkoy and his mate to being used by a solo user.

He was disturbed by someone banging on the hatch. He opened it, assuming it was Milkoy or one of his family members with water.

'I am going to talk with others who are stronger. Do you want to try and listen?' Milkoy asked as he walked into the shuttle.

'How many minds are you going to talk to at the same time?'

'I won't know until we start but it could be as many as twenty. It depends if all the relevant family members are present or if only one is there and echoes the conversation to the others.'

'I don't know what that means.'

'Among immediate family, the telepathic link is very strong; one family member can be in the conversation but will open up his or her mind so the others can hear but not participate. If a family member is not in the conversation and wants to ask a question, they can only do so through the person in the mental conversation.'

'This could be a difficult conversation for everyone. If someone has a large family they could be trying to deal with two conversations at once.'

'I doubt it. This will be the largest group I have had to talk to. But when we can't hide what we are thinking or feeling from each other, it tends to make us considerate. You know what questions are important and what can wait.'

'I am not sure I can cope with so many minds. It is much harder talking to you than my own kind.'

'The minds won't come all at once, they will join the link one at a time. If you are in at the start, you can see what you can take. If you can't take the volume of minds, I will try and echo them to you. It is important for you to be a part of this if you can. If not, I will try and speak for you.'

'This is nothing that I have tried before, but I will give it my best, when will this conversation take place?'

'Now.'

David followed Milkoy off the shuttle and into his home, they sat down together and David opened his mind up to Milkoy's and was reassured by the familiar feel. It was not long before others joined them, all of them strange. As the number grew, he found it harder to maintain control. He was just about to tell Milkoy that he was not capable of taking any more and withdrawing, when it was announced that everyone was present. David sighed with relief; maybe he would be able to cope.

As the conversation started, David followed most of what was said. But as it progressed, the conversation made references to things he could not understand, mostly about their kinetic ability and how they could achieve the best defence. He gained more from the images in their minds, but still he struggled to comprehend everything. Milkoy looked at him and he knew he would be filled in afterwards. Gradually David found it harder and harder to maintain the connection and his head started to pound; for the first time he was the weakest mind. It was a relief when they started to withdraw, leaving him pale and shaking as a result.

'Are you alright, David?'

'I will be in a minute. It was a lot harder than it is with my own kind.' David rubbed his clammy face with his hands. A cup of water appeared in front of him; he picked it up with shaking hands and drank it with relief. 'Thank you.'

'Feeling better?' Milkoy asked and when David nodded his head he continued. 'How much did you understand?'

'A lot of it, I think. I understood what you plan to do but not how you are going to do it. You were using references I had not heard before. By the end, the volume of minds was getting too difficult to filter and translate.'

'You did very well; it is never easy talking to so many, even when you understand everything that is being said. But you seem very upset by your reaction.'

'I know. I am one of the strongest telepaths among my kind so it is rare that I encounter anyone stronger than me. As a result, I am used to having the advantage. I was the weakest in that meeting and found it very humbling.'

'You would be stronger if you used your ability as much as we do. We talk mind to mind more often than we do with our mouths. We have avoided doing it out of respect for you.'

'I never knew that. Unfortunately the majority of our kind are not telepaths and we are not generally liked, so telepathic conversations are not acceptable.'

'Would you have a problem with us and the other families having telepathic communication with you?'

'No, I would be honoured.'

'Good, because if you can communicate easily with the other families, it will make it much easier when we practise sending energy for them to use.'

'How many have agreed to try?'

'All of them. They all know people who have been killed and want it to stop.'

'When do we start?' David really hoped that it was not immediately.

'Tomorrow, as the suns rise over the peak. Concern was raised that, depending on where you are, it varies if the suns are in the sky or not.'

'I may be able to put some measures into place that could help. I should have enough materials with me to build a second machine that can be used on the opposite side of the planet, adding extra resilience.' David's mind was already on various plans. 'I will leave you until you are ready tomorrow to practise with the others.'

David did not start work when he got back to his shuttle but lay down and immediately fell asleep. When he awoke, his head had stopped spinning and the ideas that had started to develop earlier were now clear. When Milkoy called him mentally some hours later, saying that it was time to start practising with the other families, he was taken by surprise.

'I am sorry, you said this was alright,' Milkoy said.

'It is, I will meet you on the peak.'

David sat in the pilot's chair and made sure than neither Milkoy nor his family were near when he started the engines. Soon he was landing on the peak and waiting for Milkoy to join him, which he did shortly afterwards with his mate.

'What are we going to try?' David asked.

'We are starting with the five strongest families; they are at varying distances from here. We will send them energy, starting low then slowly increasing in power. They will direct it into the sky until they cannot take more. Tomorrow we practise with others, until all the families have tried. Then we start with the original families again.'

'You have thought this out well.'

'I just followed your idea: start small and build on it. The others are in position and ready to start.'

'Then I will start monitoring to make sure everything goes well.'

'All our communication will be telepathic,' Milkoy warned.

'I will do my best to keep up.'

⁜

The training was going well. The stronger families had practised both as a mated pair and as a family unit with very good results. Milkoy and Karra were able to send power through various families to the far side of the planet, so no area was totally unprotected though the further away they were, the less strength there was because of the position of the suns. Little was lost in actual energy transfer as the pair or family could add their own strength when they passed it on. The problem was, the position of the suns changed the further away they went, reducing their capability.

David looked at what spare parts he had left. He had finally managed to prevent the machine from overloading and negated the need for the failsafe but as a result he could not build a second machine.

'I have not been able to find a second couple as strong as Karra and I. Would a decrease in power cause much of a problem?' He had been so engrossed, he had not heard or sensed Milkoy's arrival and jumped at the question.

'It would depend on how much weaker, but anything would be better than nothing. At the moment it is irrelevant. I don't have what I need to build a second machine. I had hoped to get something together to help, but I used too many parts.'

'A second machine would mean that there would always be someone in sunlight. Can't you take bits from somewhere else?' Milkoy asked, indicating the shuttle.

'I would if I could, but the shuttle is too different. To build another machine, I would have to leave here to get what I need,' David said.

'You came here to help us. If that is still what you want to do, the important question is: is there anything else you can do to help us by remaining here?'

'No. The machine is working well and you and the other families know what to do to defend your people. What you need is more machines and I must leave to achieve that. It would also be beneficial to update my friends and find out what is happening at home.'

'You also have to look after yourself. You are getting sick again.'

'How did you know?'

'Your skin is starting to look as it did when you were first here,' Milkoy said. 'When do you plan to go?'

'I think I need to go as soon as possible. The sooner I go, the sooner I can get back with what I need.'

'I will miss you; do you know how long will you be gone?'

'I don't. I have to assume the attackers know that I'm here and will be looking for me so I have to be careful how I get the things I need. But I'll be back as soon as I can,' David said. 'I hope that they do not return while I'm away.'

'I know what to do if they do.'

'I'll be back as quickly as I can.'

⁕

David left the planet with a heavy heart. He knew he had to be careful not to do anything to draw attention to himself and with what he needed to get, that would not be easy. Once back into FWN controlled space, they could pick up the tracking signature of his shuttle. He knew his best chance was to enter in another ship but he had no idea how he was going to achieve that.

Chapter 36

MARK walked into an overcrowded, dark room and looked around him. Like most rooms on this starbase, it was badly lit and ventilated. He had docked out of necessity; it was one of the oldest stations and he tried to avoid it when possible, but for once fate had intervened.

They had been in dry dock for a month having the life-support systems cleaned out. When a week after they had left warning indicators had started to show, they had headed to the nearest starbase to have them checked out, the same starbase where there was someone he could trust to help him.

As he scanned the tables looking for someone specific, Mark moved further into the café. It did not help that he had not seen his cousin in several years and nearly everyone was wearing an FWN uniform. When he had heard that the *Chicago* was docked here, he took the chance and contacted the bridge, only to be told the captain had gone for lunch on the base.

Mark knew the main places where the bridge crew went to eat. The first two had been a negative and this was his last option. He was just considering that he might have missed his cousin when he saw him, sitting in a corner with two other people. Taking a deep breath, he walked up to them.

'Hello Nick, it has been a while.' The trio's conversation stopped and they all looked at him.

'Mark, I heard about your father. I am sorry for your loss, he was a good man.'

'Thank you. Do you have a few moments for us to talk alone?'

Nick nodded and the other two stood up and left. Mark took one of the empty seats.

'I wish I could have made it to the memorial service but I could not get back in time,' Nick said. 'I thought about sending a message, but it's been so long I was not sure how it would be received.'

'I know. I didn't make it back either. The FWN would not wait to dispose of his body.'

'I'm sorry, I know you were very close.' Both men sat in uncomfortable silence for a while before Nick continued. 'It's been years, Mark, and you did not come to me so you could hear condolences. What do you want?'

'I need your help.'

'You are having a laugh, aren't you? We don't speak in years and then you come looking for me when you need something? I thought you have lots of high-powered friends you could turn to.'

'Not for this. I don't know who I can trust.'

'What makes you think you can trust me after everything that has happened between us?'

'We used to be not just family but very good friends. I have to trust that, although we followed separate paths over the last few years, you are still the same person. Other than my crew, there is no one in the FWN I can talk to.'

'All right, I'll listen but get to the point. What's so important that you're coming to me?'

'I think someone killed my father when he started asking some uncomfortable questions.'

His statement was met with silence then Nick said, 'Come again? He was killed? I thought there was nothing suspicious about his death.'

'It was made to look that way, but at least one person

did not like what he was doing and killed him to stop it. Everything he was trying to push through the fleet was stopped suddenly on his death.'

'It could be a coincidence, Mark'

'No, not with what my father knew. It is not a coincidence, it is a cover up. I have been in deep space, following orders and not asking any questions. It would not be easy for them to get to me and I think they are waiting to see what I do next.'

'What was your father working on? What have you got yourself into, Mark?'

'Father noticed that there was abnormal activity in a certain area of uncharted space. When he tried to get ships to check it out, the orders were cancelled. If he knew by whom, he never said. He was just told it was an inappropriate use of resources. At first he didn't think too much about it but curiosity got the better of him. He dropped the matter within the FWN but asked a good friend of mine, a scout called David, to check it out for him. What David found was awful and not what either of them expected.'

'Are you going to get to the point?' Nick asked when Mark paused.

'Are you sure you want to know everything? There won't be any going back?'

'If they killed my uncle, then yes, I want to know. I always liked and respected him and Mum was devastated by his death. As you say, regardless of what passed between us we are still family.'

'The ships that are going into uncharted space were going to a planet to kill the inhabitants. They are skinning them alive and cutting the off their wings. The skins are brought back and made into clothes. I don't know if you have heard of Lismarian fabrics?' As he saw Nick's face pale he continued. 'We believe the wings are used in industry and that is where the real money is made.'

'How is this allowed?'

'I don't know but that is what my father was looking into. Without knowing who I can go to, I don't know what to do and I can't help my friend.'

'And you think I can find out for you? That is the favour you want?'

'No, I want you to take a few of my crew and a shuttle, take them to Starbase Shu and leave them there.'

'Are you mad? What will they do once they get there?'

'David went back to the planet, I have heard from his father that people are looking for him. If they are, they will have his shuttle's frequency. As soon as he returns into charted space, they will know. Hopefully they won't be looking for a *New York* shuttle so far away from our ship. They can cross over, wait for him and bring him back to the starbase undetected. From there his father has the money and connections to get him safely to any planet.'

'If they are paying that much attention, surely they will be monitoring communications? Looking for individual shuttles is not easy unless you have specific frequencies, as you believe they have with your friend. Unless your friend knows when and where to meet up, it will be like looking for a needle in a haystack. How do you know he even plans to return?'

'The planet is very hot. He can't stay there for too long so he has to return at some point,' Mark explained. 'As to how we will find him, David is a level ten telepath. The crew, if you are willing to take them, will also be telepaths and they have found him in deep space before.'

'I'm as convinced as you that a *New York* shuttle won't be picked up so far from the main ship. They can come on board with me. I'm posted to border control and as we pass Shu they can dock and claim they have taken some leave. I also have a few telepaths on board that you can use if you need them.'

'Why is a ship like the *Chicago* on border patrols?'

'I was wondering the same thing. Now I think it is because they want to keep me away from you. Did you purposefully look for me here?'

'No, we had an unexpected problem with our life support and this was the nearest base. I actually avoid this place when I can. Our coming here was pure chance.'

'Did you only ask for my help because I was here?'

'The plan was in place, I just did not know how to ask. Communications are easily monitored.'

'We leave tomorrow. Make sure your crew are on board before 0900 hours.'

'Thank you.'

'What is family for?' Nick said as he stood up.

'How is Reni?' Mark asked just before his cousin walked off.

'She is good, so are the kids.'

'Father said you now have two little girls. Congratulations.'

'Thank you. Good luck with this, Mark. If you need anything else, let me know.'

Chapter 37

DAVID returned back to charted space several weeks later and, as expected, it was not long before the FWN *Liverpool* contacted him and demanded he follow their orders. After being scanned to ensure he had no weapons on board, he was instructed to dock and cut his engines, then wait. He followed the instructions and opened his hatch when told to do so. A few minutes later he was not surprised when a security team walked on board as he sat there calmly in the pilot's chair. He watched them raise their guns.

'How can I help you officers?'

'Please stand up and place your hands on your head.'

David stood patiently as he was searched. Scans would show any weaponry attached to the shuttle but not any personal firearms or knives. Once they were happy that he was not armed, they relaxed slightly. 'Please disembark peacefully, sir. The captain wants a word with you,' he was told.

'Of course,' David said lowering his arms and walking towards them. He could guess what was going to happen next.

He had been contacted several days ago, before returning into charted space by telepathic members of the *New York*. They were looking out for him on Starbase Shu with a shuttle from the *Chicago*. The crew had flown out in the shuttle so they could talk properly. David found it hard to listen to so many minds at once, especially since they had not been trained to do so. The distortion gave him a headache but he imagined it was worse for them. The other concern was that they might have been overheard by another telepath and reported to the FWN. The two shuttles flew as close to each other as possible and although neither shuttle had the equipment on board to transfer a person over, it did mean that David could talk to one person and not many, and at this distance from the starbase and other ships no one would overhear them.

'*Where is the* **New York**? *I don't feel them?*'

'*They are following their orders. We were dropped off at Shu unofficially to try and contact you before going into charted space,*' Paul, Elen's brother, responded. Of all the FWN telepaths, David was pleased they'd sent Paul.

'*Why would the captain do that? Surely there are rules about separating crew like that?*'

'*There are. However, I think he is hoping no one will find out.*' David smiled at the comment. '*We were brought here by the* **Chicago** *and they lent us one of their shuttles. The captain is worried that when you return into charted space you will be arrested and in the control of the FWN. He sent us to find you and bring you in undetected. With your father's help, we will relocate you somewhere out of their reach until he can find out what is going on.*'

'*How much do you know?*'

David felt Paul's agitation at the question. '*The captain has not told us much but I know more than I should,*' was his honest reply.

'*I won't ask anything more.*'

'*We will have to find somewhere that you can board this shuttle so we can take you to the starbase. After that we will arrange for you to be collected but unfortunately your shuttle will have to be disposed of so it won't be found.*'

'*Thank you for everything you and the captains of the* **New York** *and* **Chicago** *have done but I think it will be* *better if I proceed as normal.'*

'Why?'

'If they are looking for me, they won't stop. When they can't find me, suspicion will fall on the **New York** *and my father.'*

'You don't know what they will do to you once they have got you.'

'Once they have hold of me, I might find some of the people involved.'

'Sure you will! Like they won't have members of the UTA present to block you.'

David laughed. *'Good luck to them finding a telepath stable enough to do that. I suppose they could get several in, but how do you think the FWN can stop me from explaining everything to them? Trust me, they want as few people as possible to know.'*

'They could just kill you!'

'That would raise further questions and problems for them. The UTA would demand their own investigation, as would my father. They are both powerful and independent of the FWN.'

'I don't know what your father is capable of but the withdrawal of the UTA's support would be a blow to them. It would raise a lot of questions that they won't want to answer, and companies and organisations reliant on telepaths would also want to know for their own reasons. The political pressure would be immense,' **Paul said as he worked though the possible repercussions.** *'They can't afford to kill you.'*

'I know. Please relay your conclusion to the captain and your sister. It might stop her from killing me the next time we meet.'

Paul explained everything he knew before withdrawing back to Shu. David changed his route and entered charted space via a different starbase. He took on supplies and completed routine maintenance before continuing his trip.

One day later he was stopped by the *Liverpool* and now he was following the security team to talk to the captain. He just hoped he was right that killing him would cause too many problems.

David was taken to a meeting room and told to sit. He waited with the security officers until the captain decided to come and talk to him. He was surprised when, a few moments later, a female walked in and introduced herself as Captain Bauer.

'Do you know why you have been detained Mr Wilhelm?' she asked.

'No, all I was told was that you wanted to talk to me.'

'A warrant for your arrest was issued. You will have to stay on board until we reach the nearest starbase where you will be transferred and transported to FWN headquarters.'

'What is the arrest for?'

'Illegal movement outside FWN space.'

'All of this for such a minor offence?'

'I am just executing the warrant Mr Wilhelm.'

'What will happen to my shuttle? It's my livelihood.'

'It will be transported with you but for now you will be confined to a cell.'

'Thank you,' said David and stood up. 'I take it there is nothing else?'

'No. The officers will escort you and I will ask the doctor to make sure there are no medical concerns that need to be addressed.'

David followed his escort to the cells, a small area with a bed and wash area. Once he stepped into it a barrier was activated. He would not be able to leave unless he was let out.

'There is a call button should you need it, otherwise

you will be checked on every few hours and receive three meals a day,' he was informed. Smiling in acknowledgement, he lay down and closed his eyes.

After a few hours a doctor came to see him for a full medical. He lectured David about not taking his supplements and the damage to his skin from UV radiation. David refused to answer questions about the latter. He was given a shot to counter the deficiencies caused by long-term space travel and a cream for his skin; other than that, he was given a clean bill of health.

For the rest of the short trip, David only saw the person who brought him food. This was not a telepath and, other than to ask if there was anything he needed, he did not speak. David spent his time catching up on sleep and seeing if there were any telepaths on board; there were but he decided at this time not to contact them. He did not want to stir up tensions that could be detrimental to him on such a short trip.

David had started to get restless when the *Liverpool* docked at a starbase. He was not told where he was, but it was not hard to find out. A security team transferred him onto the *Madrid* and into their holding cells. He asked for something to read but was refused; he asked if his father had been informed about his arrival and was told that he had been. David knew that they were lying, which gave him the challenge that he needed to keep him occupied.

It did not take him long to find out that there were no telepaths on the *Madrid*; that was probably why the ship was chosen, he thought cynically. But his range was not limited to this one ship; did the FWN seriously not know how far he could reach?

It took him a few days of scanning before he picked up the first telepaths. They were all low grade and he did not know whether they would do as he asked, so he waited.

Then he heard it: the *London* was passing some distance away and Henrik Gregson, Tali's cousin, and his friend was on board. Together with Paul Winters, Henrik had been one of the first to sign up when the FWN opened its doors to telepaths. The *London* was a long way off and he could only hope that Henrik's mind was open and listening.

'*Henrik, Henrik!*' he shouted, stretching his mind as far as he could.

'*Seriously David, do you have to shout so loud?*'

'*Sorry, I was not sure you were in my range.*'

'*Well I am. How are you?*'

'*Not great. I have been arrested by the FWN and the* **Madrid** *is transporting me back to FWN headquarters. They are lying to me. They have told me that my father has been informed and I know he has not. I need you to contact him for me.*'

'*What have they arrested you for?*'

'*Illegal movement outside FWN space.*'

'*That is a space byelaw. If it is used at all, it is for nuisance craft and they normally just get a hefty fine. What have you got yourself involved in that they are going to so much trouble?*'

'*A lot, but you are moving away and soon I won't be able to talk to you. Please can you tell my father I have been arrested - and be careful.*'

'*I don't understand this, David. They must tell anyone you nominate if you're arrested.*'

'*I know the law. Please tell him and don't let the FWN know you have done so.*' Their paths were crossing and it was getting harder to talk.

'*I will do my best,*' Henrik promised and then there was nothing because he had moved too far away. David could only hope he still had enough loyalty to him to do as he asked.

✴

Several weeks later, the *Madrid* finally docked. David had not thought he would be relieved to arrive at his destination when he did not know what was going to happen, but the days he had spent alone with nothing to occupy him were driving him crazy. When scanning space started to wear thin, he paced the small cell. The only company he had during the trip was when he was brought food and the crew member never spoke to him and ignored his repeated requests for something to read. He got so bored he was tempted to pick through the minds of the crew to find out what they knew, but his principles stopped him.

David was again met by a security team which transferred him to the FWN headquarters and placed him in another cell, just like the last one. As he lay on the bunk, he smiled; he could feel his father, feel the lawyers Viktor had brought with him, including telepathic lawyers from the UTA. They knew he was here. The FWN would have to let them see him; they could not risk the UTA denouncing them and causing major political and financial repercussions.

The hours ticked by and David knew the FWN were stripping the shuttle's systems for information. He had downloaded everything about Milkoy, his people and the machine, and left the file behind with instructions to keep it safe and out of the sun. David had told Milkoy that if he did not come back but others of his kind arrived then he should read their minds to see if they could be trusted with the information.

After he had downloaded the information, David carefully deleted everything and replaced it with old half-formed projects he had once worked on. He had told everyone he wanted to go back into space to experiment, so old experiments were what they would get. They would not find anything on the shuttle that would incriminate him. Yet the hours dragged into days and the FWM still delayed the lawyers, they still tried to deny that David was there and at the same time they tried using FWN telepaths to read his mind illegally. None of them had the strength to get anywhere near him.

⁜

David sat opposite two FWN officers in an interview room. He could feel a telepath trying to break through his mental barriers and smiled at their ineffective attempts. Over the last few days they had been trying at random times hoping, David thought, to catch him unawares. After the UTA members had failed they were using untrained minds and David was horrified by their poor, sloppy attempts. Now they were trying several together; he did not know their ratings, but he knew they wouldn't get what they wanted.

'Do you know why you are here?' he was asked.

'I was told I had been arrested for illegal movement outside of regulated space.'

'That is correct. I know you have asked for legal representation but this is an offence where you do not have that right.'

'I have been arrested for a minor offence which is normally dealt with by a fine. If the person is a persistent offender, there's a court summons which is why legal representation is not applicable. The only reason to arrest me would be because there was no other way to find me. My father is well known; all you would have to do is tell me to stay with him until the matter is resolved.'

'As a scout, there is concern over your movements through space so it was deemed necessary to detain you.'

'It is normally scouts who fall foul of this law. I have never heard of any of them being detained and transported in a cell to a planet for further interrogation.'

'There is no interrogation, this is just a friendly conversation.'

'So I am mistaking the minds that have been trying to read mine since I arrived?'

'I don't know what you are talking about. What you are suggesting is illegal.'

'I know it is. I should warn you that I will defend myself against the next mind, or minds, that try an illegal read.'

'What is that supposed to mean?'

'None of the telepaths you have been using are strong enough. If I defend my mind, other than block as I have been doing, the people trying to read me will be brain dead very quickly. I am legally allowed to do that; you just need to talk to the UTA.'

'We will.'

'Of course you will, just to appease your curiosity,' David said. 'Are you going to ask me what you really want to know, because you are going to an awful lot of trouble for a minor offence?'

⁂

After David left the planet, Milkoy started working on his advice. Milkoy stayed where he was as he and his mate were the strongest and the only pair who knew how to use the machine which David had left on the mountain top. The others moved further away, near areas that had the greatest population, but there were still many small communities that were unprotected. They would remain that way until other strong couples could be found, but that would take time. The families expected to spend many nights out in the open until they could create a crude shelter and later, if they stayed, a proper home.

Milkoy spent a few hours each day practising with the machine and passing power to the others, who then experimented with creating shields and creating energy blasts. Those who had moved to different communities caused some curiosity as families rarely moved unless there was a good reason to do so. When they were questioned, they indicated that they had come to offer protection against the people attacking them. Most thought this was funny - until they saw the newcomers practising. Then people showed up with materials to help them build a cabin and went out of their way to make them feel welcome.

∗

Milkoy woke up suddenly in a cold sweat. Karra jerked awake beside him.

'They are coming,' he stated.

'I will ask Hirra to look after the young ones,' she said. Then, a moment later, 'she is coming.'

Milkoy started calling the others, warning them. He knew they were coming but he could not say with any accuracy where they would attack; he hoped that he would know in time.

'I am here,' Hirra shouted as she came in. Milkoy and Karra went to meet her. She was standing at the entrance with her own baby in her arms,

'Are you alright to look after them all?' Karra asked, meaning Milkoy's younger siblings who had stayed with them after the death of their parents.

'Of course. Go. I will get the other residents to come here. The smaller area we occupy, the easier it will be for us to defend it. Don't worry about us, look to the others.'

Milkoy and Karra flew up the mountain as fast as they could. As soon as they landed they uncovered the machine; David had insisted that it was not left uncovered. They powered it up and concentrated. They could feel the ships in orbit and the shuttles coming down, more than Milkoy had ever felt before. Now they were moving he could tell where they were going; they were spreading themselves out which would make it difficult to target them all.

'This is not going to be easy, Karra.'

'We will just have to do the best we can.'

Milkoy started to call the others, warning them that the attacks were coming in from different locations and they had to be ready. There would be no time once they were close enough to do anything but act.

They waited until the shuttles were nearer and started to pull the energy out of the machine. Milkoy called those who would have the power first, Karra those who would come second; they just had to hope there would be time for the third group.

'Ready,' Milkoy shouted both mentally and verbally and let out the first burst of energy. There was no time to make sure it was being transferred properly before they sent the second burst. As they started to pull in for the third blast, Milkoy called out to warn that it was incoming; then he felt the first pains started and knew they had not succeeded in saving everyone.

The pains that started to course through their bodies made it difficult to concentrate and isolate who needed extra energy. They were able to get another blast to the third location before everything became too confused. To send any more could result in them killing their own people.

※

'What the hell happened down there?' the captain asked the leaders of the three teams that had gone down to the planet.

'Sir, as we broke orbit we were fired upon. They were able to take down three shuttles before we landed and then the attack stopped. We tried to identify where the shots were coming from but we only got a rough location, which was too far away to walk to. I considered diverting a shuttle there, but we could not risk losing another one if it was attacked. We scanned the area and there was nothing of note on the readings, no indication of any technology, not even any metal.'

'Sir, my team's experience was the same. However, we were able to get a better location for where the shots came from. I sent a team and all they found was a half-built cabin and a pair with very nice skins which should bring a large profit.'

'Did they put up any fight?'

'No, sir. Like a lot of them when we arrive, they seemed ill and they were easy pickings.'

'And you?'

'We lost two shuttles. We heard the others being attacked and thought we were safe when no shots came as we broke orbit. They came a short time later as we were close to landing and they did not stop until we landed. We had no chance to find out where they were coming from.'

'It seems that they only have a short window when they can attack us, from when we break orbit to landing,' the captain said.

'So it would seem, sir. Once the shuttles are unloaded, do you want us to get ready for a second run?'

'No. We will return and replace the shuttles and men. If we try again and lose any more shuttles, we won't make any profit on this run. We will come back with a second ship. I want a detailed account from your pilots to devise a tactical flying plan.'

'Yes sir,' the team leaders said and left.

When he was on his own, the captain cursed in anger and frustration. He was warned that a previous ship's shuttles had been attacked and he had laughed at their incompetence. How could you lose shuttles on a planet with no technology? He had scanned the planet surface and found nothing that would cause concern, so how were these people doing it? He would go back and talk to the other captains before deciding how to proceed.

⁜

'Enough of this. We want to know where you have been and what you were doing.'

'I have already told you. I left charted space to work on my experiments in peace and quiet. I have not been anywhere.'

'You are lying.'

'Do you have evidence of that?'

'We believe you have been supplying technology to a people we do not have a treaty with.'

'That is a serious charge but, as I have already asked, what evidence do you have?' David pushed.

'The intelligence is sound. You claim to have been conducting experiments that needed zero gravity. That is fine but there was no need to leave charted space for peace and quiet. So why did you?'

'I thought my licence was still valid to leave charted space. I wasn't informed that it had been cancelled. But you are right: if I stayed off the trade routes then I would be left pretty much alone. I would still have to monitor communication frequencies as required by law, a law that does not apply in uncharted space as you should know. If I was wrong then I apologise profusely, but supplying technology? I am sorry, I have no idea where that allegation comes from. I mean, seriously, I have a small shuttle. Where would I have room to store anything other than the experiments I was working on?'

'If you have nothing to hide then tell us what you were doing.'

'I have already done so several times. If you think I have been supplying technology illegally then I have the right to legal advice.'

✳

'I know David Wilhelm is here. I can tell you what room he is in. If you continue to refuse to follow the rules, I will have a telepathic conversation with him,' June Jones, the UTA lawyer, threatened.

'David has been arrested for an offence where he does not have the right to legal advice,' she was advised.

'He has been arrested for an offence where you can't legally hold him for questioning. You can only send him to court, which you have not done. So let us talk to him or, as previously stated, we will do so telepathically.'

'We can't allow you to do that and we will use our telepaths to stop you.'

'If you think you can then you are very naive. Both Mr Wilhelm and I are stronger than any telepath you currently have on base. If you include the power of the UTA, you do not have enough telepaths in the FWN to stop us having a mental conversation when we want to.'

'Are you threatening us?'

'No, just stating a fact. Telepaths might work for you, but they also belong to the UTA. They will all have divided loyalties.'

'If you can talk to him any time you want to, why have you not done so?'

'Because unlike you, we respect the law. We talk regularly among ourselves telepathically, we are very good at it. However, the law restricts us from doing this during legal proceedings as the conversations can't be recorded. If you persist in breaking the law, then we will follow your example.'

'The FWN want to talk to David first.'

'The FWN do not have the legal right to do that. I am David's legal representative. If I'm not let in to see him in the next five minutes, I will contact him and start our legal representation.'

'I need more time.'

'If I give you more time, you might do something even more illegal! You now have four and a half minutes. I suggest you talk to your boss quickly.'

An hour later, David was led out of his cell to the UTA lawyer. 'Hello, David,' she said. 'My name is June Jones. I'm here to represent you and get you out of here. *Be warned, this conversation is recorded.*'

'Thank you, it is a relief to finally talk to someone. *Thank you, how much do you know*?'

❉

David lay on his hard, narrow bed wondering what the FWN planned next. He felt them coming before he heard and saw them. As the door opened, he turned his head. 'Good evening,' he greeted the guard. 'How can I help you today?'

'You can get your things, you are free to go.'

David looked at him for a moment then sat up and swung his legs over the side of the bunk. 'Just like that?'

'I was just asked to release you and bring you to the reception desk.'

David believed that the guard was telling the truth but it was still with a great deal of suspicion that he packed the few items his father had been allowed to give him. At the reception desk he saw his father, his lawyer and an FWN officer. 'Gentlemen,' David said.

'You are being released while we make further enquires. I advise you not to leave the planet and to let us know where you will be residing in case we need to talk to you again.'

'He will be residing with me,' Viktor said.

'Good. Talk to you soon, David,' the officer said and turned and walked away.

David went straight home with his father and June. They did not speak until they were in the house and the door to the study was closed.

'So what was my sudden release about?' David asked.

'I don't know. They said they had no further leads at present.'

'It would have taken them twenty-four hours to go through the shuttle's computers. Nothing was encrypted, so why after all this time have they decided that they don't have anything?'

'We have been putting pressure on them,' June said. 'We ordered all the FWN telepaths on the planet back to the UTA. Those who have acted illegally will be severely punished to make sure no one does it again. We have threatened to leak the news that the FWN were making illegal use of telepaths, news that would seriously undermine them politically if you were not released.'

'Thank you, June. Can we call you if we need you again?'

'Are you going to tell me what this is all about?' When both David and his father paused, she continued. 'Don't worry about it, maybe it is best that I don't know. If you need me again, please call.'

'I feel rude for not telling her,' David said after she had gone. 'But I do feel that the less she knows the better. As soon as I have found somewhere else to live, I will get June to inform the FWN so they can't accuse me of trying to hide.'

'Why would you leave? Anja had one of the guest rooms redecorated for you. She is so looking forward to showing it to you.'

'Admiral Yoland is dead, they arrested and kept me in

lock up as long as they could. My being here could hurt
you all.'

'Do you think we have not thought about it and
discussed it? Because we have. They did not come for us
after you left. If they think we are a threat, they will come
for us whether you are here or not, so stay.'

'I wish I had never brought this on you. If anything
happened to you, Anja and Catina I would never forgive
myself.'

'How many people have you saved? Would you prefer
to have their deaths on your hands?'

'Of course not!'

'We have made a well-informed decision and we have
taken precautions. The best security system has been
installed and I have the house checked regularly to
ensure there are no hidden devices.'

'You have told Anja everything? I thought you did not
want her to know.'

'I didn't want her to know for petty reasons, because
she was so happy about her wedding dress, but I realised
that was not good enough. I didn't want to lie to her.'

'How did she take it?'

'I am no telepath but I would say that she was horrified.'
When David raised a questioning eyebrow, Viktor
continued, 'She buried the dress, burnt the wedding
photographs and redecorated your room.'

David could not help smiling. 'I can't wait to see it, if it
is all pink with princesses. I know she now hates me for
ruining her wedding.'

'I will take you up there now.' David followed his
father to the room he had occupied the last few times he
stayed at the house. Anja appeared just before his father
opened the door and David knew she had been hovering
close by, anxious to see his reaction. David walked in,
not knowing what to expect; the last time he had had a

room decorated for him he was a young child. The walls
were neutral and showed framed pictures of starships,
from the original *Phoenix* the first deep spaceship, the
first of the FWN ships, the *Athens*, to the *New York*. The
celling was dark blue with constellations painted onto it.

'The zodiac, very appropriate.'

'What do you think David?' Anja asked nervously.

'It is perfect, thank you.'

Chapter 38

DAVID laughed as he went after his toddling half-sister Catina in a nearby park. He should have been surprised at how quickly she was growing but, compared to Hannoki's children, her development was slow. Never having been around children before, David had not questioned too much about how quickly Mesrra and Kelac grew. Watching her made him wonder how much older Milkoy and his family would be when he returned. He had never asked how long they lived for; their life expectancy could be a lot less than humans.

Although he was glad he had this time with his family, he was desperate to get back to his friends. With Anja's help, he was checking the designers who sold Lismarian clothing. It was still coming into the shops but in much smaller quantities which was making the price rise even further and was causing a lot of speculation. David had asked his father to look into certain companies and see if they were having any trouble with production. He was anxious for a response but as there was nothing he could do at the moment, he was trying to enjoy the here and now.

Having caught her, he picked up his sister and spun her around, revelling in her shouts of pleasure.

'I never knew you were so good with children,' someone said behind him.

Taken by surprise David stopped and turned round. 'Elen, I did not know you were back! When did you get here?'

'The orders for the *New York* to return were last minute. I thought about sending a message when we docked but then the FWN would know when and where we would meet.' Elen walked towards him and Catina started wriggling in his arms in protest at his lack of attention. He lowered the child to the ground and she clung to his leg, shy in front of someone she did not know. He gently stroked her head in reassurance.

'Then should you be here?' David asked.

'Why not? Our orders brought us here and our relationship is well known. It would be expected that we meet. I just did not want to be followed.'

'So you are here just to keep up appearances?'

'Of course,' she said, smiling.

'Then would you like to join us for lunch?' David asked as he took hold of Catina's hand.

'Lunch would be nice.'

'Let me introduce you to my sister. Catina, this is a very good friend of mine, her name is Elen.'

✻

Elen went home with him after lunch. Catina was fractious and he suspected that she was tired, a suspicion that proved correct when Anja immediately took her daughter upstairs to her room.

David took Elen into his father's study. 'I am very happy to see you,' he said, 'but aren't you taking a risk in coming here?'

'I discussed it with the captain. We don't believe that my visiting will cause any problems. As I said, our relationship is well known.'

'So are you here to keep up appearances, to pass a message or because you want to be?'

'We have not seen each other in a long time.'

'We always knew that would be the case. I could not

stay on the *New York* and you could not leave,' David said. 'But I never expected to miss you as much as I did.'

'I missed you too,' Elen admitted walking up to him and placing her hand on his chest, knowing that through the contact he could easily pick up what she was thinking and feeling. 'I came because I wanted to see you.'

He covered her hand in his. 'There is also another reason.'

'I have to pass on a message. The captain wants to know what has been happening and what the FWN have on you.'

'How much does he know?'

'He knows you were arrested and that the FWN are still keeping a close eye one you. He thinks he has been called back so he can be questioned about your activities and any involvement he might have.'

'Does he have a plan so that I can talk to him? In the circumstances, I don't think it would be a good idea to meet up.'

'Paul.'

'Of course! How is your brother?'

'He is well. We are still wondering if you were right to let yourself get arrested.'

'It had to happen. I could not have got the parts I needed and returned without being found. This way I was prepared and had nothing on me that could be used against me. I don't know when I can go back out into space, but this way it might be possible. It also gives me the chance to try and find out what is happening here,' David explained. 'Is there a pre-set time for Paul to contact me?'

'No, you just need to call him. But be careful. We don't know if there are any other telepaths who will be trying to listen.'

'I know and that is not much of a problem as the UTA

have recalled all FWN telepaths, those on the *New York* are probably the only ones left on the base,' David said. He focused his mind. '*Paul, Paul.*'

'*I'm here. It is good to hear from you again.*'

'*I know the feeling, I' glad you got back to the* **New York** *and not left stranded on that starbase. Is the captain there?*'

'*He is still on the ship. I am making my way to the bridge as we are talking.*'

'*Do you know why you have been called back to Europa?*'

'*No, though I expect it has something to do with you. Stand by, I will be with the captain in a moment.*'

Paul did not break the mental connection. David was aware when he walked onto the bridge, and followed the captain into his briefing room.

'David, I wish we could talk in person. How are you?' Captain Yoland asked.

David could hear the question as clearly as if he was in the room with them. '*I am fine. I don't know what I need to tell you or how much you know.*' He heard Paul transmit his question.

'I know you were arrested by the FWN for supplying technology, and I know I am here because they want to find out if you or my father told me anything.'

'*I would be happy to tell you everything but the FWN have been using telepaths for illegal mind reads. The UTA telepaths have been called back but they have others who could pick out the information from your mind.*'

'I know. I have already felt them trying to read my mind but they have not had much luck.'

'*How do you know?*'

'I have been practising with Paul and the other telepaths on board how to shield my mind. I am getting good at it and can block Paul, even when he has merged with some of the other telepaths on board.' David felt

Paul confirming what the captain had said.

'*I am very impressed. Most people who can do that are family members of telepaths because they are around them so much.*'

'I only wish I had thought about it before you left. That would have been the real test.'

'*I would have been honoured to train you. Fortunately the need for you to block your mind didn't exist when I was on the* **New York**,' David pointed out. '*You already know a lot about what has happened to me. Since then, I went back to the planet with a device that allowed them to amplify their natural ability. Because of technical problems, I could only make one machine and that left the other half of the planet vulnerable. I came back to get parts for a second machine. Hopefully if these people can defend themselves, they will be left alone.*'

'How much does the FWN know?'

'*I am not sure. They got nothing from me but I don't know what your father said or what files he kept. My arrest was an excuse to find out what I've been doing, I think they know I've been to the planet.*'

'What reason did you give for being in uncharted space?'

'*I said I wanted peace and quiet to work on experiments.*'

'That is pathetic, you could easily do that in charted space!'

'*I know, but it was the only excuse I could think of. As I'm not in custody, I don't think the FWN can prove anything to the satisfaction of the lawyers. I don't think your father revealed everything that I knew, otherwise they would never have let me go.*'

'What have you mentioned about the *New York*'s involvement?'

'*They know that you saved me but the official record states that you were told that I got lost and after that we had no contact.'*

'Thank you. I have been refusing to comment because I did not know what to say. Now I can deny everything, though I doubt they will believe me.'

'There is a big difference between believing and proving.'

'I will try and let you know what is happening but for now, keep safe, David.'

'Keep safe, Mark.'

Chapter 39

MILKOY woke up on the floor by the machine. Karra was slumped on top of him. He lifted her gently off him and checked that she was alright before moving her into as comfortable position as possible, but he did not expect her to stay asleep for much longer. He knew many had died; his mind still rang with all the deaths and he could not determine if there was anyone that he knew.

He reached out to Hirra to make sure his family were still alive. '*We are all alright,*' she reassured him. Relief swamped him. '*They did not come here. How are you?*'

'*My head is killing me, but other than that I am fine. Karra is still asleep. We will come down once she wakes up.*'

'*Just make sure that they are gone before you come back. I will let you know if we need you to return sooner.*'

'*Thank you. I will update you shortly on what we plan to do.*'

Once he had finished talking to his sister, he checked the machine as David had taught him. Everything seemed to be in order. He tried to see if there was anything that he could sense; there was not so he knew that there was no imminent attack. Were the invaders still up there, waiting before coming back down? Not for the first time, he wished David was with him; he would be able to tell him if they were still there.

'Milkoy,' his mate called him as she stirred.

'I am here,' he said, going to her side and helping her sit up.

'Everything is mixed up. I don't know... I can't tell...' She rubbed her temples in frustration.

'I have spoken to Hirra and they are all fine,' he reassured her.

'Oh...' she said, embracing him. 'It is a shame we do not have a home in this place, we spend so much time here. After today, I do not relish the flight back down.'

'We could always build something in the rock,' Milkoy said and Karra laughed at the suggestion.

'I was joking,'

'Why not? Then we would know earlier if an attack is planned and we would not have the frantic flight up and the tired flight back down.'

'You think it is possible?'

'I hope so, but unless we try we won't know.'

After confirming with Hirra that she would be fine for a while, Milkoy and Karra started to think about how best they could create rooms to stay in. 'There is nowhere to build,' Karra said. 'The solid rock means that whatever we build will be blown away very quickly.'

'We could build down into the rock, open up the side of the mountain to let in the light.'

They started to blast down at the rock near the side of the mountain, first creating a crude cave. Then they reduced the force behind their expanded energy so they could smooth out the walls and opened it out at the side. When the edge of the plateau did not give way, they made the opening bigger.

'It will do for now,' Milkoy said. 'We can bring up a few things to make it more comfortable. We would not have to worry about our family if they all moved up here. David described the home where he lived and they had something called stairs. We could try and build them and have another space below here.'

'It is a nice idea and it would certainly be useful, but we

can't live up here permanently. There is no land to farm or water to drink. It would just be a place to stay after attacks to rest and make sure they don't come back.'

'Water would not be a problem. It rains here and the water that runs off the mountain feeds the streams below so we could collect it easily. As for food, we need so little we could ask the others to supply it. If we are up here we will know sooner when an attack is coming and we can warn the others so it would save lives.'

'It is worth trying. We need to talk to the others and see what their thoughts are and if they are willing to support us. It will be interesting to see what their experience was and if the extra time would benefit them.'

'The suns will go down soon. We should get back to Hirra and see what she thinks as well.' They knew that they were tired but the flight down was harder than they expected because they had used the energy from the suns to build the room.

'*If they attack again now, I don't think I could get back up the mountain,*' Karra said telepathically as they flew.

'*It would make no difference. I have no energy left to send to the others before the suns come back up.*'

'*We were fools for creating that room now, we should have waited.*'

'*Until when? We never know when another attack will come. There will never be a good time.*'

When they landed at their farm, Hirra and the children ran out to them. It was a while before they were able to rest. Hirra wanted to know what had happened and the children were scared and needed to be reassured.

Finally they lay down together and slept, conserving what power they had left, until the suns rose again. Once the suns had risen and everyone had had a chance to rest, Milkoy contacted not only those who had been involved in yesterday's attack but everyone who might have to help in the future.

'*It worked well while we could see the shuttles but as soon as they landed and were out of our sight, there was nothing else we could do,*' Villimarr said.

Ovala agreed, adding, '*I think they killed Gilima and her mate. I have not been able to contact them and when I search for their minds there is nothing there.*'

'*I could not get hold of them for this meeting,*' **Milkoy confirmed.**

'*I am nearest to where they are. I will go and see what happened.*'

'*Thank you, Ovala.*'

'*If they have discovered that there is only one couple defending the people in the area, they could easily attack us before going on to kill everyone else. We could take out a few of the shuttles but it would only take one to kill us,*' Villimarr said.

'*We need to find a way a way to protect you during an attack,*' Milkoy said.

'*Also how to improve how far we can see so we can continue to protect the people once the shuttles land,*' Villimarr added.

'*Gaining height would help and maybe somewhere to shelter from a counter attack?*' Milkoy suggested.

'*The height aspect we can work on now. We can build mounds*'

'*We can build higher as well. David explained to me how his people build.*'

'*The local people where I am are more than willing to help us. We could build quickly.*'

'*The same here. We just need to know how to do it,*' Ovala said, and the minds of the others who had not been involved expressed their agreement.

'*This is what David showed me,*' Milkoy said, and showed them the things that David had shared with him.

Chapter 40

IT was not until the next day that David heard from Mark again. As they'd expected, the FWN wanted to know everything about their relationship and David's recent activities. Mark denied any knowledge, saying that he had not been in contact with his friend for months. As the last recorded communication was when Mark had sent a message about his father's death, the FWN could not prove otherwise. Mark did not need to be a telepath to tell they were angry and frustrated with his responses and, judging by their behaviour, he assumed that he was successfully blocking them mentally as well.

'*How long are they going to keep you here for*?' David asked Mark through Paul.

'I don't know, they want to talk to several of my crew, including Elen, her brother, Jon and my engineering team.'

'*Paul is a strong, well-trained telepath. He can block a mental intrusion from the untrained telepaths they are using.*'

'Elen knows how to block a telepathic read the same as you do, sir.' Paul broke into the conversation.

'*Really? She has never tried with me.*'

'I doubt anyone could block you, but she trusts you. Why are you surprised? She grew up with me.'

'Can we please get back to the point,' the captain said. 'So they will have the same problems with Elen as they did with me. What about the others?'

'*I never discussed with Jon or any of the engineers*

*what had happened. Unless you spoke to them, they have
nothing to tell.'*

'No, I always felt the fewer people who knew the better,'
Mark said.

*'Do you know who ordered you back? It must have
raised some questions within the FWN.'*

'My orders came from Admiral Mathers. What he
told others, I don't know and I don't know who else is
involved,' Mark said. 'David, it is no small thing to call us
in to answer questions. They are desperate to get you for
something.'

*'Do you think I could get close to the admiral to see what
he knows?'*

'If he was here. Paul has already tried to find him
mentally and could not. I requested a meeting to discuss
the orders and was told he was on Pallas. I don't think
you will find anything here.'

'Do you think I should leave?'

'I think that you should if you can.'

'How would my leaving affect you?'

'We have not spoken, they can't tie us together for
months.'

*'They can through Elen. They could accuse her of
passing messages when she returns to the ship.'*

'Damn it, I thought that there would be questions if
I stopped her going to you. I did not think far enough
ahead.'

'Can she come with me?'

⁜

After David had finished talking to Mark, David sought
her out and found her with his stepmother and sister.
'Elen, can I have a word?'

'Of course.' After excusing herself to Anja, she followed
him out of the room. Once they were alone she asked,

'what is wrong?'

'The FWN have interviewed Mark and now they want to talk to a lot of his crew, including you.'

'I would not tell them anything, you must know that.'

'I know. What concerns Mark and me is that we have been careful not to communicate in any way that could be recorded.'

'I know. You have been going through Paul.'

'You are with me here and will be returning to the *New York* once it is due to leave Europa.'

'They will think that I will pass the information verbally once I return to the ship.'

'Yes and admittedly they would be right. But we don't know what problems it would cause for you and our friends on the *New York*.'

'They might find a reason to stop me going back to the ship.'

'Can they do that?'

'Yes, they could change my orders while I'm on the planet.'

'How important is the FWN to you?'

'It has been my life since I was eighteen, you know that. Why?'

'Mark and I don't think the FWN will give me permission to leave. They are looking for a reason to arrest me again. Mark thinks I should use my connections and leave. I was wondering if you wanted to come with me.'

'You could just go? I mean this is a nice house but I doubt your father has the money or connections to do as you suggest.'

'My father bought this house when he married my mother and he was first starting out. He has not sold it because he considers it to be my home. He and Anja only live here when I am back now, most of the time he uses the mansion on Eros.'

'Your father has a property on Eros? Why have you never taken me there?'

'To be honest, I have never been there. It does not have a FWN port. When this is over, we will both stay there,' he promised. 'But for now, you need to decide if you are going to stay with the FWN or come with me.'

'When will you leave?'

'As soon as my father can help me arrange it,' David said. 'I don't expect an answer now. I know this is a lot for you to think about.'

Elen hesitated. 'I will think about it,' she said.

✳

'You were right,' Viktor said later. 'The companies we suspected of using items from the planet are all suffering from supply problems.'

'The product is still being supplied, though,' David pointed out.

'Yes, but supply has dropped by a third and the price for what is available has soared,' his father said. 'Whatever you did is working.'

'No, it isn't. If it had worked, there would be no supply. This just means it is just getting harder for them.'

'If it gets much harder, the price will rise too high.'

'No. They will get more aggressive about how they get what they want. If they work out how the planet is defending itself so successfully, they will retaliate. No, this is a temporary inconvenience to the companies. I need to go back and help Milkoy. I can't do anything from here.'

'I doubt the FWN will let you leave.'

'I have looked into it and have it on authority that they won't. That means no shuttle, no permission to buy a new one and no permission to leave, so I can't book a ticket to somewhere else.'

'I can try to get you off planet on a supply ship.'

'A supply ship is not going to get me to the planet and I won't be able to get the parts I need to build a second machine or another space suit.'

'I might be able to arrange something, let me ask around.'

'I have asked Elen to come with me.'

'I will make enquires for two people just in case.'

Chapter 41

'I want to come with you,' Elen told David later that day. When he said nothing she continued. 'I expected something more than silence. Don't you want me to come with you anymore?'

'I do, but I didn't think you would decide so quickly.'

'It was not a hard decision. I have missed you and many a time wished I was with you.'

'You never said.'

'You never asked,' Elen laughed. 'And to be honest, when you first left I don't know if I would have gone, I did not realise how much I would miss you. You have to love the irony that even with telepathy, we were both still clueless.'

'With you giving me permission to read your mind, I consciously tried as hard as I could not to. I did not, and never would, want to take advantage.'

'I know you would never abuse the right, but I thought you knew more than you did.'

'I think we need to stick to verbal communication so there can be no doubt where we stand with each other.'

'That would be a good idea. When do you plan to leave?'

'I have just spoken with my father. I don't know how long it will take to arrange. As far as I know he has never had to sneak someone off a planet before. I can't find out who is behind the attacks - I have tried but there are too many minds, so it is like looking for a needle in a haystack.'

'Your contacts in the FWN can't help?'

'My main contacts were Admiral Yoland and his son and crew. Mark put me in touch with Lieutenant Jervis, who worked with his father. He told me everything he knows. I suspect Admiral Mathers, but he is off planet and I have no way to get close to him. The other senior FWN personnel here are so locked down that Lieutenant Jervis has not been able to find out anything else.'

'Is there anything we can do to stop the attacks permanently? Or are we hoping that their losses will become so high that they will give up.'

'I doubt that they will. They are making too much money and they have a lot of resources; that is why I need to go back to help Milkoy and his people improve. Mark is making enquires in the FWN and my father in the business world, I have to hope that between them, they can find the answers.'

'So tell me about the planet and its people. What can I expect?'

'Just promise me you won't change your mind once I do.'

'I do deep space missions with limited amenities; you are not going to scare me off.'

﹡

'I believe that I can arrange your departure from Europa and your onward journey. Give me a list of what you are going to need. Is Elen travelling with you?' Viktor asked.

'She will be coming.'

'Good. Hopefully she can keep you out of trouble.'

'Do you know when everything will be in place?' David asked, choosing to ignore his father's last comment.

'Nothing definite, but I should have a better idea in a few days.'

'Is helping me to leave going to cause you trouble?'

'If everything goes to plan, the FWN won't know how

you left and won't tie your departure to me.'

'They will be suspicious when they discover me missing.'

'You report us as missing to the authorities,' Elen said, as she walked into the room and closed the door behind her. Both men turned and looked at her. 'Sorry, the door was ajar and I heard what you were taking about.'

'If I report you, they will look for you sooner.'

'You can't help us or find out more about the companies using Lismarian body parts if you are under arrest,' she pointed out. 'David is not under house arrest and is free the leave during the day if he wants. We have been going out most days. I suggest on the day we plan to leave we go out as we normally do and don't come back. You raise the alarm late at night. Europa is a major space port; they might be able to work out what ship we left on, but it will take time. Anyone searching the property will find that all our things are here, which should reduce the suspicion on you.'

'Then we will get you off the planet on one ship and change you to another as soon as possible. If you keep hopping ship, it will make you harder to track,' Viktor said.

'What about our things?' David asked.

'They will be safe here. I doubt the FWN will want to take them.'

'No, I mean we will have no clothes or wash items.'

'Seriously, David? Just add them to the long list of things you need me to get,' Viktor said.

⁜

David and Elen made a point of going out every day, either picking an activity to do or just for lunch and always taking a day pack each. They did not do the same thing twice so when they finally left their change in routine would not be seen as anything unusual.

The summons for Elen to be interviewed was delivered to David's home address. 'Are you worried?' David asked her.

'No. I have been keeping Paul out of my head for years so, unless they get several telepaths to gang up on me, they won't get anything.'

'I doubt they will do that.'

'What makes you say that?'

'They did not try it on Mark and as the captain it was likely that he knew the most. Besides, there are significant differences between a telepathic brain and a normal one. Two level five telepaths working together would not make a level ten, so you need several people to get that level and the more minds that merge, the more unstable they become.'

'So what are you saying? That the FWN does not have enough telepaths to read my mind?'

'No, they definitely have enough but the UTA have recalled all the FWN telepaths on the base to be investigated and I doubt they have transferred many back. They are reliant on the ones who have avoided the UTA and have not been trained – and they will be scared of being found out. If the FWN try to read you, it will be with someone who has learnt as they went. Most would not be strong because they would have gone mad otherwise. And a mind merge is not an easy thing to do if you are not trained.'

'The UTA can do that? Demand their return?'

'Yes. The UTA have absolute authority over telepaths. I suspect that those who have previously been undetected now fear being discovered so they may not be helpful.'

'You think telepaths are more scared of the UTA than the FWN? After everything the FWN are has done?'

'Ninety per cent of telepaths that have been chemically

stripped after the UTA trained them commit suicide within six months.'

'The UTA don't do anything about it?'

'No. Once you've been mentally stripped, you are no longer considered to be the responsibility of the UTA. It is basically a death sentence - and a very unpleasant one. Until the FWN are prepared to torture someone for months and if they survive will live with a permanent disability, then no, the UTA and their rules will take precedence.'

'I never knew they were capable of such cruelty. Paul never said.'

'When our abilities emerge, we are taken to a UTA facility and kept in shielded accommodation. We are given a choice of training with them and following their rules; the punishment and repercussions are fully explained. Alternatively we can be chemically stripped and at that age the side effects are minimal because the body can easily adapt. It might sound bad but imagine the chaos if trained telepaths did what they wanted because they did not fear the punishment.'

'It means big companies and organisations cannot easily corrupt a telepath.'

'Exactly. I gave the names of those that tried to read my mind to the UTA, but they recalled everyone on Europa because of the fear that others had acted illegally and are looking for knowledge of unregistered telepaths. Depending on the results, they could order all FWN telepaths back to be checked.'

'Which is why they have not been able to get any information - they now can't find anyone from the UTA willing to do an illegal mind read.'

'That would be my guess.'

'Well, I will find out tomorrow if someone tries to read my mind.'

❖

'How was it?' David asked her when she returned home and joined him and his father for a drink before dinner.

'It was fine. The FWN were very frustrated with the lack of information they were getting.'

'Hopefully they will soon give up and let the *New York* return to space, Mark is really angry about being made to stay here during the investigation.'

'Have you spoken to him recently?' Elen asked. 'Has he found out anything?'

'I spoke with him this morning. He believes he is making some headway but he has nothing substantial to report. Everything seems to be taking so long.' David sounded frustrated.

'It probably feels worse for you as you can't do anything at the moment.'

'I just need to get out of here.'

'You will tomorrow,' Viktor said. 'I am not taking your desperation to leave personally, you understand.'

'Sorry, Father. Being with you, Anja and Catina is the only positive thing about being here.'

'I am not one of the positive things?' Elen asked jokingly.

'You are coming with me so you don't count,' David retorted. 'What did you mean about tomorrow?'

'I have you both on a cargo ship heading for Ares, where you will change onto a second ship. There will be several more changes until you arrive at a location where a shuttle will be waiting for you with the items on your list. It is not a great shuttle in comparison to your last one, but it will get you to wherever you need to go and back to the nearest space station. I got you new IDs and everything else will be paid for in credit chips, so hopefully the FWN won't be able to track you easily.'

'They could send out alerts with our pictures,' Elen said. 'We could be recognised at any starbase while we waited for the next ship.'

'I thought about that, which is why I bought these.' He showed them what he had. 'They should help disguise you for the limited time you are off ship. The only time I can't help is when you are in the shuttle. I can't stop the FWN looking for you and they must know where you are heading.'

'It will be a risk but the area of space is large. My telepathic range is greater than their scanners. I hope it is enough to keep us ahead of them.'

Chapter 42

DAVID and Elen joined others at the long security queue to enter the space port. They had left home as normal in the morning, found somewhere they could alter their appearance by changing their hair colour and style, then made their way to the dock.

'It has never taken this long before,' David whispered to Elen.

'The security for scouts and FWN personnel is different from the crew of most other ships. All cargo and liner crews have to enter from here which is why it takes so long.'

'I can't believe it is so inefficient.'

'Your previous status gave you privileges. You are now being a snob, so shut up and put up with it before someone hears you complaining and reports it as unusual.'

'Alright,' he responded and did not say anything further as they slowly inched their way to the security station. By the time they reached it, David was starting to worry about the level of scrutiny their fake IDs would receive. When it was their turn, they were barely glanced at as he was asked about his post. Satisfied with the response, he and Elen were waved through.

They made their way to their assigned ship. The fake IDs showed them to be a married couple and, as far as anyone was aware, they were employed by a company called Space Temp to bridge the staff shortage which was going to be rectified on arrival at Ares. Viktor said gleefully that with them both being qualified and experienced spacefarers, they had the perfect skills that would allow them to provide cover on board the various ships. If the FWN came looking, they would find nothing out of the ordinary. The director of Space Temp was a good friend of Viktor's and had a strong dislike for the FWN, so he had happily forged their employment records. As temporary employees they needed to bring very little with them, just the clothes they were wearing and a change, as well as personal toiletries. Everything else was supplied by the ship they were working on.

The sleeping area they were assigned to was a long room of single bunks stacked three high, with a small metal cabinet for their personal items. They were glad they had nothing but the basics with them and nothing of value. There were no married quarters on this ship, nowhere where they could be alone; they were not even able to get beds near to each other, making it almost impossible to communicate verbally.

'*Not like the* New York,' David said into Elen's mind as he put his few items away.

'*That is because you never saw where the non-officer ranks slept,*' she retorted, framing the response in her mind so he could pick it up easily.

Over the next week, David was thankful that Elen was experienced at forming mental questions that he could pick up easily. FWN training meant that Elen could fill several roles, while David kept to engineering. They did any task they were required to do quietly and efficiently and, if they were off duty together, they kept to themselves; they had no interest in trying to make friends and risking questions they did not want to answer.

When they left the ship at Ares they picked up a few items that they needed, paying from an account set up in their false names, before going to meet the next ship. In this way, they slowly travelled towards uncharted space until they finally arrived at Starbase Isis, where they were expected to pick up the shuttle that would take them the rest of the way.

'How much do you know about this person we are going to meet?' Elen asked.

'Nothing. I was only told his first name and where we are supposed to meet up with him,' David replied.

'I just hope that, having come this far, that we can trust him.'

'My father vouched for him, but I'll soon know if we can't.'

They made their way to the bar Viktor had told them to go to. It was reasonably busy, but they got a table to themselves. They were giving their orders for a second round when a male approached the table and sat down with them. 'Can you bring me a beer?' he asked the waiter.

The waiter looked at David. When he nodded his consent he said, 'Be right back,' and left.

'I honestly did not expect you to be here. I was sure at least one of those ships you were on would run late.'

'We have been fortunate,' David replied.

The conversation stopped when the waiter returned with the order. David handed over the credit chip to pay for the drinks and, once the waiter had left, the conversation started again.

'The shuttle is at Dock 15 and everything you want is on board. It is fully fuelled and ready to go. It's expected to leave the dock tomorrow at 0600 hours and you are both shown as the crew, so there should be no problems. There is enough fuel in the tanks to get you to your destination without stopping at a perimeter base, but not enough to get you back again, I have loaded extra fuel containers on board. Your father said that you would be landing, so there might be a chance you can top them up to get you home again. Here are all your documents. The only thing I could not get was a permit to travel into uncharted space - all permits have been temporarily stopped by the FWN. I wish you good luck.' He downed his beer, stood up and left them.

'What do you think?' Elen asked.

'I think we finish our drinks, buy any personal items we need and go to Dock 15 where we can go through what is on board and try and get anything that is missing. If the FWN are looking for us here, they will find us at the shuttle whether we go now or tomorrow to launch.'

'Do you think they are looking for us here?'

'I think they are looking for us everywhere, but more so at one of the starbases by uncharted space. Here we have more chance of keeping below the radar and slipping past them.'

'They will still know when we have gone over.'

'They will know that a shuttle has gone through. We won't be the only ones breaking the law, it is just the first time the FWN will care about it. I can sense a ship before most ships' scanners can pick us up. Once we are over that border, they are going to have a hard time finding us.'

'They know where we are going.'

'I know. I am counting on the fact that whoever is behind this in the FWN does not want to announce that and show their involvement with what is going on.'

They finished their drinks then left. As they approached the shuttle, David could see what his father had meant by it not being up the standard of his previous scout shuttles; it was going to be a cramped trip. Releasing the door hatch and walking on board, he saw that it was worse than he'd anticipated. Most of the room was taken up by the machinery and other supplies he had asked for.

'Well, this is cosy,' Elen said.

'Yep, and I don't think we can unload all of this to check we have everything and restack it before we need to leave.'

'There is certainly a lot. We are going to have to trust your father's contacts and hope everything you wanted is here.'

'I hope so, but I swear that there is more here than I asked for. What I wanted should not take up this much room.'

'We have to trust everything is here if we want to make it off the base in the morning. We will have to wait until we land to see if there are any added bonuses.' Elen walked to the bunk and released it; two singles, one on top of the other, came down.

'Looks like we can't even enjoy tonight,' David said, looking at the narrow bunks.

'Oh, trust me, we can.'

⁜

It had been weeks since he had been told that David had disappeared. He remembered his anger when they had been forced to release him before getting the answers he wanted, but he had been reassured that there was no way he would be able to leave the planet, as a result the *New York* had been recalled. He had kept his distance from Europa as he did not want to risk being anywhere near that meddling telepath. Then he had been told that Viktor Wilhelm had reported his son missing, together with that female crew member from the *New York* and a whole world of problems opened up again.

Officers had immediately gone around and questioned the family. They were unable to get anything from Mr Wilhelm as that UTA lawyer was there. Viktor had allowed the officers to search the property but all of David's and Elen's property was still there, including their true IDs.

Enquires with the ports revealed numerous ships had left that day; several had taken on new crew, both male and female. The ships heading in the direction of the planet were checked first, but discreet enquires came up with no answers.

Elen's picture was circulated as an AWOL FWN officer and David's as a possible illegal arms supplier, but still he had got no further. He sent ships to patrol the border of uncharted space where David was most likely to cross and the starbases where he would need to refuel, but nothing was reported back.

The decision now had to be made, should he take the risk and send the FWN ships out to the area of space he knew they would be in? The rogue ships he was using had been given modified cloaking technology designed to evade the FWN, and they could be warned over the increase of patrols, there would be very little risk of them being discovered. Having made his decision he gave the order, the captains were only told that the apprehension of David and Elen was of the utmost importance, dead or alive.

Chapter 43

WHEN Elen woke him for his shift and he checked their position, he knew that they would soon reach the planet. For weeks they had crept closer and finally they were there.

He opened his mind up as he always did to make sure there were no FWN or rogue ships nearby and then started to call to Milkoy. David knew he was probably still too far away but he was keen to hear his friend's voice again, to know he was alright.

'*Milkoy*,' David called again as he brought the shuttle into land a few hours later.

'*David! It is good to hear your voice.*'

'*Yours too. Is it alright if I land at the same place as before?*'

'*I am on the mountain. I have been living up here with Karra for a while now.*'

'*Is there still room for me to land?*'

'*We have kept that area clear.*'

'*I will see you very soon.*'

'*Before you come down, do you sense anything up there?*'

'*No, I am not picking anything up either mentally or with the ship's scanners.*'

'*Good, I will see you soon.*'

⁜

'Elen, Elen, wake up,' David called. When he did not get a response, he gently shook her awake.

'What is it?' she asked, looking at the time. 'Have the FWN found us?'

'No, we have arrived and are about to land.'

Elen climbed out of the bunk and into a jumpsuit before taking the seat next to David. 'Are you going to land at your friend's farm?'

'No, he has not been living there, he has been up on the mountain. He assures me there is still room to land.'

'You have spoken to him already, from here?'

'I have spoken to telepaths from further than this.'

'I know, but they were strong or merged with others.'

'Milkoy is a stronger telepath than me in many ways, but he won't pick anything up from us unless it is focused towards him or the planet,' he explained, as he brought the shuttle down through the atmosphere.

'You never mentioned that before. Do they have the same problems with strong telepaths as we do?'

'No. When I tried to explain mental illness to Milkoy, he got very confused. I don't think it is something they have encountered. Their race is telepathic; some of them are stronger than others and they communicate just as much on a mental level as a verbal one.'

'How am I going to understand what they are saying?' Elen asked, worried.

'Milkoy is fluent in our language and the rest of his family are learning quickly. They will be our main contacts. I have been learning their language. I am not that good at it, but I left all the files about the planet with Milkoy so they could not fall into the wrong hands. Otherwise I would have given them to you to look at during this trip.'

The shuttle started to judder then stopped as it landed and David cut the engines. Elen reached for the hatch but David stopped her. 'Check the outside temperature first. If both the suns are up, we will need to find the environmental suits before we go outside.'

David had just finished talking when they heard banging on the hatch. 'Milkoy,' he said, smiling. 'Release the hatch - though looking at the outside temperature, be prepared to get hot quickly.'

The rush of hot air made Elen gasp in surprise. Having spent most of her adult life on a ship, a starbase or a planet like Europa where the climate was temperate, this extreme heat was a new experience. 'Do you get used to this heat?'

'No. It is always hot. The best you can hope for is not to be surprised by it. Let me introduce you to my friend Milkoy,' David said as Milkoy walked on board. 'Welcome, Milkoy. Can I introduce you to my mate Elen?'

'Hello, Elen. It is good to meet you.'

'It is good to meet you too, Milkoy. David has told me a lot about you.'

'This is smaller than the last two shuttles and you have brought a lot with you. Enough for another machine?'

'We had trouble leaving,' David said, 'and my father had to arrange the shuttle and parts. Hopefully everything I asked for is here. We did not have enough time or room to check.'

'The suns go down soon. I will come back with Karra and we can help you unload then we can talk about what has happened since you left.'

'Sounds like a plan, Milkoy.'

Milkoy left the shuttle and David closed the hatch, breathing a sigh of relief as the temperature started to drop.

'Why could we not talk now while we waited?' Elen asked.

'Milkoy does not like being in the shuttle. He can tolerate it if the hatch is open but he knows we would be too hot, so we wait until the suns go down and it is cool enough for us. It will still be hot and this high up the UV radiation is very damaging, so we need to find the environmental suits if we stay up here.'

⁂

When Milkoy banged on the hatch a short while later with his mate, David and Elen barely had any room to move. 'I am so glad we decided not to try this before we got here,' she said as she climbed over the cartons to get out. With Milkoy and Karra's help they were able to unload the shuttle and have a proper look at what had been packed.

David checked everything as it was carried off, separating the survival equipment from the mechanical parts. Once satisfied that the suits were there, together with sun creams and clothing for when the suns were not so intense, he turned his attention to the mechanical parts. 'Everything we need for a second machine is here,'

'How long will it take you to build it?'

'Not long if I follow the previous design. But before I start, I need to check the other machine to see if it is still operating correctly or if there is anything I can improve on.'

'It is where you left it.'

David started to walk off but Elen called him back. 'I appreciate you want to start work as soon as possible but can you help me get this up first?'

He looked at the large, bulky package lying on the floor. 'What is it?'

'A climate tent.' At his confused look, she continued, 'I take it this was not on your list.'

'No, I have never heard of one.'

'Well luckily someone thought it would be useful. We can attach it to the side of the shuttle and it will keep the suns' UV rays off and some of the heat out, and the shuttle's cooling system in. It will give us more room but we should get it up before the suns rise.'

Following Elen's instructions, they erected it fairly quickly. Milkoy and Karra helped to bring in their supplies so they could get to them without putting on an environmental suit. Meanwhile David checked on his machine before the suns rose.

The climate tent made it more comfortable on the mountain top. David muttered several times over the next few days that he wished he had known about them the last time he came to the planet. Elen tactfully refrained from mentioning that it would have taken very little research to learn about them.

As the days passed, Milkoy told them everything that had happened. There had been several more attacks; people were still dying but not in such large numbers, and each time they had destroyed some of the shuttles. But more kept coming.

They had discovered that if the person who was using the energy was higher up, they had a better field of vision and could sometimes hit shuttles after they had landed. Everyone had helped to build bigger, taller stone buildings; a lot of experimenting was taking place and they discussed what worked well and what failed. Stone was being blasted out of the mountains and transported to where it was needed. A lot of people were giving up their homes and collecting near to the couples who could protect them.

Word spread quickly and more strong couples took on the role of protectors, but the further they were from the mountain, the less energy could be passed to them. That made them vulnerable and that was where the last attacks had been. A second machine would hopefully resolve the problem. One thing was clear: every time they attacked now, the shuttles suffered losses.

David worried about what would happen if the enemy worked out where the main threat was and blew the mountain range to pieces from space.

Milkoy showed David and Elen around his new home. David was amazed at the individual caves that had been blasted out of the rock. 'We thought we would see if we could use our abilities for a more practical purpose,' Milkoy explained. 'Each room opens onto the mountain and is partially exposed to the suns. The only part that is enclosed is the stairs between floors, which we can use when the winds are too strong to fly.'

'I can't believe you have achieved so much so quickly.'

'There is still much to do, but it has become home.'

'Why did you decide to move up here?'

'It is easier to detect the threat from up here and we don't need to worry if we will make it up the mountain in time.'

'But you can't farm up here. How do you manage for food and water?'

'The water is easy. It rains up here and there are several natural pools we can collect from. We are brought food from the farms below, though up here we need to eat very little.'

Chapter 44

MILKOY stopped working as the hostile feelings and images of skinned bodies came into his head. He was getting to know the feelings very well and knew what they meant. He turned around and saw that his mate was also aware of them.

'Milkoy, they are coming again.'

'I know, I can feel them. I hoped that with David back we would have had a break. I will call the others to let them know that they need to be ready.' He started to make his way to the machine, Karra following him. As he emerged onto the plateau he saw David standing outside with his eyes closed, concentrating. Elen was nowhere to be seen; he assumed she was in the tent or shuttle keeping out of the suns.

'Can you tell where they are going to land?' Milkoy asked.

'Not yet. Elen is trying pick up anything on the shuttle's scanners. I will let you know when I have something you can use,' David said. 'The suns are down. If they come now will you be alright?'

'We have absorbed as much as we can. We can definitely get off a few good shots, but nothing more.'

❈

'Boss, I think I've found the shuttle.'

'How sure are you?'

'I'm getting metallic readings that were not there the last time we were here. I don't know what else it could be, boss.'

'How close to where the energy spikes are they coming from?'

'Exactly where the energy spikes have been coming from.'

'Can we take him out from here so we don't risk any of our shuttles?'

'We can hit the area with the weapons we have on board, but we won't just take out the shuttle we'll destroy most of the mountain range as well. The dust cloud from such an explosion could be devastating to the people.'

'Thus undermining why we are here. Very well, send the shuttles to these co-ordinates for now.' The captain gave several references. 'They are areas we have not been to for a while so they may not be as well defended. In the meantime, I want tactical options about how to take out that shuttle and whatever is causing those energy spikes.'

⁂

Gerric received the warning from Milkoy when he knew the enemy was coming. As soon as the conversation finished, he and his mate ran to the top of the building and waited to see where the shuttles would come down. It was not long until they came into view.

'*Gerric are you ready to receive?*' Milkoy asked.

'*Yes, they are heading to us now.*'

'*Sending it over now.*'

It was not long before they saw the energy like an arc of light coming towards them. They absorbed some to boost their strength and the rest they deflected towards the shuttles that were coming into land. The first two were direct hits and they felt a certain amount of satisfaction as they watched them break apart in the air. The third shot only clipped the shuttle but it was enough to make it turn and head back into space, leaving behind a stream of black smoke. The other two shuttles were able to land, Gerric tried to hit the nearest one but missed. He could not try again because the shuttles were now too close to the cabins.

The invaders immediately disembarked and started to kill people, causing Gerric and his mate to collapse in pain. Desperate to try and stop it, and thinking that even if he accidentally hit his own people it would be a quicker and less painful death than to be skinned alive, Gerric tried to pull himself up but he could not get the focus he needed.

'*I am sorry, Milkoy,*' **Gerric said.**

'*It is not your fault, it is so much harder with the suns down.*'

'*I think they are stopping.*'

'*You are right. The others are reporting the same at the other locations. They don't usually leave so quickly.*'

'*What do you think it means?*'

'*I don't know. I will see if David can find out anything. For now, conserve your strength in case they return.*'

⁂

The shuttle broke orbit, though the engines were straining and everything was rattling with the vibrations. Warning lights showing system failures were lighting up the pilot's dashboard as they headed back to the main ship.

'We have to dock as soon as possible. The life support is out. All we have is what is in the shuttle and the engines are failing fast,' the pilot informed the team leader 'I'm struggling to hold us steady.'

'Understood, *Falcon*. *Falcon* receiving from Shuttle 2,' the leader hailed the ship.

'Why are you coming back so soon, Shuttle 2.'

'We've taken heavy damage. We need permission to dock immediately.' There was a pause. '*Falcon* are you receiving us?'

'We've scanned your shuttle, the damage is too extensive. You can't dock. Move away from the ship.'

'Our life support has failed, we must dock now,' they responded as they moved closer. A transmitter on the shuttle allowed them to pass through the ship's shields.

'Move back now. The shuttle docking doors will not be opened for you,' they were ordered but they just moved closer. 'Move away from the ship,' the order was repeated.

'Let us dock,' the group leader demanded. They were so close to the ship now, moving parallel to it.

It was the last transmission before the shuttle's systems failed and it exploded, ripping a hole in the side of the ship. Alarms came on automatically on the ship, screaming out warnings and filling everywhere with a red flashing light. An automated voice came over the tannoy, warning people to stay away from Docking Bay 1 and that the emergency system had been employed.

'Captain, the explosion has caused a tear in the hull. We'll have to return to a starbase for repairs immediately. The emergency system has closed the Docking Bay down but it will continue to be a huge strain on the ship's systems.'

'Can we get a crew in there to fix the damage?'

'No, boss, the sensors are reporting a hull breach, we will need a dry dock for the repairs.'

'God damn it,' the captain swore. 'Will the other shuttles be able to dock?'

'It depends on how many will be returning. We can only fit ten in the other docking bay.'

'Call them back. Tell them what the situation is. If they need to leave a shuttle or two on the planet, then so be it. As soon as they are all back on board, take us out of here.'

⁜

'Captain, we are reading a merchant ship, the *Falcon*, travelling towards the boundary. Sensors show that it has damage due to an explosion by the shuttle docking bay.'

'Are the ship's files correct?' Captain Lyon asked.

'Everything is showing correct, sir.'

'Ensign Rush, can you sense anything from the ship?' the captain asked the telepath on the bridge. They had been patrolling this area of space for a while now, looking for shuttles entering or leaving uncharted space in the hope of catching the AWOL officer and her arms' supplier partner. This sort of damage was unusual; was this merchant working for them?

'The thoughts are jumbled. There's panic about the damage and if they will make it back for repairs in time. There's also anger and fear. They have detected us and don't want to be stopped by us.'

'Change our route to intercept them. Put the crew on amber alert and open communication,' the captain ordered. Then, when he was in contact with the merchant ship, he continued, 'This is the FWN *Madrid*. Can we be of assistance to you?'

'FWN *Madrid*, many thanks for the offer but we are alright and heading in for repairs.'

'Our scans indicate that the damage was due to an external explosion. You have to report the circumstances to the FWN.'

'Thank you for the warning. We will do so as soon as soon as we reach a starbase.'

'You will report it now,' the captain ordered. 'Be prepared to receive our shuttle on board for inspection of your databases and damage.'

'FWN *Madrid*, there is no need. We will report as soon as we dock. We cannot afford to be delayed due to the damage.'

'We won't delay you. You can continue on your way while we board and report on the damage. I will send the crew from engineering - they may be able to assist you in essential repairs. The shuttle will be with you shortly.'

'Sir, they are accelerating away from us,' Ensign Rush said. 'They really don't want us to board the ship. There is something on board they don't want us to know about.'

'Do you know what it is? Weapons?'

'I don't think it is weapons. I can't sense what it is at this distance. I'm sorry, sir.'

'Increase our speed to match. *Falcon*, cut your engines and prepared to be boarded.' The captain turned to his crew. 'Get security to prepare to board that ship. '

'Sir, they are continuing to accelerate.'

The captain sent out another message. 'To FWN from the *Madrid*, we have a ship with damage from an explosion. They are refusing to comply with instructions to be boarded and report the damage. We are now following and preparing for a forced boarding.'

'Received, *Madrid*. The *Dublin* is in your vicinity and is changing direction to assist,' the FWN ensign replied.

'Sir, the shuttles are ready,' Rush shouted.

'Keep them on standby. With the *Falcon's* acceleration, the shuttles won't be able to keep up.'

'Yes sir,' Ensign Rush said. 'They are planning to fire on us.' The warning came as the ships sensors indicated the arming of the *Falcon*.

'Shields up and sound red alert,' the captain ordered. '*Madrid* to the *Dublin*, the ship is now responding with force. How far out are you?'

'We should be with you within fifteen minutes.'

'Direct hit sir, but our shields are holding,' Ensign Rush said.

'Return fire. Aim for the weapon systems and engines. I want to bring in this ship intact. I want to know what they are hiding.'

'Yes, sir. Returning fire now.' Ensign Rush said.

'Release counter measures and maintain firing,' the captain ordered as the ship shook again with a direct hit. 'Damage report?'

'Sir, we have lost thirty per cent of our shields. Their weapons are more powerful than ours. We won't be able to sustain this level of attack for long.'

'That is no damned merchant ship, they must be involved in arms trade. We just need to keep going and prevent it from escaping before the *Dublin* gets here.'

Time seemed to slow as they took further hits. They retaliated but the other ship's shields were degenerating more slowly and they were able to fire faster and harder.

'Sir, their shields are down to twenty-five per cent but ours could go with another direct hit.' As the ensign spoke, the ship vibrated with the force of the blow and the power flickered. 'The shields have collapsed and they are powering up again and coming around.'

'Get us out of here. The *Dublin* will have to go after them. Sound a general alert and make sure non-essential crew start making their way to the escape pods in preparation for evacuation.'

'Sir, they are following! We don't have enough power in the engines to outrun them and they are about to open fire again.' Everyone tensed, waiting for the blast that never came.

The control panels lit up suddenly with activity. 'Sir, the *Dublin* has arrived and is attacking the ship.'

'Not a moment too soon. Move us out of range. We can't afford to take another hit.'

It did not take long for the *Dublin*, a bigger and more heavily armed ship, to finish what the *Madrid* had started and collapse the *Falcon's* shields and its weapons systems.

'*Madrid* from the *Dublin*, apologies for the delay. What is your status?' Captain Palimore asked.

'Shields are down and power is low. Injuries are minimal on the ship and there are no fatalities.'

'What do you know about the ship?'

'Very little. It came to our attention due to the damage to its docking bay. When I said I would send over a shuttle with a crew to report and assist, they tried to leave and opened fire when we went to follow. My telepath said they were hiding something. I don't know what is going on but I am sure their registration is false, I suspect they are involved with David Wilhelm and the weapons trade. Why else would it be here now?'

'I agree, I am sending my security over in shuttles. Do you want your security to join them?'

'After the attack we have just sustained, it would be a pleasure.'

'Mine are deploying now. If we force the port hatch, can you take the starboard docking bay?'

'I will instruct them now.'

⁜

The request came though from those on board the *Falcon* an hour later for a joint communication between the captains of the *Madrid* and the *Dublin*. As they all logged on, a three way communication could be seen between the bridges of the *Madrid*, *Dublin* and *Falcon*.

'Congratulations on a quick and successful takeover of the ship. We both got your initial reports. What has happened since then?' Captain Palimore of the *Dublin* asked.

'Sir, the ship took a lot of damage and several corridors were blocked. When we boarded, several men were trying to get to what we now know were the cargo bays. We stopped them and detained all the crew, then completed a full search of the ship. We have started a download for the ship's logs. At the moment they just show the ship was in orbit of a planet they call Lismar, which is well into uncharted space. It will take a while for the files to be properly interrogated.'

'What are you trying to tell us? Please get to the point.'

The tactical leaders looked at each other before they continued. 'Once we cleared the corridors, we were able to gain access to the cargo bays. They had skins and what looked like giant bug wings in there. We think they were trying to get to them to destroy them.'

'Skins? Like our skins?' Captain Lyon of the *Madrid* asked, rubbing his arms in an unconscious movement.

'Yes and no. From the shape of them, they are from small humanoids but in appearance they look like the Lismarian fabric.'

'Are you saying that clothing we wear is made from skins from living beings?'

'It looks that way, sir.'

'How many skins are there?'

'A hundred or so. We did not like to count them.'

'The Lismarian fabric can't be from these skins. The haul is not sufficient to supply the demand for it. Maybe these skins inspired the design?'

'Then why take them? Supply has dropped significantly over the last six months and prices have gone up.'

'Sir, the ship is missing a large number of crew and shuttles,' the *Dublin* tactical leader said. 'I think they must have been attacked before the *Madrid* challenged them. It would account for the damage.'

'Preserve everything. I will send specialists across to see if they can pull anything further out of the computers. Where are the crew now?'

'We have them locked in this ship's brig.'

'You said the logs showed that they had been in orbit of

a planet. Do you have the co-ordinates?'

'Yes, sir.'

Chapter 45

THE news of what was found on the ship spread quickly among the crews of the *Madrid* and *Dublin* and was met with shock and revulsion. At first people thought it was a joke but, as the first crews came back and told their friends what they had seen, reality set in. Most of the crew had heard of the Lismarian fabrics but struggled to understand how real skins had made it into shops for people to buy. Any animal-based products, including meat, had been outlawed for generations. Some argued that the rich fabric might only be copies of the skins but others said that if that were the case, why were there so many in the cargo hold? What purpose did they have? And what about the massive fly wings in the hold? No one seemed to have any answer.

Several hours after the firefight, the *New Delhi* arrived to offer assistance and help with the repairs to the *Madrid*. Everyone on board wanted the engines and shields operational again as soon as possible. This was just one ship but there had to be others out there, finishing off what the *Falcon* had started before it got damaged. How many ships was anyone's guess. If they came looking for the missing cargo, would three ships, one of which was badly disabled, be able to hold them?

⁂

It was the worst news he could have received, and his fists balled in frustration. The *Falcon* would have destroyed one FWN ship and it would have been written off as an unfortunate event, it could have been blamed on David, but to have had the *Dublin* so close by! He had overplayed his hand. He had directed the FWN to the area to find that bloody, interfering telepath. With their improved cloaking technology and telepaths on board, his rogue ships had been easily avoiding detection from most FWN ships for years. The fact that this one got badly damaged! That it could no longer cloak! When he had sent FWN into the area was the worst of luck.

That trader ship was going to come in and there was nothing he could do about it. All he could hope was that he would be able to silence any remaining crew before they had the chance to talk. For now he had to do damage limitation, contact his broker and make sure he no longer had any financial investments in the companies that would shortly be going under when the Lismarian trade finished. It was only a matter of time before that planet was found and then everything would collapse.

Chapter 46

THE crew of the *Falcon* were split between the *Madrid* and the *New Delhi* and placed into their holding cells. The head of security on each ship spoke to each crew member but the response was always the same: utter silence. In the meantime, engineers who were not needed in fixing the *Madrid* were working to gain access the *Falcon's* computers to try and discover where it had come from. The work started slowly but, as other ships arrived in response to the situation and were able to supply their own crews to assist, it meant that work could continue non-stop, and it was not long before they were successful.

'What were you able to find out?' Captain Palimore asked the crew on the *Falcon*, during a conference call with all of the captains.

'We have found out where the ship came from. It appears to be a regular route for them.'

'So this was not a one-off?'

'No sir. It appears to have been going on for a considerable length of time.'

'Were you able to find out who they are supplying?'

'No sir. All we know is where the *Falcon* dropped off their cargo. We managed to get the information from their navigation records. Unfortunately we don't think there is anything else to find.'

'You have not been over there for very long. What makes you say that?'

'We have not been able to go through everything but

early indications are that multiple records have been deleted. If that is the case, our only hope of retrieving them would be back at a tech lab.'

'Thank you, good work.' Captain Palimore ended the communication with the engineer, leaving him with the other captains. 'What are your thoughts?'

'We need to go to that planet and see what the hell has been going on,' said Captain Lyons.

The next day the *Dublin* and *New Delhi* made their way to the planet the *Falcon* had come from, while the *Madrid* went back to charted space along with the *Falcon* and the other FWN ships.

⁜

'*Milkoy, do you sense that*?' David called to his friend, who was working on the caves.

'*I sense nothing. Have they come back*?' Milkoy replied. A moment later he flew back with his mate to join David and Elen.

'There is a ship up there, but they are still too far away for me to get anything definite.'

'I will go and check the shuttle's sensors,' Elen said. The others joined her and waited in nervous silence while she worked. 'It is the FWN.'

'What are they doing here?' David wondered aloud.

'I am not the telepath. How would I know until I am told?'

'How long until you can read them?' Milkoy asked.

'It depends how close they come and how many people on board know what's happening. It might be a while.'

'We need to hide the machine. We can claim that what we have with us is the first technology we have brought here,' Elen said.

'We could take it back to one of the farms,' David suggested.

'The FWN scans are top of the range. If they start investigating, they will ask why we suddenly left the mountain and came back. If they check the area, they might find it. It would be better to hide it here, where the technology we are declaring can mask it.'

'We could create an alcove in the mountain then cover the front with the rock,' Milkoy ventured.

'How long would it take you?'

'Not long.'

'What will we do if we are attacked while the machine is hidden?' Karra asked.

'You won't be attacked with the FWN here,' Elen said.

'Why not? What is the FWN?'

'It is like the police force of charted space,' Elen said. It was clear Milkoy and Karra did not understand her. 'In charted space the FWN, or the Federation of Worlds Navy, enforce the law. Your planet is in uncharted space so it falls outside the area they patrol, but if anyone came here to attack you the FWN still have the authority to protect the planet.'

'Then why did they not come before?'

'We did not know who we could trust.'

'You thought this FWN were involved?'

'They keep order in space and ensure only authorised supplies are brought into the ports. We had to assume there were some FWN personnel involved and if we told the wrong people we would not have made it back here.'

'Can we trust the ones here now?'

'I think so. If they were hostile towards you, you would know by now. I think we need to wait and see why they are here,' David said.

'He is right. The FWN is huge. It is more likely they have tracked us here,' Elen clarified.

'Will they make you leave?' Karra asked.

'They may, but they will also have a lot of questions

about why we are here.'

'I am confused. Is it good or bad that they are here?' Milkoy asked.

'We don't know,' David admitted.

＊

The shuttle's communication unit started bleeping a short time later and David hit the receive button.

'I am Captain Palimore of the FWN *Dublin* calling the shuttle on the planet.'

'Captain, this is David Wilhelm.'

'Mr Wilhelm, please come up to the FWN *Dublin*. There are numerous matters I need to discuss with you in person.'

'I'm sorry, Captain, I'm not very trusting of the FWN at the moment. I'm happy to talk in person but please come down here.'

'Very well, Mr Wilhelm, but what makes you think I can trust that my crew are safe on the planet?'

'Why wouldn't they be? I'm sure you have run your scans. We are not armed and neither are the people here. Your crew can come down with weapons and they will have the advantage,' David said. The *Dublin* was near enough that he could read the crew and he felt their concern. They had found the trader ship badly damaged and they had no idea how it had happened. They wanted answers. They knew they were missing something big.

'Captain, please believe me,' David continued. 'If your crew mean no harm to the local people then they will come to no harm, but I will not come up to you as I need to do what is best for my friends here.'

'I will think on what you have said and call you back shortly with my decision,' said the captain and the communication cut out.

'The captain seems to be considering it,' Elen said.

'He is, but he is worried as he does not know what is happening.'

'Do you think he will agree to come down here?'

'Yes, because all the information he will be given is that there is nothing, other than the climate, that will harm his crew.'

❖

It was not long before the captain called them again and agreed to come down in a shuttle. David advised him about the effects of the suns and the need for environmental suits. Now David stood with Elen looking up, waiting for the shuttle to break orbit. They had spoken to Milkoy and he wanted to meet the captain but would wait until David called him to join them.

'Keep your mind open. If you sense anything from them let me know straight away.'

'Of course, but won't you be able to read them better than me?'

'They may bring their own telepaths with them, which might cause me trouble,' David said, not wanting to go into the politics of the matter.

It was not long before the shuttle landed near to David's. The hatch opened and David both felt and heard the occupant's reaction to the heat. He smiled at their cursing. 'I did warn you to wear environmental suits,' he shouted, and Elen jabbed him in his ribs.

'The readings said the UV radiation and heat were at acceptable levels for short exposure,' Captain Palimore said as he walked off the shuttle, shielding his eyes with his hand.

'That is correct but it does not mean the experience is pleasant. Please follow us and we will go straight into the environmental tent.' David did not wait to see who followed him as he walked away. After the crew of the shuttle entered, he sealed it up. Elen went into their shuttle and came back with water for them to drink.

'I'm sorry, I should have taken your advice. I didn't expect it to be so hot,' Palimore said.

'What we can tolerate and what is comfortable are two different things. The levels are only just acceptable for short-term exposure. Trust me, the suns can do a lot of damage very quickly. This is as cool as we will get until the suns go down - unless you all want to squash into a shuttle.'

'No, we can cope with this.' Palimore sat down on one of the packing cases and, once the rest had settled themselves as best they could, he continued. 'What are you doing here on a planet with no technology?'

'How did you find me?' David countered.

Captain Palimore raised his eyebrows. 'You expect me to explain everything to you? I don't know you and I don't know your crew.'

'You don't trust us?'

'Not yet.'

'Then walk with me.'

'You will need to put something on your skin, otherwise you will burn within minutes.' Elen pointed out.

'We won't go far.' David said.

David looked at Elen; she shrugged then nodded. She did not understand what was going on but trusted the captain and so did he. Palimore stood up and followed David out of the tent and onto the *Dublin's* shuttle.

'I hope you don't mind but here we can talk in private and comfort,' David said.

'Not at all,'

'I have a lot of reasons for distrusting the FWN at present, I want to trust you so please explain how you found us and why you are here.'

'In the circumstances you are asking a lot, all

intelligence suggests you are a criminal'

'Yet here you sit alone with me. You know what you have been told does not correlate with what you know. Both of us are suspicious of each other, I am here with Elen and both of us are unarmed, you have a six armed crew and a fully weaponised ship in orbit. I'm just asking for the curtesy of you explaining why you are here before you force us to return to FWN space.'

'Alright, we were patrolling space looking for you and Ensign Winters, you have both been circulated as wanted for supplying illegal weaponry, when the *Madrid* found a rogue ship, the *Falcon*, with heavy damage. When they were stopped the crew opened fire on the *Madrid*. Investigation showed that the crew had started deleting files and there was a cargo hold full of skins that looked like Lismarian fabrics. All we were able to find out is that they came from here. And here you are, allegedly supplying weapons - and yet there are no weapons. So I want to know what the hell is going on here.'

'The *Falcon* was here. Its crew were coming down in shuttles and skinning the people alive for their skins and wings. The skins are sold as Lismarian fabric and the wings go to various industries. I have never supplied weapons to the people here, they just worked out how to protect themselves.'

'I have so many questions to ask that I think it best to start at the beginning. How did you find this planet?'

'With what has been happening here, I am not very trustful of the FWN.'

'If these people are being attacked and killed for their skins, the FWN would never countenance it.'

'You say that but there are those in the organisation who do, otherwise Admiral Yoland would not have asked me to look into suspicious activity when he could not get the FWN to investigate. The other admirals were not interested and openly considered it a waste of resources. To cut a long story very short, the admiral was killed and I was arrested on trumped-up charges. While I was under arrest, the FWN tried illegal mind reads. Unfortunately for them, I found out more than they did. I don't know who in the FWN is involved, but I know they are trying to cover it up.'

'You are telling me an awful lot for someone who does not know if they can trust me or not - or are you illegally reading my mind?'

'No, but the local population are. Though their minds work in a different way to mine, they are very aware when any attention is directed to them and they are not sensing you or your crew, so they don't consider you to be a risk. I believe you have no idea what is happening here.'

'If that is true, and you don't believe I am a threat, explain it all to me.'

David thought about everything he knew, then took a deep breath and started at the beginning. When he finished, the captain sat in silence. 'Are you going to say something?'

'I am not sure what to say. Admiral Yoland was a good man and I know Mark well.' Palimore rubbed his brow in frustration. 'Members of the FWN would have to be involved, otherwise these ships would have been stopped before now and the merchandise could never have passed customs. But why go to so much trouble for clothing? Surely there could not be enough profit in it.'

'The skins are a nice perk. We think the wings are being used in various industries which is where the real money comes from.'

'I would love to see one of these people.'

'It could easily be arranged.'

'It would break a lot of laws and would probably upset

them.' Palimore had just finished talking when someone hammered on the hatch; he leaned over and opened it, assuming it would be one of his crew.

'Come in, Milkoy,' David said. The captain's jaw dropped. 'May I introduce you my friend, Milkoy.'

'Hello, I am pleased to meet you.'

'A pleasure,' Palimore said, staring in amazement.

'Milkoy is a leader among his people and is interested in why you are here.'

'Of course, as I have said, we located a ship with heavy damage which, according to their navigation records came from here but what I still don't understand is how the rogue ship received the damage it did if there are no weapons or technology here?' Palimore said.

'We can defend ourselves,' Milkoy said. Turning to David, he asked, 'Shall I show him?'

'Please do.'

They went out on to the plateau and Milkoy let out a blast of energy.

The captains personal intercom buzzed 'Sir, our sensors picked up a sudden energy spike at your location. Are you alright?' Captain Palimore's ship called down.

'We are fine,' he responded.

'The shuttles came down and we defended ourselves as you just saw. We think one shuttle was damaged and went back to the ship then exploded,' David explained. 'I have brought parts with me in the hope of building a machine to increase the energy they expand.'

'So they can protect themselves more effectively,' the captain clarified.

'Yes. So what happens now?' David asked.

'The crew of the *Falcon* have been arrested and they and the ship are heading back to Europa with the *Madrid* and the *Paris*. Three FWN crews saw what was on the *Falcon* and others arrived later; there are now two ships in orbit of this planet. Once I have the facts I have been ordered back to give a full report but I will arrange for the *New Delhi* to stay to ensure there are no further attacks. I have been told to bring you back with me.'

'I can't leave them.'

'They will be safe, David. You know the most of what is going on, so the admiralty will want to talk to you,' Captain Palimore told him. 'Whoever is involved in this trade needs to be found and punished. Too many people know about now it to try and cover it up. The best they could hope for is to distance themselves from it. All machinery will obviously have to be removed as well.'

'I guessed that.'

⁂

The next day David said his farewells to Milkoy and his family. He expected it would be for the last time and, as a result, he told his friend to read everything he could from his mind as quickly as possible so he would know how to repair the machine if he needed to, and anything else he would find useful later on.

Now the FWN were aware of the planet, David doubted he would ever be allowed to return and he wanted to leave them as prepared as possible, when he had left before it had always been hard, but he always knew there was a chance of returning. This time he knew the planet would be carefully monitored and managed as per regulations.

Chapter 47

WHEN he was told he could not fly his shuttle back but must have it loaded into the shuttle bay, David half-expected, that he and Elen would be placed in the ship's cells. Instead they were led to a cabin.

'We are wanted for supplying arms. I expected to be arrested,' Elen said.

'If we had found weapons you definitely would have been.' Captain Palimore smiled. 'But with everything we have found out, I will give you both the benefit of the doubt.'

'Being on that planet and having that technology are also offences.'

'Elen, do you really want to do the trip back in the brig? Don't remind him,' David said.

Captain Palimore laughed. 'Unfortunately all the machinery found on the planet got mixed up with our own spare parts. My report states we found you on a mountain away from the population. You had done nothing, yet, to help progress these people, so why cloud the bigger issue here?'

'Others will know what we went there to do.'

'Anyone who comes forward with more information will be subject to an investigation. I don't think you need to worry about it.'

'Thank you.'

'If I receive any updates I will let you know. For now I suggest you make yourselves comfortable. You both know your way around FWN ships so I will leave you both to it.'

✢

The trip back to Europa was uneventful. Not wanting to cause problems with the crew, David and Elen kept to themselves as much as possible. Captain Palimore kept his promise and let them know any updates. The news was spreading through the FWN like wildfire; another ship was going to support the *New Delhi* in orbit of Lismar.

When they arrived at Europa, David and Elen were transported down to the planet. They expected to be treated as prisoners but again they were surprised; the officers who met them were polite. They were separated into different interview rooms. David waited for illegal mind intrusion, but there was nothing; the FWN were playing by the rules this time.

David was soon visited by an officer who sat down opposite him. 'Thank you for joining me here.'

'I didn't think I had much of a choice.'

'Probably not. I am Lieutenant Commander Jamison. Captain Palimore has sent us a report of everything you have told him and we are acting on the information. I need to make sure that nothing has been missed.'

'Is it just going to be you sitting here talking to me? Not telepaths trying to do a little digging?'

'No,' Jamison said. 'I am sorry about your treatment last time but I can assure you it won't happen again. Those involved have been punished.'

'I bet the UTA were not very happy about it.'

'No, they were not. It set back relations between us for a considerable amount of time.'

'I can imagine.'

'Please can we go through everything you know?'

David sat for a moment, thinking. His distrust had

gone on for so long that he wondered if he should say anything. Then he berated himself as a fool; most of what he knew was out in the open now so what good would keeping silent do?

After he finished his account, he was taken back through it but this time asked a lot of questions to clarify points. Once the questions had run out, they let him go and he discovered a car was waiting to take him to his father's house.

'Where is Elen?' he asked before getting in.

'She was released about two hours ago. She should be waiting for you at your father's.'

'Thank you.'

When he got home Elen and his family greeted him and bombarded him with questions. It was a long time before he could ask his father about what had happened to him once he had left.

It took a few days for all the questions to be answered. Though the information that the Lismarian fabrics were really skins had not been made public, the fabric had been withdrawn from shops; companies that had been earning fortunes failed quickly and that triggered an economic downturn.

'Is the stock market crash going to ruin you?' David asked his father.

'No. I made sure I had nothing invested in those I suspected of trading Lismarian products – I invested in their rivals. I expect to make a fortune out of this.'

'You already have a fortune.'

'A second one then.'

※

'I paid you very well to protect our interests Admiral Mathers,' he said slamming his fists down on the desk.

'There was no way I could have foreseen that ship

getting damaged and found.'

'FWN ships should not have been in the area. For that I hold you directly responsible.'

'You wanted me to stop the interference in your trade by that telepath, they had slipped past our security, if I didn't send ships to the area how else would you want me to stop them?'

'You have command of the FWN fleet, they should never have been able to leave Europa. Everything is your fault and you will pay for your failures.'

'I can guarantee you I will take you and your friends with me.'

'Who have you told?'

'No one, yet.'

'That is good to know.'

❋

After his release David linked in with the UTA and discovered that, as a result of the information he had given about the illegal mind reads, several FWN telepaths had their minds read, then were chemically stripped of their abilities which had led to their suicides. This had frightened others and stopped them trying anything similar, under threat of a forced mind read several names of undeclared telepaths were handed over and forced under UTA rules and regulations. The names of the officers who had ordered them to act illegally were passed to the FWN and they had been interrogated and stripped of their rank, but they all claimed they had been acting under orders of Admiral Mathers. The UTA retained control of the investigation of all telepaths and demanded that they were all recalled to ascertain what they knew, which was very little.

It was about a month later that he was asked back to FWN headquarters. He was invited into a room with comfortable chairs, not one of the interrogation rooms like before. It was not long before a FWN officer joined him.

'Thank you for coming back. I am Admiral Hiro. I wanted to inform you about the result of our investigation.' He sat down opposite David.

'Have you found out who is behind the attack on Lismar.'

'No. The crew of the *Falcon* refused to talk and although we were able to get a warrant from the court so a telepath could read their minds several of the crew committed suicide, including all of their telepaths, before it could be enforced, those left only know where the shipment was being dropped off, which we knew already from downloading the ship's systems. We went to the port but could find no record of the deliveries or anyone who was aware of them, that port is still closed and is likely to remain so.'

'There was no information about the other ships involved?'

'Vague information, but they are all illegal vessels so it does not lead us anywhere. All we found out was that there are several other ships.'

'Why don't you go public with what has been happening? People might come forward, give information.'

'Or they could be killed. The economy is unstable now and the FWN are needed more than ever before. If we advertise what has been happening, we will undermine our own authority and we can't risk the disruption that will cause. A court order is in place stopping you from going public over this. Should you release any information you will be looking at a long jail term.'

'So that is it? There is nothing else we can do? What about the admiral who authorised the illegal mind reads and the warrant for our arrest on false information.'

'Admiral Mathers authorised both and he committed suicide a week before you arrived here when the UTA started asking painful questions.'

'Did the questioning stop after his death?'

'No, the investigation will continue but whether we find anything or not is too early to tell. For now, all items from Lismar are being withdrawn and the companies investigated to ascertain if they knew where the product came from. FWN ships are patrolling Lismar's orbit while we look to expand charted space to include the planet.'

'As I asked before, so that is it? The people who organised this have got away with mass murder. What is there to stop the rogue ships going back, once the patrols are withdrawn?'

'We can't stay there forever but why would they go back? They will have no one to sell the fabric and wings to. Also from what I understand from Captain Palimore, the planet's inhabitants have worked out how to defend themselves.'

'I want to go back there. I can help them further.'

'Mr Wilhelm, we accept that you originally crashed on the planet, but you went back twice more. You have broken the law and could be imprisoned for life as a result. If you go back again we will prosecute you to the full extent of the law. We have decided not to proceed at this time as we can't prove that you gave the planet's inhabitants any technology or information that would hinder their natural development. They need to progress as best they can on their own.'

'I have friends there. You can't stop me from seeing them, it is not right.'

'You have family here. And I can and will stop you going back there,' the admiral said. 'David, see sense. Even if you managed to sneak back, you could not stay there for long. How long would you survive, you have already had cancer once and as a result you remain at high risk of it returning and killing you? Also how much damage would you cause in not letting them develop naturally and find their own way?'

'It doesn't seem fair.'

'No one ever said life was fair. Go home. The trade has stopped. Trust the investigation to develop as it should. We won't stop trying to find those responsible, but your role is finished now.'

⁜

David left the FWN with a heavy heart. Being told he could not go back to Lismar made him want to do so even more. On his arrival home he wanted to vent his anger and frustration to someone, anyone, but no one was home. Knowing his father would be at his offices he caught a taxi there.

'David what is wrong? Why are you here?'

David explained all of his anger and frustration over the lack of action for such a major law violation and his view that nothing was being done over it.

'From what you have said and what I know, everything in the FWN ties back to Admiral Mathers, who is now dead. In the private sector Petro Diaz and Theron Gallo have collapsed their businesses and disappeared.'

'What are you saying? There is nothing we can do? There were other companies using Lismarian products.'

'They are being investigated, but I would guess that they would have no idea where the product comes from and everything would tie back to Diaz and Gallo.'

'So that is it?'

'There is nowhere else to go with this, I am sorry David but from what I know those responsible have covered their actions very well. I am sure the investigation will continue but expect everything to result in a dead end, there is nothing more you can do.'

⚜

'Are you alright?' Elen asked as David came home and he explained everything that had happened between himself, the FWN and his father.

'I wish I could go back once more to make sure they are alright. I hate having to trust the FWN's word for it that they are safe.'

'I know, but too many people know the truth now. Milkoy and his family will be alright, they still have the machine to defend themselves. Let them find their own way, as the admiral suggested, and spend time with your own family.'

'How can I trust that they are safe?'

'You know what to look out for, if anyone starts using Lismarian products again, you will know that you will have to act again. If the trade has stopped as the FWN has said you could just be causing developmental damage.' Elen said, 'stay here where your family need you.'

'They don't need me.'

'They might not need you, but they want you as part of their lives. They love you,' Elen said. 'I need you.'

'You never needed me before.'

'I was never going to be a mother before. Let the future progress as it should, David.'